BLOOD FALLS

WARRIOR MAGE LIBRARIANS BOOK ONE

ANNA MCCLUSKEY

This is a work of fiction. Any resemblance to actual events, places, or persons, living or dead, is entirely coincidental.

Author website: annamccluskey.com
BookBub: bookbub.com/profile/anna-mccluskey
Facebook: facebook.com/annamccluskeyauthor
Instagram: instagram.com/authorannamccluskey

Cover art by Sleepy Fox Studios
www.sleepyfoxstudios.net

Acknowledgements:

Y'all wouldn't believe the struggles I had writing this series. And in actually finishing it, despite everything going all crazy-like in my life and in my brain, I must give credit to a plethora of fantastic people:

The regulars at my twice-weekly writers' group, particularly Courtney Nelson, Jay Wegehenkel, Vanessa Frazon Nelson, and Greg Ranzoni, who showed up each week and gave me encouragement and feedback.

Co-workers at my day job who put up with me jabbering on and on about plots, characters, and cryptids and who gave me ideas or let me bounce ideas off of them. In particular, Rose Giacomini, Johnny McFadden, and John Standeven. Special shout-out as well to Connor Woods for giving me the idea for potato-based divination, which opened up a whole plotline of other prophecy ideas for me.

Asher Olson, you get your own section with most effusive thanks. Legitimately could not have done this without you and your consistent feedback, relentless emotional support, and general amazingness.

Sarah Biglow too. You stand alone in the many, many messages of encouragement, the forever-willingness to bounce ideas off each other, and the accountability. You are a great friend and an inspiring author.

Sandra Almeida Junca, who helped me with the Portuguese names and phrases in Book 3, and Krista Garcia whose expertise in ancient American cultures was likewise invaluable in the same book.

My subscribers on Ream, who help keep the lights on and remind me that I do have readers who enjoy my work, even when I'm sinking into depression. Jay Wegehenkel, I owe you special thanks as part of your Ream rewards tier, but I need to shout out the rest of you too. Thank you for being there.

And finally, Kickstarter backers. I know I'm late with these books. You have been so supportive and understanding. Thank you so much for your patience.

-Anna

Chapter 1: Trevor

Trevor dropped his sword and dove to the ground, rolling in a perfectly executed somersault to avoid the demon's outstretched claws. He danced in place as Sister Margaret distracted the creature by piercing its hide with her twin swords and then pulling them out swiftly.

He saw his opening and darted back in, stooping to grab his greatsword with both hands and then using his upward momentum to plunge the weapon into the demon's scaly underbelly, twisting and dodging before using a stitching motion with his left hand against the sword hilt to teleport himself three feet away, avoiding any skin-to-scale contact with the beast.

The creature spun, reaching blindly for him again, its grotesque mouth gaping open in a bellow as its talons swished through the air, groping through the spot Trevor had just vacated.

Glancing at the elderly mage who stood off to the side, Trevor hoped the Scholar Mage Exorcist was almost ready to send this bastard back to its home dimension.

The man's hands glowed, and his face was entirely occupied by an expression of intense concentration.

"Focus, please," Sister Margaret called out as she aimed a kick at the creature's shin with her heavy brown combat boot. "And remember — don't let the demon touch you! That's how possessions happen."

Trevor turned his attention back to the demon, skipping backward as its tail lashed out toward him.

It spun around to face Sister Margaret, and Trevor let out a wordless bellow of his own to confuse it. The demon's eyeless head swiveled as it shifted its weight from foot to foot, its ears extending like satellite dishes as it struggled to figure out where its enemies were.

Moving his hands in a complex gesture, Trevor used his mage powers to move a heavy table from where it lay on its side a few feet away to right above the demon's head, dropping it with a CRASH right on top of the foul creature.

Finally, a beam of light shot out from the exorcist's hands straight at the demon, and it disappeared with a *POP*.

Trevor lowered his sword, transferring it to his left hand as he swiped at his sweaty face with the short sleeve of his black t-shirt. He had declined to wear armor for this task, opting instead for the agility granted by simple work-out gear.

"Thank you for your assistance," said the exorcist gravely as he approached the pair. He offered a towel to each of them, which Trevor accepted with a grateful smile.

Sister Margaret demurred, instead pulling a small black folded cloth from her leather bandolier. Her eyes turned from seer white to their ordinary dark brown as she shook it out and sat down cross-legged on the floor, avoiding a puddle of demon-blood, and began cleaning one of her swords, laying the other neatly across her lap.

"You're welcome," Trevor wheezed. "Happy to help." As he focused on catching his breath, he vigorously rubbed the towel over his close-cropped black hair. Then he began carefully running it down the length of his sword, pushing the blood and guts off to join the considerable amount already on the floor.

"That demon has been plaguing this room for months," the man continued. "Truly the bane of the librarians who live and work here."

Trevor glanced around the room, which was in shambles. The kind of shambles that happened when someone accidentally summoned a demon in a reading room and then couldn't get anyone in to take care of it for three months.

"We're working through the backlog of Warrior Mage Librarian tasks as quickly as we can," said Sister Margaret. "Before our hire, the department was short-staffed for a long time, and you know there are dozens of these secret Vatican libraries scattered around the world."

The SME nodded. "I wasn't blaming you, by any means. If anything, our exorcism branch is just as hard-pressed."

"I hope none of the the books in here were irreplaceable," said Trevor. He picked up a volume that had been essentially shredded beyond repair. He could barely make out the words on the cover. Something about stitchers in ancient Greece?

"At least the historian who accidentally summoned it got out in time," said Sister Margaret. "Lucky he was a stitcher — the ability to teleport does come in handy. As a seer, I'd have been fucked."

"That's why you should learn all three disciplines," said Trevor, trying to keep the exasperation from his voice. This was a familiar argument.

Sister Margaret looked up from her weapons and rolled her eyes at him. "You know why I don't. You spread yourself out like that, and you're not as powerful in your primary discipline." She pointed a dagger at him. "If you didn't use seeing and spelling, you'd be one of the most formidable stitchers in the entire Warrior Mage dicastery, if not *the* best."

He shrugged. "As it is, I'm no slouch, and I have the other skills at my disposal."

Trevor finished cleaning off his sword and carefully flipped it around, sheathing it at his hip and adjusting the belt to lay comfortably flat.

The exorcist cleared his throat. "Both paths have their place," he said. "Personally, I am set in my ways. I'm a speller, I've always been a speller, and damned if I won't be a speller until the day I die."

Sister Margaret stowed the last of her now-clean weaponry — a five-pointed throwing star — back into its pocket in her leather bandolier and gracefully pushed herself up into a standing position. She cocked her head and lifted an eyebrow. "Ready?"

Trevor grinned ruefully, dropping the subject. "How's the beer here?"

She shrugged. "Your guess is as good as mine. You think I've been to a haunted fortress in India before?"

"I don't know your life," he teased.

"The beer is serviceable," said the exorcist. "The wine is better. And the food is fantastic."

Chapter 2: Sister Margaret

Full of serviceable beer and fantastic food, Sister Margaret left Trevor to his after-dinner poker game with three of the resident Scholar Mage Librarians and headed back to the stark room she'd been assigned in the dormitory wing of the Bhangarh Fort Library.

Her baggage was still on the narrow bed where she'd thrown it upon arrival that afternoon. She glanced around the room. "Weapons rack, weapons rack," she murmured. "There you are."

She eyed the rack dubiously. "Why so tiny? Isn't this a warrior room? Well, I suppose I can make do."

Sister Margaret unbuckled her sword belt, carefully hanging the twin swords that were her main weapons on the end closest to the bed, so she'd be able to easily grab them if something happened in the night.

Next, she pulled fifteen knives and daggers out of various hiding spots around her body, arranging them on the rack, packing them in as closely as she could. Then she moved on to miscellaneous potions, from pepper spray to drugs and poisons to mystical elixirs. Most of these she pulled out of pockets in her bandolier. There wasn't a good way to store them on the weapons rack, so she stashed them in the top drawer of her dresser.

Finally, she divested herself of her projectiles: a set of blow darts, four throwing stars, and a handful of smoke bombs. She carefully slipped the throwing stars under her pillow for easy access and then placed the rest on her nightstand. If someone broke into her room, her best bet was always to kill or disable them while they were still at the door, rather than give them time to engage in an actual fight.

Sister Margaret lifted her bandolier off over her head and folded it neatly on a nearby chair. She unbuckled her arm bracers, and then her torso armor, letting her breath out with a whoosh of relief as her ribs expanded fully. "This must be how normal women feel when they take off their bra after a long day at the office," she muttered, running a hand over her ribcage.

She peeled off her leather pants and rummaged in her duffel bag for a pair of black leggings to pull on in their place, then exchanged her sweat-soaked black undershirt for a clean one. For the final touch, she loosened her long hair from its tight braid, allowing it to float around her face in a wavy black cloud.

"Holy, fuck, that feels good," she breathed, massaging her sore scalp. Maybe she should just shave her hair all off. That's what a true warrior did.

"This is how I pay for my vanity," she murmured. "And to what end?"

But as she gazed at herself in the full-length mirror that hung on the wall, she couldn't help but feel a spark of joy at the beauty of her thick, waist-length hair. "I am allowed some small measure of vanity, am I not? I'm only human," she told herself. "Besides, it would break *mi abuela's* heart if I came home to St. Louis with a shaved head next Christmas."

Sister Margaret laid out her travel yoga mat and began to run through her nightly stretching routine, starting with her extremities, seating herself on her knees with her feet flexed underneath her rear, toes tucked against the floor.

As she moved up through her body, she focused on clearing her mind of vanity, of thoughts of far-off family, of stressors and day-to-day minutiae. Clearing her mind of all thoughts. Just using the movements and the breath to clear her mind altogether.

Tomorrow they would head back to the Vatican for their next assignment.

Chapter 3: Trevor

Back in Vatican City, Trevor strode into a familiar conference room and stopped short. Cardinal Neubacher, the newly-appointed head of the Warrior Mage Librarian Department, was seated at the table, absorbed with reading from a file folder laid down in front of him.

Cardinal Neubacher looked up and gave him a reassuring smile.

Trevor smiled back, nervously.

That this debriefing was being handled by someone so high up the chain of command could be either a good sign or a bad.

"Have a seat, young man," said the Cardinal, his voice smooth and benevolent.

The man's voice was *always* smooth and benevolent, though, always had a faint tinge of kindly humor. And sometimes he used that veneer of amity in very scary ways.

Nevertheless, there was nothing Trevor could do but take his seat. He cleared his throat. "Sorry I'm a few minutes early. I hope I didn't interrupt your reading."

"Not at all," the cardinal said mildly. He pushed the file back a few inches and leaned forward, steepling his fingers in front of his face.

That didn't help the feeling of menace that he exuded.

"I appreciate your punctuality."

"I'm sure Sister Margaret will be here soon," Trevor babbled. "She's very punctual herself. Just maybe not as neurotically early for everything as I am."

Cardinal Neubacher's eyes crinkled as he smiled. "You can relax, Trevor. I'm not here because of any kind of problem. Quite the opposite, in fact."

The door flew open and Sister Margaret bustled in. "I'm here, I'm here! I'm not late! It's just now— Oh." She covered her mouth with her hand as she spotted Cardinal Neubacher. "Your Eminence. I didn't expect to see you here. Apologies. Even though I'm not late."

"You are not," he confirmed. "Please, have a seat."

She gave Trevor a sideways look as she made her way to the seat across the table from him.

He shrugged back at her.

"I will get straight to the point," Cardinal Neubacher began. "As I can see that you are both a bit nervous at my presence. We have a special assignment for the pair of you."

He paused for a split second before continuing. "As you are undoubtedly aware, over the past couple of years, we have made the paradigm-shifting discovery that we are not alone on this Earth."

Trevor blinked. He raised a hand.

Cardinal Neubacher nodded. "Yes?"

"I, uh, am not sure what you're referring to, actually," Trevor said carefully. "When you say 'we' and also 'not alone,' um. Well. What?"

"Cryptids," said Sister Margaret, as though that explained everything.

Trevor waited for either of them to elaborate on that. "Like . . . Bigfoot?" he hazarded.

"Bigfoots, yes," said Cardinal Neubacher. "And dragons, merfolk, various shifters. . . . Has nobody told you about this?

In the entire year you've been here?" His voice carried pure astonishment.

"Surely we've talked about it," said Sister Margaret.

"No," said Trevor. "Not a word."

"But it's all anyone was talking about last year," said Sister Margaret.

"You mean last year, before I worked for the Vatican, when we were busy dealing with an ancient, corrupt secret society?" said Trevor. "I guess I must have been distracted."

"And by the time you started working for the Vatican, things had calmed down a bit." Cardinal Neubacher nodded. "And you were thrown straight into your training, and kept busy with more standard Warrior Mage Librarian tasks."

"So, maybe you could tell me now," said Trevor.

"With pleasure," said Cardinal Neubacher. "The Church has always suspected the existence of cryptids, although that has never been our term for them. We have evidence that early medieval knights fought fire-breathing dragons, for example. And we have further evidence that suggests the existence of such creatures as unicorns, vampires, and others. So, while we were surprised when an emissary from the Cryptid Collective approached us about eighteen months ago, we were not shocked."

"Eighteen months?" said Trevor. "About the same time I was learning about magery."

"Yes," said Cardinal Neubacher. "This created quite the stir among the Church mages. Outside of the mage departments, of course, this has all been kept very quiet. But at first we were understandably concerned that it would result in conflict."

"And did it?" Trevor asked.

"Despite the best efforts of some of our more zealous Cardinals, who had trouble understanding the difference between dragons and demons, no," said Cardinal Neubacher. "Since the cryptids came out of the woodwork, we have been able to maintain a cordial relationship with them, even bringing some witches into our employ. While we have been aware of witches' existence for some time, we were a bit peeved to discover that they've been a part of the Cryptid Collective for centuries and never mentioned it. Our understanding is that the Cryptid Collective has reached out to several other powerful groups of mages as well as the Church, with the expectation that we join their ranks and work together to keep magic from affecting humans and humanity from affecting magic and cryptids."

"How does humanity affect cryptids?" asked Trevor with a frown.

"Well, for one thing," Sister Margaret cut in, "we, as a whole, seem dead set on populating every inch of the planet. And equally determined to destroy said planet."

"Yes," said Cardinal Neubacher. "One large contributing factor for approaching groups with political power seems to be the hope that we will help reverse the climate catastrophe overtaking the Earth." He paused. "There's something else, though. Something we haven't been able to really get a straight answer about. There has been an odd thread of . . . desperation in the communications from the Cryptid Collective throughout this entire process."

Trevor frowned. "Desperation?"

"As though there were a deeper underlying motive behind bringing us in. But of course everything is buried beneath layers of diplomatic language and it could very well be simply that the cryptids have been as nervous as we about this rather enormous step forward." Cardinal Neubacher shook his head abruptly. "No sense in borrowing trouble, but I urge you to keep your eyes and ears open for anything that might shed light on that."

Trevor exchanged a glance with Sister Margaret.

"I take it our next assignment will involve cryptids?" said Sister Margaret, leaning forward. Her voice overfilled with excited anticipation.

"Ah, yes," said Cardinal Neubacher. "I apologize; I'm getting ahead of myself. Your assignment. The collective's annual summit is coming up. We have been asked to send a delegation of two mages."

"And you'd like us along to serve as bodyguards?" Sister Margaret guessed.

"We would like the two of you to be our emissaries to the Cryptid Collective."

There was a long moment of stunned silence. Cardinal Neubacher waited for them to process, steepling his hands again in front of his serene face.

"I don't think I heard you correctly," said Trevor slowly.

"I believe you did," said Cardinal Neubacher. "You will represent the Vatican's Warrior Mage Dicastery at the Cryptid Collective summit in two weeks' time."

Sister Margaret jumped to her feet. "Two weeks? Are you fucking kidding me?"

Trevor stared at his boss in stunned silence. This felt far above his pay grade.

He supposed there must be a reason they were being sent. But what were the odds Cardinal Neubacher would tell them the truth if he asked?

Only one way to find out.

"Why us?" he asked. "We have no experience in diplomacy. We're the greenest WML's you have. I'm not even Catholic. It doesn't appear to make any sense."

"Perhaps not on the face of it," Cardinal Neubacher admitted. "But we have our reasons."

"I think it would help us to know what those reasons are," said Trevor, carefully choosing his words in an effort to remain tactful.

"Perhaps," said Cardinal Neubacher. "Allow me to be blunt, as the dragons certainly were. Not all of the cryptids are entirely welcoming of the idea that humans will be attending this summit. We needed to send someone who comes across as inoffensive."

Trevor's eyebrows shot up and he nodded toward Sister Margaret, who was pacing the room, muttering curse words under her breath, alternating English and Spanish and occasionally throwing in some Italian for good measure. "So you picked her?"

"Yes, actually. Sister Margaret is intelligent and likable. As are you, Trevor. You are also more diplomatic and it is to be hoped that you will keep her . . . reined in somewhat."

Sister Margaret pivoted on her heel and sat down again, leaning toward Cardinal Neubacher. "If you want someone easily reined in, why send warriors? Why not scholars?"

"Your average Scholar Mage Librarian is insular. Awkward. Not a people person."

"Okay, so that's SML's. What about another kind of scholar? An SMH seems like an excellent choice. Why not send a historian, who might be more versed in the historical evidence you mentioned of previous interactions with cryptids?"

Cardinal Neubacher shrugged. "Trevor, you do have a background in history, do you not?"

"Yes," he admitted. "My doctorate was in medieval history, focusing on comparing European customs with those in Asia and Northern Africa."

"There you are," said Cardinal Neubacher. "So you are perfectly qualified. You two are the team for this job. Besides, if things do go south, we'd like our representatives to be able to defend themselves."

Sister Margaret shook her head and leaned back in her chair, folding her arms across her chest. "Nuh uh. There's more to this. What aren't you telling us?"

Cardinal Neubacher nodded. "There is one more piece to this. I mentioned that the cryptids have approached other groups as well. One of those groups is Aurora."

"Oh!" Sister Margaret's eyes widened and she sat upright, her chair skittering a little on its wheels at her abrupt movement.

Trevor frowned, feeling more lost than ever. "Who or what is Aurora?"

"Haven't you been in contact with anyone back home?" asked Sister Margaret.

"Not enough, I guess," said Trevor.

"Aurora is a new, emerging secret society," said Cardinal Neubacher. "Combining the remnants of the Auditors with the former Foxes and Harpers — the groups who aided you in your fight against the Auditors. It is being led by your old friends Chameleon and Coyote."

"Ah." Understanding dawned. "So you want us to go because we have experience with some of the other emissaries."

"I think there's a good chance they'll send someone who you know, perhaps someone like Nicole Poe or maybe another high ranking member of the former Foxes," Cardinal Neubacher agreed. "Even if their representative turns out to be someone you don't know personally, you're familiar with their leaders, and can potentially leverage that into an ally relationship. There are two other groups sending delegates: Pala and the Illuminati."

"The Illuminati?" said Trevor. "The Illuminati are real?"

"Of course the Illuminati are real," said Sister Margaret. "Get your head out of your ass."

Trevor ignored his partner. She had a tendency to get snarkier when she was under stress. "And who is Pala?"

"A bunch of hippy mages," said Sister Margaret. "Social justice types. The Vatican has worked with them in the past when our ideals lined up. Why not send someone who has worked with them?"

"We're not as concerned about making connections with Pala," said Cardinal Neubacher. "As you said, we've worked with them in the past, and while they do have high connections in the UN, they're not particularly intimidating as a group. We're more concerned about navigating relations with this emerging Aurora group. They seem determined to become major world players, in ways that the more insular Auditors were not. We'd like to make sure they're on our side from the start."

"And the Illuminati?" Trevor was still trying to wrap his mind around the fact that they were actually real. Somehow that seemed less probable than vampires, unicorns, and dragons.

Cardinal Neubacher waved a hand. "The Illuminati are not as important as they think they are. Let them play around with their boy's club, their meaningless posturing and mystical symbols. Their presence at the summit is more about the perception that they have any political pull than the reality of it." He cleared his throat. "So, what do you think? Do you accept this position?"

Sister Margaret raised an eyebrow. "Do we have a choice?"

He shrugged. "There's always a choice."

"What happens if we decline?" asked Trevor.

Cardinal Neubacher lifted an eyebrow, mirroring Sister Margaret's expression. "Nothing much. We give you another, more typical assignment. We could send you to Russia, perhaps. There's a book of spells that has somehow come to life in the library in the Valley of Death. Smothered three scholar mages before the librarians managed to lock down the room. We could give you that assignment; assign someone else to this emissary.

"But maybe the next time a prestigious assignment like this comes along, we don't even consider you. We assume you're not interested in jobs like this one. And then, maybe, after you've done a lot of plodding, ordinary assignments, just maybe, someday, you'll be recognized once more as a valuable team and maybe you'll be offered potentially career-advancing assignments again. Or maybe not. Maybe you just carry on as you have, remaining junior WMLs for decades until you finally retire, wondering what might have been."

Trevor's lips quirked. "That's quite a pathetic picture you've painted there."

"We'll take it," said Sister Margaret, jumping to her feet.

"Wait, that worked?" Trevor stared at her.

"I don't know," she shrugged. "I want to take the path more adventurous, don't you?"

"Well, yes," he admitted.

Cardinal Neubacher cleared his throat. "So, it's settled, then. You'll go to Antarctica."

Trevor's eyes widened. "Did you just say *Antarctica*?"

Chapter 4: Sister Margaret

Sister Margaret left St. Adrian Hall and jogged over to the next building in the complex, shooting off a text as she went.

Once inside, she headed straight for the stairwell and took the steps two at a time, rushing toward a particular office. Her phone dinged as she pulled open the door on the second floor, and she glanced at it.

Sister Margaret grinned at the response, and strode down the hall, stopping in a doorway and rapping lightly on the doorframe.

"Well, that was fast," said the woman behind the desk, looking up.

"I was already on my way here when I texted you," Sister Margaret admitted. She stepped into the room and Mother Eleanor gestured toward a chair. "Thanks for agreeing to chat."

"Anytime," said Mother Eleanor. "You said you have an important decision to make? I am always happy to assist one of my sisters in a time of need."

"Thank you." Sister Margaret sat down and regarded the Mother Superior of her order. When she had first come to Rome and met Mother Eleanor, she had been shocked that someone so young held the position of Mother Superior to the elite Sisters of Saint Joan.

Then she'd learned that Mother Eleanor, who didn't look a day over forty-five, was actually in her mid-seventies.

Sister Margaret was confident in her own fighting prowess, but she was equally certain that Mother Eleanor could best her in a spar with one hand tied behind her back.

"Cardinal Neubacher has asked me to accept an unusual assignment," Sister Margaret began.

Mother Eleanor waved her hand. "The Cryptid Collective summit? It's already approved," she said. "In fact, I was hoping you'd stop by. I have a little . . . side quest to add."

Sister Margaret leaned forward. This sounded interesting. "What are you talking about?"

Mother Eleanor's eyes sparkled as she gave her a wide grin. "Saint Joan's sword," she breathed. "I have reason to believe that the sword of Saint Joan of Arc herself is in the custody of the ice dragons in their city at Blood Falls."

Chapter 5: Trevor

The next morning, Trevor and Sister Margaret reported back to the conference room. Standing at the head of the room, fiddling with a laptop, were two senior WMLs, a duo known colloquially as the bishops.

The bishops were not actually bishops, per se, or at least not currently. Trevor was a little hazy on the hierarchy of Catholic clergy, but his understanding was that if you were a bishop, you were specifically in charge of a bunch of churches.

These two used to have that job, in neighboring territories, but had to leave their posts because a few of the priests who served under them . . . disappeared.

Trevor's understanding was that these particular priests were bad men who did bad things and when the bishops found out, they took matters into their own hands.

Which, honestly, Trevor couldn't fault them for. And it seemed that the Church didn't either, because rather than disciplining the pair, they had moved them to Rome and promoted them to Warrior Mage Librarian, which was apparently somehow a higher rank than bishop.

Father Max looked up from the laptop he was fiddling with and gave them a cold smile. "Trevor. Sister Margaret. Take your seats, please. We'll be ready to start shortly."

Before Trevor could sit down, however, he found his hand being pumped enthusiastically by the other former bishop, Father Nicholas. "Well done, my boy," he said. "This is quite the assignment for you! Are you excited to be going to Antarctica? I would be so excited!"

"Yeah," said Trevor, blinking down at the short, balding man. This was the most interaction he'd ever had with the bishops, who usually kept to themselves. "I mean, before yesterday, I didn't know dragons existed, and now I'm going to their city, on a continent most people never even think about going to."

"You are going to learn about dragons, young man," said Father Max. It sounded like a threat. "And all of the other cryptids."

"They're so fascinating, don't you think?" said Father Nicholas. He released Trevor's hand and lunged over to Sister Margaret, who stood up to have her own hand vigorously oscillated. Her wide eyes met Trevor's and he cleared his throat, stifling a chuckle.

Father Nicholas dropped Sister Margaret's hand and bounded to the front of the room, beaming toward the pair of them.

Trevor and Sister Margaret resumed their seats just as the first slide of Father Max's presentation appeared on the wall behind him.

"Oh, fuck," muttered Sister Margaret. "Power point."

Trevor shrugged. He didn't mind a good power point presentation, as long as it was interesting and helpful.

Father Max turned and pulled down a screen, allowing the slide to spring into better focus. Emblazoned across the top were the words *Cryptid Collective Summit Objectives:*

Below was a bulleted list:

- *Survive with few injuries and zero casualties*

- *Make alliances, focusing in particular on witches, dragons, and unicorns, as well as Aurora*
- *Avoid merfolk*

With no preamble, Father Max launched into the presentation. "In two weeks time, you will be attending the Cryptid Collective summit as the emissaries of our organization."

Father Nicholas reached behind a podium, and the lights in the room dimmed.

Father Max didn't seem to notice, continuing his speech without pause. "Your objectives are as follows. Don't die. Don't get too injured. Don't allow your partner to die. Don't allow your partner to get too injured. Make alliances. Particularly make alliances with witches, dragons, unicorns, and the mage group known as Aurora."

Trevor tentatively put up a hand to ask for clarification on what kind of alliances they would be making.

"Save your questions until the end," Father Max barked.

"Chances are, they'll be answered anyway," said Father Nicholas. "The presentation is very thorough."

"Avoid merfolk," continued Father Max.

A new slide appeared, the words *Injuries and Casualties* emblazoned at the top. "Now, we know that things do happen in this kind of situation," said Father Nicolas. "So you won't be penalized if you get injured or your partner gets killed."

"What a relief," Sister Margaret muttered.

Father Max fixed her with a stern glare, and she slumped slightly in her seat.

"We expect both of you to do everything in your power to prevent this from happening, however," said Father Max, his gaze never leaving Sister Margaret's face.

"Yep." She nodded vigorously. "Got it."

Trevor coughed to cover a laugh, only to find himself pinned down under Father Max's regard.

"Everything. In. Your. Power," Father Max repeated.

"Yessir," said Trevor. He sat up a little straighter.

Father Max pushed a button and three more bullet points appeared on the screen.

- *Do not challenge anyone to a duel*
- *Do not accept any dueling challenges*
- *Stay together as much as possible. The buddy system is not just for school children*
- *Avoid merfolk*

"I think all of these points are pretty self-explanatory," said Father Max. "I do not think we need elaborate further, do we?"

Trevor found himself shaking his head vigorously, even though he actually did want to know about the whole merfolk avoidance clause. Not as much as he wanted to avoid Father Max's ire.

"Good." Father Max moved on to the next slide, which read *Alliances* at the top with another bullet list underneath:

- *Witches*
- *Dragons*
- *Unicorns*
- *Aurora*

Father Nicolas took over speaking. "We are particularly interested in making alliances with these three cryptids and this particular mage group. As you know, witches and mages have a long and bloody history—"

Trevor lifted his hand halfway up. "Excuse me?"

Father Nicolas raised his eyebrows.

"Sorry," said Trevor. "I know you said no questions, but you also just said 'as you know,' and I'm afraid I don't know."

"Ah." Father Nicolas nodded. "You haven't been around for very long, have you? Very well. Our story begins in the ninth century of Our Lord—"

"I hardly think we need to go into the entire history," interrupted Father Max. "All you need to know is that mages, as we know them today, originated in the Roman Empire and magery spread throughout Europe during this time, growing in popularity even among the pagan peoples as far west as Britain and Ireland."

"How is this a shorter story than mine was going to be?" scolded Father Nicolas. "Look, in the ninth century, the Vikings invaded the British Isles, bringing witches with them."

"Many of the witches stayed there, rather than returning to Scandinavia with their boats," added Father Max, glowering at Father Nicolas.

Father Nicolas ignored his partner, continuing as though he hadn't spoken. "Witches began to spread throughout Europe, often clashing with mages."

"Mages, particularly those connected with the Church, began to out witches to the general population, often exaggerating the extent of their magic and fabricating intentions of evildoing," added Father Max.

"Which started the witch hunts of the middle ages," said Father Nicolas, stepping forward to stand slightly in front of Father Max.

Father Max reached forward and pulled Father Nicolas aside."Which made the witches, understandably, hate mages even more, and they began to actively fight against mages, attacking monasteries, nunneries, Church libraries, and so on."

"And the rest is history," said Father Nicolas quickly. He turned and gave Father Max a triumphant grin.

There was a loaded pause as the two bishops locked eyes.

Trevor glanced at Sister Margaret, who seemed to be holding in laughter. He cleared his throat. "Thank you. That was very illuminating. You are both excellent storytellers."

Father Nicolas turned and beamed at Trevor. "Young man, you will make a fabulous diplomat. Now, we would like to use this summit, this joining together in the same harmonious organization of magical beings, to begin to mend fences, as it were. We would like you to approach the witch delegations with offers of alliance and you will be given complete power of negotiation."

"Give them whatever they want, essentially," said Father Max. "We want the witches on our side, we want them to stop attacking our strongholds, and ideally, we'd like more of them in our employ."

Trevor dutifully wrote this down on the notebook in front of him.

"Dragons," said Father Nicolas. "Another group of cryptids to whom we may owe some reparations."

"St. George?" suggested Sister Margaret.

"Among others," said Father Max. "Much of the history there is lost. The dragons have been friendly so far. So don't bring it up if they don't. But if they do, we are, again, prepared to negotiate, and you will, once more, be given full discretionary powers."

"And what do we want from dragons?" asked Trevor, pencil poised.

"Their good will, essentially," said Father Nicolas. "And information as well. It seems that dragons hold the respiratory of much of cryptid history. We would like to know more about cryptids and the collective."

Sister Margaret raised her hand. "Is that all they hold? What about artifacts?"

Father Max stepped forward, peering intently at her from beneath his formidable eyebrows. "What do you know, young lady?"

"That is between me and my Mother Superior," she said.

Trevor looked back and forth between the two, holding his breath.

Finally, Father Max nodded shortly. "Fair enough. I will not ask for the secrets of your order."

"As it so happens," said Father Nicolas, smoothly. "The dragons do hold many artifacts of both cryptid and human origin. If you'd like to look into that, we certainly won't stop you."

Sister Margaret sat back in her chair, a thoughtful look on her face. She caught Trevor's eye, and he raised an eyebrow. She shook her head minutely.

"Moving on," said Father Max. "Unicorns."

"We would love to add some unicorns to our payroll," said Father Nicolas. "They will be most helpful in our own WML department. Additionally, we'd like to negotiate passage through some of their territories and maybe even permission to expand our library system into them."

"And Aurora," said Father Max. "Our understanding is that the two of you have some experience with them?"

Trevor shrugged. "More with the organizations they sprang from."

Father Nicolas bounced up and down on the balls of his feet. "I've heard rumors, but never actually knew what happened to you all last year."

Trevor exchanged a glance with Sister Margaret. "It's kind of a long story," he said.

"I do love a good long story!" Father Nicolas pulled up a chair and sat down at the table across from Sister Margaret, leaning his chin on his hands and looking back and forth between the two with an expectant look on his face.

"Well," said Sister Margaret. "It all started with the Auditors."

"Actually, it started with my friend, Tillie," said Trevor. "At least for us."

"Right." Sister Margaret nodded vigorously. "As you know, it is largely believed in the mage world as a whole that a mage can only practice one of the three disciplines. Can only be a speller, a seer, or a stitcher."

"I always thought that before I joined the Church," said Father Max. "I have now studied the three, but have chosen still to mainly focus on my primary discipline."

"As it turns out, the source of that fallacy was a mostly self-contained secret society called the Auditors," said Trevor. "Which had taken upon itself the mission of wiping out any outside mages who use multiple disciplines."

Father Nicolas made a tsking noise with his tongue. "You'd think people could just mind their own business, wouldn't you?"

Trevor shrugged. "Long story short, Tillie was a seer, and she started spelling and stitching. The Auditors caught wind, came after her. Her sister and I went looking for her, stumbled across the whole world of magery, which we were previously unaware of, and ended up embroiled in a fight against the entire organization."

"My convent got involved when an influential local mage put out a call for warriors to fight against the injustice," put in Sister Margaret. "We ended up working with a couple of other societies who had good reason to go against the Auditors. Aurora is made up of the remnants of those groups."

"So you've worked closely with the mages at the top of Aurora," said Father Max.

Trevor nodded.

"Excellent," said Father Nicolas, rising to his feet once again, a broad smile on his face. "We're looking for mutual aid agreements with them, as well as non-interference in political spheres. Do you think you can get that?"

"We'll do our best," said Sister Margaret.

Trevor jotted down a few more notes as Father Max moved on to the next slide:

Avoid Merfolk
- *Merfolk are rumored to be Bad News*

- *Most deaths at past summits were caused by merfolk*
- *Don't try to negotiate with them until we're more established in the collective*
- *They are not happy that humans have been invited to join the collective*
- *Just stay away from them*

Father Max raised his eyebrows and regarded Trevor and Sister Margaret. "Just stay away from merfolk," he reiterated.

"Got it." Trevor dutifully wrote that down as well.

Chapter 6: Sister Margaret

After the bishops' presentation, a Scholar Mage Librarian named Holly came in for another presentation, this one all about the various known species of cryptids in alphabetical order, including customs, fighting styles, and how the reality seemed to compare with the lore.

"And that is the last of them," she concluded, the screen going black as she snapped her laptop closed over the slide on werewolves. "Any questions?"

"Yeah," said Sister Margaret, tracing circles on her temples. "How is it possible that we know so fucking little about all of these cryptids? Two hours of slides and you used the phrase, *and we really don't know for sure, but we think...* way too many times for my comfort."

Holly shrugged. "We're hoping you'll be able to fill in a lot of those gaps after the summit and continue to do so as you work with the cryptids more."

"I'm sure you're doing your best." Trevor's voice was mild, but the look he shot Sister Margaret was full of reproach.

She sighed. "Sorry. I'm just not one for sitting still and absorbing information."

"Understood." Holly's smile was sympathetic. "The good news is that you have time to break for lunch before your next presentation." She glanced down at the notebook in front of her. "Be back in this room at two o'clock and I'll be giving a complete history of everything we know about what goes on at these summits. There will be even more gaps in knowledge in that one than the last."

Sister Margaret followed Trevor out of the room.

"Join me for a quick bite at Del Panino?" he suggested.

She shook her head, which was starting to feel like it was stuffed with cotton and far too much knowledge. "I need to process."

"Fair enough. See you in a hour." Trevor started off down the hallway, and Sister Margaret turned in the other direction, jogging back toward her order's headquarters.

She headed straight for the second floor of the large stone building, peering through the windows into a few rooms as she walked down the hallway. Finally, in the third sparring room she checked, she saw one of her sisters alone, doing some stretching exercises.

Sister Margaret knocked on the door and waved to Sister Renalda through the window.

Sister Renalda grinned at her and opened the door. "Feel like getting your ass kicked?" the other woman taunted.

"Hardly," Sister Margaret snorted. She walked into the padded room and grabbed two practice swords from the rack by the door, hefting them to check that their weight was comparable to her own twin short swords.

She discarded one and selected another, swishing it through the air. Satisfied, Sister Margaret turned back toward Sister Renalda and activated her seer powers. "Got some real aggression I need to work through today."

Sister Renalda bared her teeth, and lifted a wooden version of the deadly one-handed flail that was her own weapon of choice.

The two women circled each other warily. A flail was an unusual weapon, and Sister Margaret always enjoyed the challenge of going up against it. Especially in the hands of Sister Renalda, who was an absolute genius with it.

Add to that Sister Renalda's skills with her own discipline of magery, and—

Sister Margaret forced herself to focus as her seer sight showed her Sister Renalda's first move, a combination of weapon-work and use of her magical stitching powers. A moment later, she swerved to avoid the flail as it swung toward her head, then immediately wheeled around as Sister Renalda disappeared from where she'd been standing, reappearing directly behind Sister Margaret, her foot raised to kick her forward.

Instead, Sister Margaret skipped to her left, using the action to slash toward Sister Renalda's midsection with one sword and stab the other toward her opponent's throat.

Sister Renalda evaded both swords and stitched herself back to her original position, but closer to Sister Margaret, attempting to wrap the flail's chain around Sister Margaret's neck.

Warned by her seer sight, Sister Margaret took three running steps forward, swinging back around again to intercept the flail at the intersection of her two swords.

Before she could twist to disarm her opponent entirely, the other woman used a gesture to move her flail magically from her left hand to her right.

Sister Margaret stabbed one of her swords toward Sister Renalda's right hand, and Sister Renalda dropped the newly recovered flail with a curse, tucking her body and diving into a roll just in time to avoid Sister Margaret's other sword, which was heading for her throat.

Sister Renalda was moving too fast for Sister Margaret's seer sight to effectively give her the future, so she switched it off, relying instead on her fighting instincts.

"Heard you're getting some kind of promotion," said Sister Renalda as she dodged one of Sister Margaret's swords and blocked the other with the shaft of her flail, punching forward afterward toward Sister Margaret's belly.

Sister Margaret danced backward and spun around, out of range of Sister Renalda's weapon, then lunged forward, crossing her swords at Sister Renalda's throat, only to find the other woman had stitched out again. "Not a promotion, exactly," she said, whirling around again and landing a flurry of blows on Sister Renalda, forcing her backward with her flail swinging wildly. "Just an unusual assignment."

Sister Renalda stitched herself away again, this time all the way back toward the wall, out of Sister Margaret's reach, then immediately back again to directly behind Sister Margaret.

Sister Margaret staggered as the flail's head caught her in the back. She turned it into a low spin, slashing at Sister Renalda's legs.

"Mother Eleanor seemed pleased about it anyway," said Sister Renalda, dancing backward.

Sister Margaret pressed her advantage, aiming for Sister Renalda's hands again, this time focusing on her stitching hand. She landed a chopping blow right on the other sister's wrist. "That's disabling," she crowed. "No more stitching."

"Fair enough," Sister Renalda rushed at her, forcing her back again. Her flail struck Sister Margaret in the chest, hard enough to knock her on her ass.

She was up on her feet again in an instant. "She gave me a secondary task, actually, but I'm not sure if I'm at liberty to divulge it," said Sister Margaret, circling her opponent carefully, looking for an opening.

Sister Renalda was favoring her left side, respecting the premise that in true combat, Sister Margaret's blow would have severely injured her.

"The sword," said Sister Renalda. "She told me, actually. I have some expertise on the matter, after all."

"You do?" Sister Margaret saw her chance and danced forward, ending up with swords crossed at Sister Renalda's throat.

"Yield," said Sister Renalda, raising her hands.

Sister Margaret grinned and lowered her swords. "What kind of expertise?"

"I'm the one who found the text about the sword that led us to believe it might be in the hands of the dragons," said Sister Renalda. "Back when I was the order's archivist. An illuminated manuscript that hinted at the existence of dragons and that this one rogue sister had made a deal with them and that the timing coincided with the disappearance of the sword from the order's vault."

"Fascinating," said Sister Margaret.

"There's more," said Sister Renalda, dropping her practice flail on the weapons rack. "The reason I was brought back to Rome last year. I gather when cryptids first came forward, Mother Eleanor remembered that we had texts that dealt with them, and set a few of our more scholarly number to pull them out and seek out more. On a hunch, Sister Chantal searched through some more . . . ordinary tomes from Saint Joan's time."

Sister Margaret raised her eyebrows as she began to pace the room, focusing on cooling down her body and letting her heart rate gradually slow. "I take it they weren't all ordinary after all?"

"No, they were," said Sister Renalda. "Just diaries of people who might have come into contact with the blessed warrior. Nobody special, really. But one of them was a mage-blacksmith."

Sister Margaret stopped moving, her eyes widening as she stared at Sister Renalda. "And you think this blacksmith may have crafted Saint Joan's sword?"

"Maybe," said Sister Renalda. "The manuscript is in terrible condition; Mother Eleanor has me restoring it now. In a few weeks, it may be ready to start analyzing. We may actually be able to unlock the secrets of the sword."

"Secrets?" Sister Margaret dropped to the floor for some stretches. "What kind of secrets?"

"Well, we know it was a magic sword, of course," said Sister Renalda. "And of course the making and use of magical weaponry is knowledge that has been lost to us."

"But if we have a specific sword and the memoir of that sword's maker...." Sister Margaret breathed.

"Exactly," said Sister Renalda. "We may be able to put together some of the pieces and regain those skills."

Chapter 7: Trevor

The next couple of weeks went by in a blur. There were crash courses taught by anyone the dicastery could get its hands on who had had any actual contact with cryptids, which was unfortunately not very many.

And Trevor couldn't help but notice that a lot of what was "taught" to them seemed to be pure speculation.

Finally, the day of their departure arrived. Getting to Antarctica wasn't a question of simply getting on a plane in Rome and then getting off at a dragon city.

First they took a cab to the airport, where they used their Vatican-issued credentials to walk right past security, armed to the teeth, and hop on a private jet to New Zealand's South Island.

Next, they rented a car and drove to a little-known cove all the way down at the southern tip, where they found a small airfield that looked essentially abandoned.

But on the airstrip was a tiny plane with a staircase leading up to it.

He glanced at Sister Margaret, and she shrugged back at him. "These are the coordinates they gave us," she confirmed, looking at her phone. "I guess that's our ride."

Trevor unbuckled his seat belt and got out of the car, walking around to the trunk to gather up all of their luggage.

Much of it was disguised to look like scientific gear, as they'd be posing as microbiologists, there to study an unusual waterfall near the dragon city.

Blood Falls was aptly named, as the water that flowed over the snow was a brilliant scarlet color. Just behind the falls, the city of M'Tainla was hidden from the view of any humans intrepid enough to venture into the frozen continent.

He left the luggage piled up behind the car and strode toward the airstrip, Sister Margaret right behind him.

As Trevor stepped off the mobile staircase into the tiny chartered plane, his breath caught. Standing in front of him, face wreathed in a sunny smile, was somebody who couldn't be anything but a bigfoot.

"Hello!" said the bigfoot, who was clad only in a thick pelt of dark brown fur, stooping slightly in the cramped cabin. The plane was all one open space, with the controls on one end and three rows of three seats each behind them. "My name is Marian, and I have the very great honor of taking the pair of you over to Antarctica."

Sister Margaret strode forward and grasped Marian's hand — or was it a paw?

"It's very nice to meet you, Marian. I'm Sister Margaret and this is Trevor and you are the very first cryptid either of us has ever met, unless you count witches, and there's some debate now about whether they're cryptids or humans."

"Well, you're the first humans I've ever had a conversation with, unless you count witches," said Marian. "So, I guess that makes us about even. Seen a good few of you from afar, through the woods, but never actually met any."

She stepped toward Trevor and extended her furry appendage to him as well.

He took it, shaking it firmly. It was very handlike with five fingers and a palm, just like a human, but fuzzy. "Are we the only ones on board?" he asked, looking around.

"Yes," said Marian. She turned and sat down, flicking a few knobs as she continued speaking. "Dragonlord Ch'etwime felt that it would best that mages be brought in without any cryptid passengers. I guess he figured that I was enough of a shock for you."

"You're not very shocking," said Trevor with a smile. "I was expecting to be much more shocked, to be frank."

He looked around and, spotting a clear space in the corner of the plane, moved his hand in a stitching gesture, bringing the stack of luggage neatly into the space with his magery.

"Well, I'll have to work on that for the rest of the humans, then." Marian laughed. "Maybe instead of English, I could address them with a series of roars and growls and see if they try to communicate back in kind."

"I think Coyote would just take that in stride," said Sister Margaret. "And Chameleon would probably want to record the sounds and try to find patterns to decode your language."

"Coyote takes everything in stride," Trevor agreed. "We don't know any of the other mages, though, so I don't know how they'd take it."

"Most humans would freak the fuck out," said Sister Margaret. "But if they're coming to the summit, they're mages, and presumably high level ones, and if they're smart, they'll have studied up on cryptids the same way we did and they'd know in advance that you don't actually communicate that way."

That was true. Trevor had known already that bigfoots spoke the same languages as humans. This one had a very American accent and spoke excellent English, so she was probably a Sasquatch from North America. He knew that bigfoots were spread throughout the world, going by a variety of names depending on their region. Yetis, for example, lived in the Himalayan mountains.

"Better buckle up," said Marian, nodding toward the seats behind her. "It can get a little bit turbulent."

Trevor and Sister Margaret took her advice, sitting down in the first row with a seat between them.

Trevor tightened his lap belt and closed his eyes as the plane took off. He could handle dire battles, but something about being in a small metal tube that shook as it took off spooked the hell out of him.

After a few bumpy minutes, their course smoothed out, and Marian stood up, walking straight over to a tiny kitchenette against the back of the plane.

Trevor twisted in his seat to watch as she reached into the tiny fridge, pulling out a quart of milk, which she poured into three chipped white mugs, adding a powder before placing them into a microwave. "I always make hot chocolate when I have a small group like this," she said. "Humans can have chocolate, right?"

"Yes," said Trevor. "That sounds lovely." He leaned against the arm of the empty seat beside him, watching as the bigfoot swayed back and forth in an odd but dignified dance.

"Werewolves can't, you know. Something about how it interacts with their nervous system," said Marian. "And salashifters don't like it. It's the strangest thing. How can you not like chocolate?"

"Salashifters," said Sister Margaret. "Those are the fire elementals from Africa, right?"

"From Ethiopia," said Trevor. He wondered what his mother, who had been born and raised in Ethiopia, would think if he told her that a race of shape shifting lizard people with fire magic also called her native country home.

"That's right." The microwave dinged and Marian pulled it open, taking the mugs back out one at a time and giving them each a quick stir with a spoon. "Now, I won't say another thing against salashifters as a whole — only met one or two I didn't care for -- but there's something very suspicious about an entire species who doesn't like chocolate, don't you think?"

Trevor lifted his hands, palms out. "I will reserve judgment until I actually meet one."

"That's fair," said Marian. "Probably a good policy."

"So, werewolves are closely related to dogs, then," said Sister Margaret. "Dogs aren't supposed to have chocolate either."

Marian laughed. "Don't let one of them hear you say that. It's a bit of a sore topic. Now, one of my best friends is a werewolf, and I will say that overall they are a very rational people. But they do NOT like being compared to dogs. And to be fair, we bigfoots aren't fond of being compared to gorillas."

Trevor sighed. "There's just so much we don't know about cryptids. I just know I'm going to say something stupid and fuck this up entirely."

"I'm sure you'll be fine," said Marian. "They wouldn't have sent you if they didn't think you were the right mages for the job, right?"

Trevor experienced a twinge of doubt. He couldn't shake the feeling that there was more to this assignment than Cardinal Neubacher had let on. He glanced at Sister Margaret and was less than reassured to see that she looked slightly uncomfortable too.

As the awkward silence lengthened, Marian waved her hands. "I'm sure you'll be fine," she repeated. She carried the hot chocolates toward them on a black plastic tray, taking her time, balancing the mugs carefully as she took small steps, pausing between each one. "You seem like nice, down-to-earth humans, and honestly cryptids don't know that much about humans either. If you say anything that offends someone, just claim it's a human thing. Happens all the time at these summits. There's so many different species there, nobody can keep all the customs straight. You get a salashifter and a unicorn together, and the salashifter says something about horns, the unicorn gets in a tizzy, challenges the salashifter to a duel, next thing you know everyone realizes it was all a misunderstanding, nobody has to fight, it's all good."

Trevor frowned, trying to sort all of that out in his mind.

"A duel?" said Sister Margaret. "Are there many duels at these things?"

Marian finally reached them and stooped, offering the tray. "You never do know. Killing at a summit is frowned upon. Certain cultures will absolutely try to duel you, like the mer. Others will just attack off the cuff, but with those, they're usually not about fighting to the death. Merfolk and unicorns are the fiercest, and dueling is such a big part of mer culture that if you tried to get out of a properly challenged duel, you'd be up in front of the Cryptid Court for cultural suppression, which is a serious crime."

Trevor cupped his hot chocolate in both hands. He hesitated, but decided he felt comfortable enough with Marian to ask. "We were told that the merfolk weren't happy about mages being present at the summit this year. Is that true?"

The brow ridges on Marian's furry face lifted as she set down the empty tray, taking a sip from her own mug before she responded. "I don't know a lot about the merfolk myself, to be honest. This will be the first year in a while that the merfolk will be sending any delegations to the summit."

"Do you think they decided to come specifically because they were unhappy about humans being included?" said Sister Margaret.

"There are rumors to that effect," said Marian, her voice colored with reluctance.

"Any advice for avoiding trouble with them?" asked Trevor.

"Don't challenge them to a duel," said Marian with a shrug. "And don't accept if they try to challenge you. My understanding is that there is no shame in declining, even among the merfolk. But if you try to weasel out of it once you've accepted, then your life is forfeit, and since that is their law, the Cryptid Court would be unable to save you."

"Okay," said Sister Margaret. "No mer duels. Got it."

"Any other species we should be concerned about, in your opinion?" asked Trevor.

"Don't try to keep up with a bigfoot's alcohol consumption," said Marian. "Don't try to fit a kallanpa amaru into a binary pronoun – always use they/them."

"Kallanpa amaru," said Trevor. "Those are the mushroom people?"

"Yes." Marian continued. "Let's see. . . . Don't try to touch a unicorn unless they expressly invite you; that's rude. The aqrabuamelu can be a bit touchy, so try to be extra polite around them. Oh, and don't try to rescue the humans who are there with the vampires. They don't like that."

Sister Margaret raised an eyebrow. "The humans don't or the vampires don't?"

"Both," said Marian. "Oh, and—" she hesitated. "I probably shouldn't tell you this, but what the hell? I like you guys, and I'm not a big fan of, well, I happen to know that the witches sent a particular representative who hates mages and is planning to start some shit with you. Don't rise to the bait. I know witches and mages don't always get along."

"We've been warned about Matriarch Monin already," said Sister Margaret. "Current plan is to just steer clear of her. Our instructions, in fact, are to do our best to bury the hatchet with witches once and for all. Time for this fucking feud to end."

Marian cocked her head, studying Sister Margaret with a small smile. "You know, when they told me one of you was a nun, you're not what I pictured."

Sister Margaret grinned. "Sister, not nun. There is a difference. But yeah, I get that a lot."

Chapter 8: Sister Margaret

Sister Margaret enjoyed the flight into Antarctica. Marian was a delight to talk to, and made a mean cup of cocoa. And she didn't share Trevor's fear of bumpy flying.

But as she and Trevor stepped off the plane and onto the diminutive tarmac of the small research station at the edge of the Ross Sea, her mind filled with doubt again.

All of Marian's warnings kept swirling around in her head. It had felt like she'd just been cautioning them over and over to tread lightly, step around the feelings of various cryptids. Stepping lightly was not Sister Margaret's strong suit.

Maybe she had been wrong to accept this assignment. Maybe she was just going to be a thorn in Trevor's side. She had no doubt Trevor would be a fantastic diplomat.

He was suave, kind, empathetic, and thoughtful. He spoke carefully and deliberately and would never accidentally start any kind of feud or duel.

She was probably going to say something asinine or take offense at something completely innocuous and blow up and ruin everything. It was probably too late now, though.

Sister Margaret glanced backward and saw that the plane was already taking off again. Definitely too late.

Marian gave her a final wave from the cockpit, and Sister Margaret waved back before turning to observe her surroundings.

She had now officially been to all seven continents, every single one of them, in the past year. Not bad for someone who had never left St. Louis before that.

She hurried to catch up to Trevor, who was already heading toward the little hut where they would supposedly be able to catch a helicopter to the edge of Lake Bonney.

She hurried to catch up.

Chapter 9: Trevor

As Trevor hurried toward McMurdo Station, he tried not to panic. Maybe he had made a huge mistake in coming here. Sister Margaret would be able to handle all of the minefields Marian had mentioned.

Sister Margaret wasn't afraid of duels. Trevor just knew he was going to spend the next month so petrified of starting a duel that he'd either accidentally blurt out all the things he wasn't supposed to say, thus starting a duel anyway, or he'd just clam up and never get anything done out of sheer terror.

He glanced back at his partner. She had paused to wave at Marian as the plane took off, standing there looking cool as a cucumber, as usual. Nothing ever seemed to bother her.

Trevor turned back toward the station. Nothing for it but to keep on going. Maybe a little of Sister Margaret's bravery would rub off on him.

A heavily bundled person of indeterminate gender was walking out of the station and down the tarmac toward them.

Time to convince the other humans to give the pair of them a ride to Blood Falls. The dragons would meet them there.

Chapter 10: Sister Margaret

Sister Margaret whooped with pure joy, all misgivings forgotten as the helicopter swooped down toward the frozen lake below.

"First time in a chopper?" shouted the pilot over the noise of the blades as she continued to maneuver closer to the ground.

"Yes!" she called back. "It's wonderful!"

"Your colleague doesn't seem to be in agreement," the pilot laughed. She gestured toward Trevor, who was clutching at the arms of his chair.

"Sorry," shouted Trevor, his voice muffled a bit by the heavy scarf and ski mask he wore. "I just get a little motion sick."

The helicopter lurched and Trevor squeezed his eyes shut, hunching his shoulders.

"He'll be fine," Sister Margaret yelled. "He's dealt with much worse than a little turbulence."

"What are you two studying out here?" asked the pilot.

"Microbes," shouted Sister Margaret. "In the waterfall."

The pilot nodded, but didn't respond, focusing instead on bringing her vehicle the rest of the way down. She landed the helicopter about a hundred yards from the edge of the lake. "I'm not gonna turn her off," she called out. "Just toss your stuff on the ground and then be careful of the blades as you hop out. Keep low to the ground and drag your things a ways off so I can take off again."

"Sounds good!" Sister Margaret unbuckled her safety straps, slung her backpack over her shoulders, and tossed her two olive duffel bags toward the snow, jumping down after them, her body folded in half to keep low as she hauled the bags away from the chopper.

It felt strange to be able to bend so easily. Normally, her armor would have restricted a movement like that, but in her guise as an ordinary microbiologist, she was instead dressed in snow gear layered over street clothes.

She grinned at Trevor, who was right behind her, then realized he'd be unable to see her expression through the thick scarf wrapped around the lower half of her own face. The two of them went back for some weighted hard cases they'd brought along from Rome for the purpose of mimicking scientific equipment to cement their disguises.

Finally, all of their gear, real and bogus, was out of the way, and she stood back and waved to the helicopter pilot. The woman waved back and the chopper lifted back up, flying away toward the main base.

That helicopter ride had really lifted Sister Margaret's mood. She felt exhilarated and ready to take on the world. She glanced at her partner.

She couldn't see his face, of course, but Trevor's body language told her he was still a little shaken.

"You gonna be okay?" she asked.

"Yeah, fine," he said. "I don't know why that got me so rattled. I'm fine on airplanes. Mostly. The big ones anyway. Once they're in the air. It was just so bumpy, though, the entire time, not just little bits like on a plane, and the wind buffeting at us the whole time."

"Yeah, it was awesome." Sister Margaret laughed. "I can't wait to do it again after the summit!"

She sobered a little. First they had to survive a month of interacting with cryptids. And before that, they needed to get to the dragon city.

"Somebody's supposed to be coming to get us, right?" said Trevor, looking around at the desolate, icy wasteland.

Sister Margaret shaded her eyes, more out of habit than any other reason; her tinted goggles did an excellent job of dimming the sun. She scanned the horizon, pausing to look at the red waterfall in the distance. "Would you look at that?" she breathed. "It really does look like blood."

"That's so cool," said Trevor. He rummaged in his backpack and pulled out a set of binoculars, peering out at Blood Falls, across the lake. "And the dragon city is supposed to be right behind, isn't it?"

"Can you see it?" asked Sister Margaret. "What does it look like?"

"I don't think — wait, yes!" She could hear the excited smile in his voice. "It's beautiful!"

"Can I see?" Sister Margaret held out her hand and Trevor placed the binoculars in it.

"Orient yourself to the falls," he instructed, "and then look a little to the left and beyond."

Sister Margaret put them to her eyes and the blood red waterfall sprang into focus. It was breathtaking and strange, and she spent a moment staring at it before she remembered that she was supposed to be looking to its left.

She turned her head slightly and gasped. Coming straight toward her through the air were two of the fiercest, most majestic creatures she'd ever seen.

Chapter 11: Trevor

At Sister Margaret's gasp, Trevor spun around. He had been scanning the landscape, familiarizing himself with a continent he had never in a million years thought he would be visiting.

"What? What's wrong?" he demanded.

Sister Margaret lowered the binoculars. "Nothing is wrong," she said. She pointed upward and toward the falls. "Our escort is coming."

Trevor grabbed the binoculars she offered him and scanned the sky. "Holy fuck," he breathed. "The pictures just don't do them justice."

The dragons were pale blue, almost white, which made them difficult to see against the cloudy sky. Their smooth wings were spread wide as they rode the air, barely moving at all, giving the dragons an almost lazy appearance.

Their mouths were open wide, sharp teeth on display, prompting Trevor to wonder what the dragons' diet consisted of. They were obviously meat-eaters, but what meat was available in Antarctica? Penguins seemed very small for someone so large. Seals, maybe? Or perhaps even whales.

Trevor lowered the binoculars and realized that the dragons were close enough now that he could see them without the boost, albeit just as specks in the distance. "You don't suppose we'll be expected to ride the dragons, do you?" he asked. That helicopter ride had been rough on his stomach, and he couldn't imagine riding dragonback would be better.

"That seems like it would be disrespectful," said Sister Margaret, doubtfully. "Dammit, I wish we'd had more time to learn about the cryptids!"

Trevor nodded. "I feel the same, but honestly, more time wouldn't have helped. There just wasn't that much material to study. The Vatican has only had a year to collect information, and much of that was spent negotiating treaties anyway, and it seemed like the only contact they'd really had with cryptids was with salashifters and kallanpa amaru. Nobody I talked to had ever met a dragon."

Trevor found himself grinning. It did feel good to be a pioneer, even if he had his doubts about his ability to pull this off.

He was about to meet a dragon!

"Wait until Sister Regina hears about this," said Sister Margaret. "She's going to shit herself with envy."

Trevor chuckled. "That's an image I could have done without."

The dragons were close enough now that he could see their shape, unaided by the binoculars.

"Damn, they are moving fast!" Sister Margaret observed. "Where do you think they're going to land?"

Trevor glanced around and pointed to a large, flat rock plateau nearby that seemed to have been cleared of ice and snow. "I bet that's their spot."

Sister Margaret turned to look. "Stands to reason. Come on, let's get our stuff up there." She unzipped one of her bags and pulled out an ice pick. "Good thing we let them pack us some tools back at the station."

Trevor nodded. "It would have been suspicious if we hadn't. I wonder how the non-humans get here; a unicorn can't very well show up at a research station with forged papers and ask to be choppered in."

"Maybe a unicorn can make the journey overland," said Sister Margaret. "And I'm sure Marian is fine with flying them over here. That's probably why there aren't very many seats in the plane. They need room for non-humanoid cryptids. Not sure how they'd get to New Zealand to begin with, though. Where do unicorns live again?"

"On wildlife preserves," said Trevor. "A lot of them in Africa, some in North and South America. Not as many in Asia and Europe. Lots in Australia, so they probably have a way to get to New Zealand. Maybe a cryptid-run ferry boat."

The two of them arrived at the base of the plateau. Trevor glanced behind him and saw that the dragons were almost upon them, and did in fact seem to be heading toward the flat landing area.

Sister Margaret had tied her bags to her waist and was already climbing. Trevor unpacked his ice picks and carefully watched Sister Margaret. He had never climbed a sheer ice cliff before. It looked very challenging. He shook his head; he wasn't really up for risking his life if he didn't have to.

Stowing the ice picks back in his bag, Trevor crouched, lacing his arms through the handles of both duffles. Then he moved his fingers in a stitching motion and teleported himself up to the plateau top, just in time to see Sister Margaret's face peeking up over the edge.

"Cheater," she said. She reached a hand out toward him and he dropped his bags, clasped her hand in his left and stitched her up with his right. "You might have mentioned you were planning to stitch before I put in all that effort."

"It was sort of a last-minute decision," he admitted.

Trevor felt a huge gust of wind and craned his head backward to see the two dragons hovering directly above. He carefully stepped back toward the edge to give them as much landing room as possible, Sister Margaret following suit.

The frigid wind was finding chinks in his layered snow gear, so he erected a mage shield directly in front of himself and Sister Margaret. He felt instantly warmer. Not warm, but warm*er*.

The dragons gracefully lowered themselves down. Despite the wind, they didn't seem to be using their wings much, and Trevor wondered if there was a magical component to their landing mechanics.

"Welcome!" the smaller of the two dragons boomed. They both towered over the humans, but Trevor estimated that this one was about seven feet tall and maybe ten feet long from snout to tail, while the other was probably eight feet tall and about twelve feet long. "I am Dragonlord Ph'Tyblon. This is my associate Dragonlord Kh'Wafleb, and we are honored to have been chosen to assist you, our first human guests for many years, to our summit in our fair city of M'Tainla at Blood Falls on the icy continent of Antarctica."

Trevor was relieved to see that the two dragons had a lot of distinguishing features. Aside from their size, they had varying eye colors and facial structures, and Dragonlord Ph'Tyblon had a patch of pale blue scales in the middle of his forehead, while Dragonlord Kh'Wafleb's cheeks were sprinkled with a dusting of pink scales, almost like a human might have freckles.

They both had a single large, curved horn emerging from the back of their necks and arching over the tops of their heads, which Trevor knew marked them as male. Females would have two tusklike horns on either side of their mouths.

This was particularly helpful, since *Dragonlord* was a unisex title given to any dragon over a certain age.

"Thank you, Dragonlords." Trevor bowed. He wasn't sure if that was really appropriate, but some kind of formal gesture of respect seemed warranted. Dragonlord Ph'Tyblon, at least, seemed to have a very ceremonial air about him. "I am Trevor Harper. My associate is Sister Margaret Herrera."

"Pleased to meet you," said Sister Margaret. She strode forward, extending a hand to the Dragonlord Ph'Tyblon, characteristically taking the less formal approach.

Dragonlord Ph'Tyblon daintily extended a large off-white talon toward her, and Sister Margaret lifted it up and down a couple of times. The process repeated with Dragonlord Kh'Wafleb.

Trevor stepped forward and shook the dragons' talons as well, feeling exceptionally awkward.

Sister Margaret seemed completely at ease. "So, how does this work?" she asked. "How will we get to the city?"

Dragonlord Kh'Wafleb turned his back and Trevor was relieved to see that, nestled among the spines on his back was a sort of sling with what appeared to be a small wheeled vehicle, rather than any kind of saddle or anything like that. They wouldn't have to fly on dragonback after all.

"We have these for many of the land-based cryptids," Dragonlord Ph'Tyblon explained as he slit the sling with his talon and shifted to allow the vehicle to slide to the ground. "It has wheels, but has also been imbued with witch magic to fly a couple feet over the snow, which is much more efficient. The wheels are just for emergencies or in case you run into any human scientists, which does happen on rare occasions. The bigfoots make them, like most cryptid technology."

"It's very easy to steer," added Dragonlord Kh'Wafleb, "Just aim for the waterfall, then take a left. You'll come to a mountain pass. Go through it, and there will be a road to follow once you get past the area where human scientists and explorers sometimes wander." As he spoke, he removed another magic cart from the other dragon's back. "We'll leave this one here for the group of salashifters who are scheduled to arrive soon."

"How do the salashifters get here?" asked Sister Margaret.

"Same way you did," said Dragonlord Kh'Wafleb. "Except they'll be choppered in from a different research station. We have to spread them out a bit so nobody gets suspicious. But it's easiest for anyone who can pass for human to use the network of researchers who are always around, at least the ones who don't live near any unicorns."

"There are a lot of cryptids who look human, aren't there?" asked Trevor. "Salashifters, kallanpa amaru, vampires, werewolves...."

"Oh, the Werewolves run in wolf form," said Dragonlord Ph'Tyblon. "And the kallanpa amaru can shift into any form, so they tend to just fly in as eagles or seagulls or some other large bird, actually."

Trevor approached the cart, which looked kind of like a cross between a Jeep and a miniature barge. It was black and had an open, boxy black frame. Silver spikes lined the frame and there didn't seem to be any room in the front or back for an engine. There was a tiny cargo area in the back and a pair of bucket seats on the front with a foot-high wall in front of the seats.

Attached to the front wall were two steering wheels, one in front of each seat, and there were two pedals in front of each seat as well.

He hefted his luggage into the cargo area.

Sister Margaret did the same and then used the spikes on the frame to haul herself up into the left-hand seat, which Trevor tended to think of as the driver's side. He vaulted into the other side, which was apparently designed for British drivers.

"Only one steering wheel will work at a time," said Dragonlord Ph'Tyblon. "Use whichever one you please."

"I'm driving," said Sister Margaret.

"Suits me," said Trevor. That would give him more of a chance to soak up the scenery. This frozen land really was beautiful. It wasn't as featureless as one might expect. Yes, there were vast, flat sheets of ice as far as the eye could see, but it was broken up with ice formations like the plateau they were on, the mountains in the distance, and of course the lake right in front of them with the surreal red waterfall just beyond.

Trevor murmured a Latin phrase and his hands glowed as the spell took effect, forming a domed shield over the open vehicle. With another murmured word, he conjured up a small flame and set it to hover between himself and his partner. A natural speller wouldn't need to vocalize the spells, but he was a natural stitcher, and while he was comfortable using the other two disciplines, they didn't come as easily.

The dome quickly heated up, and he dismissed the flame as the dragons took off once again. With a sigh of relief, he removed his heavy hat and scarf, rubbing his face and twisting his lips around. He wasn't used to fabric covering his face and while he understood it was necessary in this frigid country, it made his skin crawl.

As Sister Margaret studied the minimalist dashboard, something teased at Trevor's mind; something the dragon had said about . . . unicorns? Right. Cryptids who looked human, but didn't live near unicorns would go through human channels to get here.

What did they not know about unicorns? He sighed. Far too much, and the dragons seemed to assume they did know it.

Sister Margaret pushed a button next to the steering wheel and the car . . . sort of . . . came to life. That was the best way Trevor could think to describe it.

It didn't make a sound; there was no engine to rev. And it didn't even move.

But he could feel that something in its aura was now awake and ready to move.

"Well, that's creepy as fuck," said Sister Margaret. "I love it."

She pushed on one of her two pedals and the car smoothly lifted off the ground and moved forward — straight off the edge of the cliff.

Chapter 12: Sister Margaret

For the second time that day, Sister Margaret found herself howling with joy as she flew over the Antarctic landscape.

The odd little car zipped down the cliff face, a couple of feet in front of the sheer wall. As they neared the bottom of the drop, she prepared to hit the brakes, but before she had a chance, the car corrected itself from vertical to horizontal, following a curving line as it straightened itself out.

Sister Margaret glanced at Trevor as they flew across the frozen lake, hoping this wasn't as rough on him as the helicopter had been. At least it was smooth, rather than bumpy. Bumpiness seemed to be his main objection.

To her relief, his face wore a broad grin, similar to her own.

"This is fantastic!" she exclaimed. "Don't you think?"

"Fuck, yes!" he replied. "How do we get this technology?"

"We live in Rome," she replied. "You want the same people who tear around on scooters to have access to this?"

Trevor laughed. "Probably not. But I want it! So fast! So smooth!"

Sister Margaret turned her attention back to the landscape speeding past. She adjusted the steering wheel slightly, turning to her right, away from the dragon city and toward the red falls across the lake. She wanted to get a closer look at this strange phenomenon, and the dragonlord had said that this was the way to get to the road anyway.

As they skimmed over the lake, Sister Margaret glanced down and noticed a long, skinny shape under the ice.

"Is that a shark?" said Trevor, pointing at the same shape. "That can't be right, can it? This is a lake. Isn't it fresh water?"

Sister Margaret shrugged. "It certainly looks like a shark. I don't know anything about Antarctic marine life. Maybe they're seals? What do seals look like when they're in the water?"

"There's another one!" Trevor gestured as a second shape appeared beside them.

Frowning, Sister Margaret watched them closely. They seemed to be following their vessel. How would a shark or a seal even sense their existence? They weren't touching the water or even the ice on top. This seemed like very strange behavior for an animal.

As they approached the waterfall, the ice began to break up a little, showing the bare water in between floes. Maybe they'd be able to get a better look.

Sister Margaret slowed the car down as she switched on her seer sight, hoping to see if there was any magic involved or if they were about to do anything unpleasant.

She couldn't see past Trevor's shield, which glowed brightly to her mage sight. She could usually see through shields, but there must be something about the functionality of this one, designed to keep heat in, that made it heavier. "Do you mind lowering that, just for a moment?" she asked. "I can't see."

He sighed, but put his mask back on and dismissed the shield.

Even through her layers, the cold hit her like a truck once the barrier was down. She ignored it, and as Trevor wound his scarf around his neck, she turned her seer eyes on the shapes below again.

The entities under the water still looked somehow blurry, and the air seemed thicker, the future murky.

These were definitely not sharks.

Sister Margaret wished she had her armor on, feeling vulnerable without it, but at least the cold-weather gear was nicely padded and had also given her plenty of opportunities to hide weapons. She kept her right hand on the wheel, flicking her left wrist at just the right angle, and a throwing star fell down into her hand, ready to be deployed if anything hostile came up out of the water.

Beside her, she saw Trevor lifting his own hands, ready to stitch. She kept her seer sight on in case it decided to start working properly.

Lowering her foot gently onto the brake, Sister Margaret slowed down further, almost to a crawl. She watched the shapes in the water carefully. They had formed a wall between their vehicle and the waterfall, still below the water, so not barring the way forward.

But Sister Margaret knew that if she had been in charge of whoever they were, and she had been feeling unfriendly, she would simply wait until her opponent was above and then move to disable the vehicle.

Since she wasn't in charge of them, and was in fact, the opponent in question, that wasn't going to happen.

Instead, she waited until the last minute and then suddenly swung the steering wheel hard to the left, spinning the hovering barge in a tight circle and then slamming on the brakes so that they stopped short, facing their ambushers.

She spared a moment to wonder how exactly a hovercraft's brakes acted so quickly with no ground to give it traction, but then again, it did seem to run on magic, so maybe that wasn't something she could really question until she had a chat with a bigfoot mage. Were they called mages?

Sister Margaret pulled her focus from planning out an imaginary meeting with cryptid mage-mechanics to the present moment. She smiled grimly. She'd been right about one thing anyway.

These weren't sharks. They had popped halfway up out of the water and they sure looked unfriendly.

"Merfolk," Trevor murmured.

She nodded. Not that she'd needed the information. She'd seen the drawings of merfolk in a few of their various shapes during the debriefings too. They hadn't really prepared her for the reality.

Merfolk in real life looked nothing like how they were depicted in movies. For one thing, they weren't any kind of half-and-half situation. There was no dividing line between fish and human, and in fact there was very little human resemblance at all.

Their bodies and faces were covered in shimmery scales like a fish, and their coloring was all fishlike as well. One of the two merfolk facing them was a beautiful forest green shade and the other was bright orange with white swirls all over.

Both had fins like a shark, and also arms with humanlike hands. Their torsos, which were about three feet long, tapered into a shoulder-less neck, which was topped with a head that did look sort of humanish, but with a forward-facing snout instead of a nose and mouth.

Their chests were smooth and flat with no hint of navels, breasts, or nipples.

Sister Margaret spotted gills on the sides of their necks, but they lay flat and still, and she noticed their chests rising and falling as though they breathed air through lungs.

Their snouts gaped open, showing an impressive array of sharp teeth, and their fingers were tipped with long, black outstretched talons. Slung across their backs were large tridents with wickedly sharp tips.

She could see short legs treading water under the surface and both of them wore kilt-like garments that appeared to be made of intricately woven seaweed.

Sister Margaret wished her seer sight was working. She couldn't see anything in the future, and in fact there was an odd shimmer in the air around the merfolk, as though they were surrounded by a light, very localized fog.

She switched off her seer sight and the fog went away. That was a neat trick.

Sister Margaret readied her throwing star, carefully grasping it between her thumb and mittened fingers in a way that wouldn't tear at the fabric and expose her hand to the cold.

"Listen," said Trevor slowly, before she could act. He stood up and raised his hands, in a gesture of good will. Of course, who knew if merfolk used the same kind of body language as humans.

Sister Margaret was not going to count on that. She kept her throwing star ready, and in fact loosened the dagger at her waist as well, ready to draw with her right hand.

"We don't want any trouble," Trevor continued. "We're here for the summit, same as you, right?"

"We're not at the summit yet," hissed the orange mer. The mer's voice sounded like a cartoon snake, slithery and menacing. "The rules don't apply just yet."

"Water is *our* territory," said the green mer. This mer spoke a little lower, but still quite hissy.

"And so many accidents can happen on the water," said the first mer.

"We'd love to talk this out," said Trevor, his voice steady. "I understand that the merfolk were not pleased that we were invited here. Maybe we can work out our differences and find some common—" he paused. "That is, some common seas."

Right. *Common ground* was a distinctly land-based expression. That's why Trevor was the diplomat. Sister Margaret's hand tightened on her knife hilt. She had talents of her own.

The orange mer's arm moved lightening fast, grasping the trident from its sling and swinging it around to point it at her and Trevor.

Sister Margaret moved just as quickly, flinging the throwing star at the mer's shoulder, carefully aiming for an area that would hurt but not kill, at least not on most creatures.

She hoped it wouldn't kill the mer; that would be a diplomatic nightmare before the summit even began.

The orange mer hissed in pain, trident falling away, although she could see that it was attached to the mer's hand via a cord of some sort.

Sister Margaret instinctively reached for the tiny grappling hook she always kept on her bandolier, third pocket from the bottom, but the bandolier was neatly packed away in a duffel bag in the back of the car, and she remembered too late that the grappling hook was stowed today in a pouch on the side of her boot instead.

The mer had already retrieved the trident by the time she remembered that, so instead she let another throwing star fall into her right hand and readied it.

"First blood is yours," said the green mer in an oddly formal cadence, as though this was a ritual of the fight.

Sister Margaret knew they hadn't been challenged to a duel, which involved the throwing of fish heads, so this must be some other kind of ceremonial battle that hadn't been covered in their crash courses.

That meant there were rules, which was good. Then again, she didn't know the rules, which was bad.

It was possible that there were words she could say that would stop them from trying to kill them. But what if she said something and it was exactly the wrong thing, and would give them the right to imprison them or even execute them as soon as they set foot in the summit?

She snuck a glance at Trevor as she waited for a hint to the next step of the fight. Dammit, she couldn't see any of his face under that fucking mask and scarf. No clue as to whether he knew what was going on or had any kind of plan.

He stood straight and tall, his hands still raised, but she couldn't even see if he was preparing a stitch or had any spells going, with his hands hidden by his mittens.

"There will be no more blood," said Trevor.

Sister Margaret held her breath. That was a pretty good guess. She watched the merfolk closely.

They remained still for a moment, simply bobbing up and down in the water, the orange mer holding the trident, the other with empty hands.

Then the green mer finally spoke again. "So be it. If you will not give us satisfaction, we will leave you be for now."

Before Sister Margaret could breathe a sigh of relief, however, the orange mer let the trident loose again, throwing it straight toward them.

Trevor raised his shield again, doming it over the car, but the trident buried itself in the front of the car, below the shield.

Fast as an eel, the cord snapped taut, and the orange mer retrieved the trident, tearing away a panel from the vehicle's front.

Without another word, the merfolk dove back below the lake waters and swam away.

Chapter 13: Trevor

Trevor sat down abruptly and let out his breath in a giant whoosh. "I guess I said the right thing," he said.

"I guess you did!" Sister Margaret reached over and clapped him on the back. "Well done, sir! I wasn't sure we were getting out of that one with our objectives in tact."

"Technically we didn't," he pointed out. "Objective number three: avoid merfolk. That has been broken."

"Hey, we didn't break it," said Sister Margaret. "Avoiding someone just means you don't seek them out. It doesn't mean you've failed if they pop out of a lake right in front of you and start throwing weapons."

"You threw the first weapon," said Trevor. He shivered. Even with the shield up, he was getting chilly. Stooping down, he realized that the trident had punched all the way through the front of the car, creating a large hole into which the cold air was streaming.

He extended the shield to cover it and conjured another flame, feeling a little bit of mage energy leaving him as he did so. Hopefully they could get to M'Tainla soon — all this spelling was taking it out of him.

Trevor turned toward Sister Margaret to see why she hadn't started driving yet. His eyes widened as he realized she was pressing frantically down on the gas pedal, and the car wasn't moving.

A stream of curse words began to emerge from behind her scarf.

"What is happening right now?" asked Trevor, interrupting her swearing.

"I don't know," she said. "Nothing. Nothing is happening. The car isn't moving. It's dead."

As soon as she said that, Trevor realized that the sense he'd had of the car being semi-alive back on the plateau had disappeared at some point. He no longer felt like it was poised and ready to go. It still hovered over the churning water, but it wasn't moving forward.

And who knew how long it would hover once it died?

"Oh, fuck," said Sister Margaret as the vehicle suddenly lurched downward about an inch.

"It's okay," said Trevor. "It's not sinking yet. We just need to get out of here."

He looked outward, scanning the shore of the lake beside the waterfall, about two hundred yards away. "There!" he pointed to a flat-looking area that looked big enough to hold all of their gear.

The car lurched again, plunging another six inches, almost touching the water now.

"Let's go," said Sister Margaret. She reached back into the cargo area, using one hand to grip the handles of three duffel bags and a backpack. "Leave the fake shit behind."

Trevor grabbed the remaining duffel and backpack and waited until Sister Margaret had a good hold on his parka, then moved his hand inside its mitten in a stitch, focusing on the spot he had chosen.

A second later, they were on the shore, watching as their magical car plunged into the icy red water.

"Welp," said Sister Margaret. "Guess we're walking."

Trevor shook his head. "I'm exhausted. I think we're camping first."

Sister Margaret nodded. "Fair enough. Thank God we've got all the gear from the research station. And for that woman who insisted on walking us through how to use it all. I've never camped in my life, and I sure as shit wouldn't have known how to assemble a tent before that."

"We'd be dead without it," agreed Trevor. "I don't have the reserves to keep us warm with spells all night."

Trevor crouched, opening one of the duffels, one that the staff at the McMurdo Station had packed for them. "Here's the tent," he said. "It looks small, but that's best anyway. The closer we're sleeping, the warmer we'll be."

"This is like one of those romance novels where two co-workers have to stop for the night unexpectedly and there's only one bed in the only room left," said Sister Margaret with a laugh.

Trevor grinned. "Except that we don't hate each other, and also we're not those kinds of people."

"I used to be those kinds of people," said Sister Margaret. "A long time ago. But you're really not my type."

Trevor raised his eyebrows in mock-indignation. "What is that supposed to mean?"

"I mean, you know I'm gay, right?" she said.

"Huh." Trevor tried to remember if that had ever come up in conversation. "I don't think I did know that. Anyway, nobody is my type, so either way…. We can probably be certain we're not in a romance novel."

Trevor snapped the collapsed tent poles together, forming two arches, then felt around for the bag of stakes. He located it underneath the folded canvas floor wall.

He tossed the floor to Sister Margaret, who got to work spreading it out across the ice, topping it with the sleeping pad, which was specially formulated to keep the cold on the other side of it.

Trevor threaded the arches through the corresponding holes in the wall fabric before setting it upright, affixing it to the floor, and hammering the stakes into the solid ice with some difficulty.

He raised an eyebrow — which, of course, she couldn't see — and gave her a small bow. "Shall we get cozy?" he suggested.

Sister Margaret laughed and tossed their high-tech low-temp sleeping bags into the tent, following them with the duffel bags and then crawling in.

Trevor followed behind, carefully cradling the small solar-powered heater in his arms. He hoped it still held some charge; if they'd been the researchers they had claimed to be, they would have set it up first, letting it charge all day while they assembled the rest of their camp.

Since they hadn't planned to need it, it had sat in the dark bag instead.

Unfolding the heater's stand, he set it aside and unrolled his sleeping bag, zipping it to Sister Margaret's to make one bag for warmth.

They arranged the sleeping bag around themselves and then zipped it shut. "It's pretty warm already, even if the heater doesn't work," said Sister Margaret.

Trevor nodded, but reached for the *on* switch, pausing to take a deep breath before finally hitting the orange toggle. He exhaled with a grin as the machine whirred to life, its coils glowing and an immediate warmth emanating from it.

"Thank God," Sister Margaret murmured.

Privately, Trevor figured it had more to do with technology, but it was none of his business who or what Sister Margaret wanted to thank for the device that would provide one more chance that they'd make it through the night.

"Good night," he said. "Here's to keeping to our objectives."

"Don't die," Sister Margaret reminded him.

"And don't let your partner die," he finished. He rolled over, putting his back to Sister Margaret, and she did the same.

A moment later, Sister Margaret was snoring, and a moment after that, Trevor was sound asleep as well.

Chapter 14: Sister Margaret

Sister Margaret woke up some time later. It was very difficult to tell if it was morning, since they were in Antarctica during the summertime, and as such, it never actually got dark. And she didn't have a watch on and her phone was buried somewhere in in the luggage, so she didn't even know what time they had set up their camp or how long she had slept.

She did know that she felt rested and very, very cold.

At some point while they'd slept, the heater had run out of juice and had stopped working. She was very grateful that they had both been comfortable sleeping in the same bag, since that was probably all that had kept them warm enough to wake up.

She nudged Trevor and for a moment she was terrified that he would not, in fact, wake up. Desperately, she shook him hard, and he came awake instantly, pushing her away as best he could in the cramped space.

"Wha—? What's going on?" he demanded.

"Oh, thank God," she said. "I thought you were fucking dead."

"Why would I be dead?" Trevor said. "I'm far too cold to be dead."

"People get cold when they're dead," she reminded him. "And sometimes they get dead because they're cold."

Trevor sat up, which, given their close proximity and sleeping bag arrangement, forced Sister Margaret to sit up as well. "I guess, since we're up, we should get moving," he said. "Let's pack up and try to find the road."

She nodded. "Moving around will help warm us up, too."

"My mage reserves feel pretty replenished," said Trevor. "I think I can manage a shield at least, although I'll save the actual flame for an emergency."

Sister Margaret thought this felt pretty emergency-tastic already, but she kept her mouth shut. The cold had always made her cranky, and she would do her best not to take it out on Trevor.

Instead, she unzipped the sleeping bag and grabbed the heater, moving it out into the sun in order to get it charging again. God willing, they'd be in M'Tainla by the time they needed to sleep again, and it would be unnecessary, but in her experience, anything you didn't plan for was sure to happen. So she sure as fuck wasn't going to count on not needing that heater.

The two of them worked in companionable silence, breaking down their basic camp. Once the tent was down, Trevor worked on packing it back up into its duffel and Sister Margaret scrounged in the other station-packed duffel for rations. Most of the food they'd sent along required the use of a stove — they had a small propane-powered one, or there was a more permanent one in the shack they were supposed to be staying at on the other side of the lake.

But she managed to dig out a box of protein bars and meal replacement shakes. She pulled out two of each and handed Trevor his portion before downing hers. The bar tasted like cardboard and the shake turned out to be too frozen to drink, but she used a dagger to cut open the top and ate it like a push-pop. It wasn't bad, actually, although it could have used a lot more sugar.

Regardless of flavor, she could feel herself waking up and gaining energy, and as she put her scarf back in place over the lower half of her face and packed up the trash from their meal, she grinned broadly.

"Could be worse," she remarked to Trevor. "We're alive and we're having adventures."

"I rather think the summit itself was enough of an adventure without getting stranded by the side of a mostly-frozen lake," Trevor pointed out.

"We're not stranded," said Sister Margaret. "We've got four good legs."

"And a mountain to get over with four duffel bags and two huge backpacks," he countered.

"Which you can spell to be lighter." She smirked at him. He wouldn't see the smirk, but he knew her pretty well, so she assumed he'd discern its existence from context.

Trevor shook his head, but his deep chuckle sounded through his scarf and mask. "Touché," he said.

Sister Margaret knew that levitation was one of the least draining spells, so it stood to reason that making something lighter would be even less draining.

She also knew that she didn't want to risk Trevor exhausting his reserves too quickly. "We probably won't need the shield once we start hiking," she said. "That should help."

"Fair enough." Trevor picked up the heater and fiddled with its stand, collapsing it in the particular way that allowed you to clip it onto a backpack so it could charge while you carried it. He clipped it onto Sister Margaret's pack and then helped her into it.

She helped him into his, and then hefted two of the duffel bags.

Once he'd picked up his duffels, she felt all three of her bags lighten to the point where it felt like she wasn't carrying anything at all.

"Nice. Thank you." Sister Margaret looked around to make sure nothing was left of their campsite and then began walking in the left-of-the-waterfall direction given to them by the dragonlords.

Trevor dropped the mage shield before she walked into it, and the wind hit like an enemy slamming into her in battle. "Oh, fuck," she muttered. "Maybe we do need that shield."

"Let's see how it goes," suggested Trevor through gritted teeth. "Maybe it'll ease up. If it doesn't, I can always put the shield back up."

Chapter 15: Trevor

Trevor followed behind Sister Margaret, struggling with each step against the wind. At least he couldn't even feel the weight of the pack on his back, and the duffels he was carrying felt almost empty.

After only about fifteen minutes of walking, he decided that he was draining more energy fighting the wind than he would by putting up a shield in front of them. It didn't need to be a full dome like he'd done the day before in the boat; just something to break the wind.

He formed the Latin words for a shield in his mind, not bothering to make it heatproof, just a physical barrier. That would take less energy too, and then if Sister Margaret needed her seer powers, it woundn't blind her like the heat shield had.

"Oh, yes. Thank you," said Sister Margaret ahead of him as soon as the shield was up.

The relief was immediate, and they both straightened their backs as they continued forward, making their way along the cliff face, the sound of the wind all around them, almost drowning out the five-story-high cascade of blood-colored water behind them.

Trevor hoped they'd be to find the mountain pass and the road the dragonlords had promised them. They were meant to have seen it from the air, after all, not the ground.

The lake beside them was getting less red, the water calmer as they left Blood Falls behind them. As they slogged along, the water gradually gave way to large chunks of ice, and then finally to solid ice once again.

Trevor breathed a sigh of relief as the water turned frozen, and he realized he'd been half-expecting another mer attack at any moment.

Now hopefully all they would have to fight off would be frostbite. And getting lost.

His footing slipped and he windmilled his arms. His mittened right hand smacked into the cliff face beside him, and the fabric caught on a rocky patch, allowing him to brace himself for a moment and regain his stability.

Excellent. Another source of danger — falling and injuring themselves.

"Are you okay?" Sister Margaret grasped his arm, steadying him further. "Maybe we should get those ice picks out again."

"Good plan." Trevor set down his duffel bags and knelt to open them. The first bag he opened proved to have only his own clothing and weapons. The other bag was filled with McMurdo Station gear, including the ice picks.

Trevor handed one pair to Sister Margaret and set the other down on the snow while he reorganized the bag. By the time he was ready to stand again, his knees were cold and damp, and he took a moment to stitch away the moisture.

Stitching took less mage energy out of him than spelling, since it was his natural discipline.

Chapter 16: Sister Margaret

Sister Margaret picked her careful way through the snow and ice, an ice pick in each hand, her levitated duffel bags bobbing behind her, tied to her waist with a length of rope.

She estimated that they'd been walking for about three hours at this point, and had fallen about half a dozen times each before she'd hit on the idea of using the picks to pull themselves along.

She pulled her front pick from the icy wall, moving it over about a foot, and then removing the back pick. She stepped carefully to her left, using the pick to keep herself braced upright, and then smashed the other pick into the ice before repeating the process.

Using their hands to walk like this meant that Trevor was now using a full levitation spell instead of simply making the bags lighter, but it also meant they had less chance of injury.

"How are you holding up?" she called ahead to Trevor. Between the shield, which now surrounded the pair of them, and the levitation spell, plus a few instances of stitching away obstacles in their path, to say nothing of the physical exertion, he was probably feeling pretty tired.

Hell, she was feeling tired, and she had used very little mage energy, only occasionally using her seer sight to make sure nobody new was coming to fuck with them.

She sure wished somebody would come to rescue them, though.

"Let me know if you need a break or anything, yeah?" she called. Still no response.

She frowned. It wasn't like Trevor not to answer her.

With a deep breath, Sister Margaret put on a burst of speed, closing the short distance between the two of them.

She put a hand on his shoulder, hanging off the cliff face with the other. "Hey. Trevs. Are you okay?"

He spun around to face her, his eyes wide under his goggles. "What?"

"I've been calling out to you for the past couple of minutes," she said. "Are you okay?"

Trevor slumped, and shook his head. "I'm sorry. I'm so tired, I must have gone into some kind of hyperfocus mode."

Sister Margaret felt a pang of guilt. She had made the choice long ago that she wouldn't use any mage discipline but her natural seer ability. Morphing, as it was called, meant that you could use more skills, but the skills you had would be spread out.

People who morphed had less power in their natural discipline because they used the others. It was a trade-off that many people found worthwhile, but Sister Margaret prided herself on having stronger seer powers than most other mages, and she didn't want to dilute it.

Now she could see the value in being able to use spells and stitches in a pinch, and she wished she had at least learned those skills, even if she didn't practice them so often.

Well, it was too late now, and there was no sense in dwelling on the past. Time to use her super sight to their best advantage.

"Stay here," she instructed Trevor.

He nodded and clung to the cliff wall with his ice picks as she passed him by. She turned on her mage sight and focused on the path — for lack of a better word —- ahead of them.

Sister Margaret plunged her own ice picks deep into the ice. This was a tricky bit of magery that she had only used a couple of other times. Most seers couldn't do this at all without a scrying bowl.

She sent her powers upwards, looking at the area with a bird's-eye view.

There! She swooped down again, looking at a wide open space just about a quarter mile ahead. It even had an overhang that would block a lot of the wind; it was perfect.

Sister Margaret switched off her seer sight and turned back around to address Trevor. "Can you make it another quarter mile?" she asked.

He lifted his head and blinked at her. "Yeah," he said. "Yeah, I can do that."

"Good. Let's go." She started to turn to lead the way, then thought better of it. "You go first so I can make sure you don't collapse. It's just straight ahead."

He nodded, but said nothing, and she couldn't see anything of his face but his eyes. No way to know if he'd taken that as humor or if he really was so drained that it was a real possibility.

Sister Margaret kept a sharp eye on her partner as they hiked, but they reached the camping spot she'd chosen without incident.

It was even better up close. The wall turned slightly here, forming a sheltered corner where parts of the rock were visible beneath the ice. She knew that in wintertime, it wouldn't make a difference, but even Antarctica had a summer, and it just meant slightly less snow.

Whatever — she'd take it.

Sister Margaret pointed to the sheltered corner. "Come on. Sit down and drop the bags."

Trevor stumbled over, and she followed. As he leaned against the rock wall, he divested himself of his backpack and dropped the levitation and lightening spells.

The duffel bags fell to the ground, and Sister Margaret staggered as her backpack suddenly dragged against her back.

She hastily unslung the pack and dropped it to the ground as well, and then began rummaging through the duffels to find the tent.

She unfolded the floor and sleeping pad quickly, gesturing to Trevor to sit down on them while she finished building the tent.

Sister Margaret set up the tent around Trevor, poking her head in to unfold and turn on the fully-charged heater as well, before taking up a crouched position outside with her back braced against the rockface and her buttocks hovering above the icy ground.

At some point, probably when he'd dropped the other spells, Trevor had also released the shield, but it didn't make as much difference as it could have in this sheltered corner.

Still, she hastened to perform her reconnaissance quickly so she could get into the tent too and warm the fuck up.

Sister Margaret took a deep breath and turned on her seer sight again, using it once more to "fly" above the campsite, looking for the mountain pass and the road.

"Oh, sweet Jesus, thank you!" she murmured. The pass was just ahead, and the road started after only a short climb of maybe half a mile.

The road was made of some kind of dark blue paving that she wasn't familiar with, but it was a distinct surface separate from the ice and snow, and it looked to have been cleared of both.

It was still a mountain pass, and it wound steeply along, but it would be easier to walk it than the wilderness they'd been trekking through to this point.

Sister Margaret continued following the road with her mage sight, scouting ahead. What was that structure?

She swooped closer, and saw it was a kind of hut made of some pale blue material. She peeked in through the window and almost cried. There was a set of bunk beds that seemed to be made for humans, a table, a small kitchenette. This was some kind of waystation. If they could get there after this sleep, they could stay there for a few hours, get some rest on a real bed, and prepare some real food and maybe get to M'Tainla the next day.

How far away was M'Tainla, anyway?

Feeling newfound energy brought on by hope, Sister Margaret turned away from the waystation and followed the road further until she saw a vehicle just like the one the dragons had given them.

It was heading toward her. Could someone have noticed they hadn't arrived and come after them?

Sister Margaret rushed her sight toward the car to investigate. Driving the vehicle was a tall dark-skinned man incongruously dressed only in a loincloth, despite the open-air vehicle and the icy surroundings.

The man's hair was fire engine red and cut in a short, layered style that fell forward over his forehead in a way that brought the word *emo* to Sister Margaret's mind. His eyes were an eerie rose color, set in a face with features that were sharp and delicate, almost catlike.

His body was decorated extensively with draped jewelry, body piercings, and tattoos.

"Salashifter," Sister Margaret murmured. She turned her attention to the two other occupants of the car, who sat in the back cargo area.

"Oh, fuck." All hope drained out of her.

Chapter 17: Trevor

Somebody was shaking him. Trevor started awake. "What? What's going on?"

He had a sense of deja vu. Hadn't this happened last time he'd woken up? He felt like he'd only had a few minutes of sleep.

"I'm sorry," said Sister Margaret. She looked disheveled, and stressed out, her scarf slipped from her face and her parka torn in a couple of places from the long hike. "I'm so sorry, but we need to get ready. There's nowhere we can hide. More merfolk are coming."

"Shit." Trevor pushed his sleeping bag off of himself. "How long was I sleeping?"

Sister Margaret gave him a sad smile. "I'm sorry," she said again. "Only about half an hour. I looked ahead, and found the road."

Trevor's eyes widened. "How did you do that? Can you scry with ice?"

She shook her head. "That's not important. What is important is that I saw a car coming toward us. It's the same kind of car we had before, so it's coming in fast. There's a salashifter and two mer."

"The same ones as before?" asked Trevor.

"Nope. Exciting new ones," she said. "Look, you're in no shape to fight them off, so I want you to stay in the tent, and I'm going to pretend I'm on my own. I'll try to fight them off, and I'll act like you're dead or lost. Be ready, though, in case I fall."

He shook his head. "What the hell are you talking about? Of course you're not fighting them alone."

Trevor pulled his weaponry bag toward himself. In the interest of discretion, he'd had to leave his greatsword behind, but he had plenty of smaller weapons.

He took out a sword that was about two-thirds the length of his usual weapon and belted it on. It probably looked silly over the down parka, but that could work in his favor if they underestimated his fighting skills.

Even tired, Trevor was a formidable fighter. Hell, even unarmed, he was adept at krav maga.

He could feel adrenaline coursing through him as he prepared for the upcoming battle.

"Here." Sister Margaret, her own twin short swords buckled on as well, was handing him an energy bar.

He took it gratefully and wolfed it down, perking up further as his belly filled. And after all, some sleep was better than no sleep, right?

He heard a shout from outside the tent, and he hastily pulled his ski mask over his head. Battle or no battle, this was Antarctica, and the cold could still kill.

Chapter 18: Sister Margaret

The newcomers were making no effort to be stealthy, shouting out something she couldn't make out through the thick canvas of the tent.

Sister Margaret switched her seer powers back on, directing the magery to her ears instead of her eyes — another skill many less powerful seers didn't have.

"Are you in there?" the voice was saying. "Sister Margaret Herrera? Trevor Harper? We've been looking for you."

"It may not be them," said a hissing voice similar to the mer they'd encountered before. "If this is the camp of human scientists, we will have to exterminate them."

"Of course," said the first voice. "Unless I can convince them I'm also a scientist."

The hissing voice laughed. "Dressed like that? You haven't spent much time around humans, have you?"

"Not as such," admitted the first voice. "At least not humans who remained alive afterwards. But we're not supposed to kill them at the summit."

"I believe that only applies to the ones invited to the summit." This voice was hissing too, but Sister Margaret discerned a slightly different quality. This was the other mer. "And this is an inhospitable environment. Humans die around here all the time without our interference."

This was proving a very interesting conversation.

"Are they here to finish us off?" Trevor whispered beside her. With her enhanced hearing and his close proximity, the whisper sounded like a shout in her ear, and she quashed a startled shriek.

"Unclear," she responded once she'd gotten ahold of herself. "It kind of sounds like they might not be, unless we turn out to be someone else."

"Well, since we're not someone else, maybe we're okay," said Trevor.

"Whoever they are, they're in that tent," said the salashifter. "I can hear them rustling."

"Come out, humans," called one of the mer. "We're not here to hurt you."

"They're saying they're not here to hurt us," Sister Margaret reported.

"Do you believe them?" asked Trevor. "Although honestly, it doesn't matter. Either way, we're probably better off out there where we can fight."

"Fair." Sister Margaret took a deep breath and in one smooth motion, unzipped the tent flap and rolled herself out of the tent and onto her feet, drawing her swords as soon as she was upright, and turning toward the movement of the three cryptids standing beside their hovercraft.

The cryptids stared at her for a moment before the salashifter stepped forward, hands lifted. "Sister Margaret Herrera?" he asked again.

"Who's asking?" she said. She adjusted her seer powers to show her the near future instead of amplifying their voices. In her vision, she saw a peaceful interaction, followed by herself tucking away her swords and shaking the salashifter's hand.

That was a good sign, but she still couldn't be sure it wasn't a trap. She knew the mer could interfere with her seer sight. Could they project a false future?

"My name is Taye," said the salashifter. He gave her a brief close-lipped smile before continuing. "I am your assigned On'Chala."

Sister Margaret lowered her weapons, still keeping a wary eye on the merfolk. Her future vision showed them staying back, still seated in the cargo area of the car.

An On'Chala, she'd been told, was a sort of guide that each delegate to the summit was assigned. She knew it was a prestigious position, on par with the envoys themselves, and that every On'Chala was of a different species of cryptids than the emissaries they were assigned to.

But nobody at the Vatican really knew what the On'Chala's actual duties were. And just because someone was randomly appointed to guide them around or whatever didn't mean they were automatically friendly.

"You know what an On'Chala is?" he asked, taking a step toward her. His hands were still spread in a gesture of goodwill.

She took a step back, but sheathed her swords. Her foresight was now showing Trevor entering the conversation and still no fighting.

Taye offered her his right hand, and she shook it gingerly.

"We have a vague idea," said Trevor. "You're some kind of guide, right?"

"It's more than that," said Taye. "My main duty is to help you navigate intercryptid interactions. I'm an expert in various cryptid cultures, and can help you to avoid offending anyone or explain to you what's happening if someone from another culture offends you. It greatly decreases the chances of fights, which before On'Chalas were introduced, often resulted in injuries and deaths at the summits."

"Why did you bring them?" Sister Margaret gestured toward the merfolk. "We've already been attacked by their kind."

One of the mer, a creature unlike any of those who had attacked them, levitated upward. This mer resembled an octopus more closely than a shark. The mer was also covered in scales, but instead of a long body with fins, legs, and two arms, they had a central body-head combo surrounded by several smooth tentacles with hands at the ends.

The mer lifted two tentacles, echoing Taye's posture. "My name is Zachary," he hissed. "We are not of the same mind as the school that attacked you."

Sister Margaret blinked. The mer's name was Zachary? Shouldn't the mer have exotic hard-to-pronounce names like the dragons did?

She turned off her seer sight; it wasn't as helpful during a conversation as it was during a fight, and it was starting to give her a slight headache, keeping all the overlays straight.

Taye stepped back, clearly startled as her eyes turned from blank white back to their ordinary mode with their dark brown irises.

He may be an expert in cryptid culture, but he must not be as briefed in mage powers.

The other mer stepped out of the car, standing on two legs, rather than hovering as the tentacled mer had.

Sister Margaret whirled toward the newcomer, and the mer raised both hands as well.

"My name is Carly," she said. Her head was enormous, her mouth filled with jagged teeth, and she had a single antenna curling over the top of her head with a light at the end like an anglerfish.

Another bizarrely ordinary name. Sister Margaret found herself relaxing. Something about the names put her at ease.

"We denounce the actions of Bryan and the Agualadron School," said Carly.

Then again, it sounded like the dick who had left them to die was named Bryan, so maybe ordinary names didn't mean friendly.

"Look," said Trevor. "It seems like you're not going to try to kill us, right?"

"That's correct," said Taye. "In fact, I am tasked with actively preventing your death."

"Fantastic," Trevor continued. "So, I'm freezing. How about you all help us dismantle our camp, and we all head back to M'Tainla, and maybe we can continue this conversation in the car?"

"A most excellent plan," said Zachary. Still hovering about three inches above the ground, he floated over to the tent. "How can I help?"

"Do you know how to dismantle a tent?" asked Sister Margaret.

"I'm afraid not," he admitted.

"You can load up our bags," said Trevor. "Except that one." He pointed to the one that the tent would be packed into.

Without waiting to see if the mer would follow his instructions, Trevor picked up the tent and began pulling out the arched poles.

Sister Margaret took the fabric from him and folded it up as he finished collapsing everything and tucked it into the bag.

When she turned around, the anglerfish mer — Carly — had folded the sleeping pad. She held out her hand and the mer handed it to her.

Taye folded up the floor, and within a couple of minutes their camp was broken, the heater stowed back onto the rear of her backpack, and all of the bags neatly stowed in the cargo area of their vehicle.

She nudged Trevor and pointed to the passenger seat before hauling herself into the back of the car among the baggage. The mer followed suit, Taye resuming his own place in the driver's seat.

Before she knew it, they were on their way.

Trevor put up a mage shield around the car, and the wind cut off abruptly.

Sister Margaret bit her lip. Should she stop Trevor from using up his mage powers? It seemed like the danger had passed, but you never knew.

She glanced outside and realized how quickly they were going. There was no way the two of them would be able to withstand the Antarctic winds at this speed in an open-air vehicle.

So that decision was made for her. Instead, she turned to the merfolk who sat beside her in the cargo area, Carly seated cross-legged in a similar fashion to herself, Zachary nestled between their duffle bags with his tentacles folded up around him sort of like a wringing mop.

Carly was dressed like the shark-like merfolk they had encountered before, in an intricately woven loincloth at her waist, and nothing else. Zachary didn't seem to have any clothing at all.

"Thank you for your assistance," said Sister Margaret.

Carly nodded, her antenna following the motion stiffly rather than bobbing or swaying as Sister Margaret would have expected.

"We represent a small faction of the merfolk who have been pushing for us to take our place on the global stage for generations," she said. "We are pleased to finally be here at the summit of cryptids, and we are pleased to be dealing with humans at last, instead of merely sinking your ships and feasting on your corpses."

"Thank you," said Sister Margaret. "We are also pleased that you are not feasting on our corpses."

Trevor twisted around and frowned at her. She shrugged back at him. Carly was the one who brought up corpse-feasts first.

Carly bared sharp teeth and it took Sister Margaret a moment to realize the mer was smiling.

Chapter 19: Trevor

Trevor eyed Carly. He was encouraged to find that some of the mer were on their side. He'd been under the impression that all of them hated humans, and it had certainly been drilled into their heads even before the attack to avoid all the merfolk.

Carly noticed his regard and bared her teeth again.

Trevor decided to assume that was a smile.

"You look different in real life," she said. "I haven't ever seen a human up close. Only on TV or on the Internet or off in the distance. We've been cut off, even from witches and shapeshifters."

"You have TVs?" Trevor said. "And the Internet?"

"Yes," said Carly. "We've been able to repair quite a lot of modern technology from sunken boats. And our own technology is very advanced as well. I think your Vatican may be interested in seeing some of it. Our school is interested in trading information such as this with various groups at the summit."

Trevor nodded. "We are authorized to negotiate such deals with any friendly cryptids. But—" He paused. How to be diplomatic about this? "How . . . official . . . is your group versus the other group? Among mer society, I mean?"

Zachary gestured from side to side with one of his hands. Trevor noticed that he had tiny suction cups lining his tentacles all the way down to his fingertips. "It's complicated. Our society is set up differently than yours. More like how primitive humans lived. In groups."

"Tribes?" suggested Sister Margaret.

"Yes, that's the word I'm thinking of. We do not refer to them as such — we call them schools. But that is how we live. Tribes within our cities, but they are less family and more about viewpoints. And each school governs itself. So, we do not speak for all merfolk, but neither does Bryan and his school."

"Fascinating," said Trevor. "It seems you know much more about us than we do about you."

Carly made an odd buzzing sound.

Trevor blinked, alarmed for a moment before he realized she was laughing. He exhaled slowly.

"It's unfair, isn't it?" she agreed. "We have so much information about your people because you broadcast it all over the world. We stay hidden. You will be hard pressed to find even other cryptids who know much about us merfolk."

Trevor thought he detected a note of sadness in her hissing voice. "Why hasn't your school come to the summits before, if you're self-governing?"

"The way has been barred," she said.

Trevor waited to see if more information was forthcoming, but instead she pulled a spray bottle out of a pouch by her side, which he hadn't noticed before, attached to her skirt. She spritzed herself all over and then handed it to Zachary, who did the same.

He felt kind of awkward about watching them, so he turned instead to the front, and realized that they were nearing an odd road that seemed to appear out of a cave off to the side and then wound up over the cliffs beyond.

He hadn't even noticed that they had reached the mountain pass.

Suddenly he saw the dragon city off in the distance, ice-colored except for a slight blue tint, and camouflaged from a casual observer, but there if you knew what to look for.

Taye pulled onto the road, still hovering a couple feet above, but now over a wide dark blue surface instead of packed snow and ice.

Trevor could see that what had appeared at first glance to be a sheer cliff was actually a series of rising plateaus. "This is Taylor Glacier we're climbing, right?" he said.

"The dragons call it L'Taergan, I believe," said Carly. "Which translates roughly to *Surrounding Plains*."

"Does their city's name have a meaning as well?" he asked. "M'Tainla?"

"Ice City," said Zachary. "Their language is very literal."

"Are you fluent in it?" asked Trevor. "Does each cryptid race have its own language? Is race the right word there?"

"I am not fluent," said Carly. "But I know enough to get by. Race or species are the commonly used terms, yes, and only the more isolated races have their own languages. Most of the others have either assimilated into the humans around them, and use their language now or never had their own to begin with and have always used human speech."

"I assume the merfolk have their own language, then?" said Trevor.

"Yes," Zachary replied. "But we all speak English as well, because we have become fascinated by American television and movies. And Chinese and Korean. Same reason. Many of us in our school also speak Spanish and French, as we like to visit the islands closest to our city — Cuba, Haiti, the Dominican Republic. We do not have contact with the humans, but we have picked up their languages while we observe."

"Your city in the Bermuda Triangle," said Sister Margaret. "Why so concentrated? I would think there would be merfolk all over the place --- the oceans are so huge."

"Huge and dangerous," said Carly. "And we are not many. Like most other cryptid races, our population is small."

"How many merfolk are there, total?" asked Trevor. "If you don't mind me asking."

Carly made a shruglike gesture, lifting her hands to her chin level before dropping them. "Maybe eighty thousand? Maybe a hundred thousand? Somewhere in between, I would say."

"And they all live in one city," said Trevor. "And all the dragons live in one city, and all the salashifters, and all the kallanpa amaru -- each of them has a fortress where they live."

"Yes," said Carly. "But many other races are spread around the world and still others are spread out but only within a general area."

"Right," said Sister Margaret. "Werewolves are all in northern Canada and Alaska, but scattered throughout. Bigfoots have small villages throughout the world. Vampires all live in human cities, many of them in underground lairs, although I understand some dwell in regular buildings, pretending to be human."

"I heard a rumor that some vampires are pushing for a move to a more localized population," said Carly.

"Really?" said Trevor. "Where?"

"New York, London, or Moscow," said Carly. "Somewhere with a lot of abandoned subway tunnels, I suppose."

Trevor blinked. The Vatican had secret libraries under each of those cities. Could that be of interest to the vampires? A point of reference with which to open negotiations?

Just then, the hovercraft crested the ridge of the glacier and all chatter stopped.

Taye hit the brakes, slowing down, which Trevor appreciated as it gave him that much more opportunity to gawk.

He stared at the vista that opened up in the valley below. The glimpses they had gotten from the other side were just the tippy tops of the ice city.

M'tainla spread out before them like a cross between a wintery skate park and a cinematic depiction of Rivendell, all spirals and sloping lines with grand balconies and buildings built into the cliffs and a network of bridges connecting spires all across.

There were also roads through it and dragons walking along them, plus a few dragons in the air. Beside the dragons on the ground, Trevor could see smaller figures, which must be other cryptids here for the summit.

"Wow," said Sister Margaret. "I don't know what I pictured, but I'm not sure this was it."

"It is beautiful," said Carly, awe in her voice, as though she herself still wasn't quite used to the sight.

Trevor nodded, speechless. *Beautiful* didn't quite cover it, but he wasn't sure what word would. It was . . . otherworldly. Ethereal. Surreal.

"It's a city of dragons," he said. What else was there to say?

The car cruised down the sloping road into the valley, between small clusters of buildings that resembled enormous, art nouveau igloos. Windows showed that many of the domes were three or four stories tall, many of them connected by the wide, curving bridges running between the upper stories.

These overpasses were well-used, dragons and other cryptids roaming along them, leaning against railings, and even seated at clusters of tables like sidewalk cafes situated outside some of the buildings.

Finally, they arrived in the valley, where the structures were more varied in shape. Aside from the slope they had just come down, the walls of the valley consisted of sheer cliff faces with caves dug into them and balconies extending off, some covered and others open to the elements.

On the valley floor was a dizzying maze of swirling towers and high domes with more familiar house-like shapes sprinkled in among them.

Trevor noticed that most of the dragons walked around rather than flying, and he wondered if that was to avoid being seen by human scientists, in deference to the land-bound cryptids coming in for the summit, or for another reason entirely.

Maybe flying was more tiring than walking and was reserved for longer distances. The past couple of days had really driven home to Trevor how little he knew about the supernatural races who shared their world.

Trevor loosened his scarf as the air warmed in the protected valley.

He found himself wondering how the merfolk stayed warm. While he wasn't a biologist, he was pretty sure fish were cold-blooded.

Taye, he knew, kept himself warm with magic, as salashifters were essentially made of barely contained elemental fire.

His musings were interrupted as Taye turned down a side street and then immediately pulled the car up to a curb near the corner. The salashifter reached down and tugged on a small lever and the hovercraft sank gracefully to the ground, turning itself off.

Trevor shivered, remembering again how their first car had died — or rather been killed — after their fight with the other mer school.

He pulled his mask back down and his scarf back up, dropped his mage shield, and disembarked, feeling extremely stiff. The soreness hadn't quite hit him yet, but he knew it wouldn't be long, after the exertions of the past couple of days.

Trevor stretched as best he could, encumbered as he was by the heavy cold weather gear, and then reached into the back of the barge to grab his backpack.

He left the two duffel bags where they were. "Just bring your pack," he said to Sister Margaret. "I'll stitch in the rest once we get to our room."

"Thanks." Sister Margaret dropped her own duffels back in the cargo area.

Carly scrambled out of the back of the vehicle, closely followed by Zachary, who balanced himself awkwardly on two of his tentacles. Trevor watched closely as Zachary spun around rapidly several times, and when he stopped, he was hovering above the ground as he had back at camp, his tentacles floating in the air about his body, much as they would if he was in water.

Trevor had missed this earlier, and had wondered how exactly the octomer had moved from being seated in a car to levitating above the ground. He still wasn't sure exactly how the merfolk breathed out of water. They must have some kind of combination gill-lung respiratory system.

Trevor turned his attention to Taye, who was pacing forward, his bare feet light on the snow, leading them to an arched door.

Trevor glanced upward and saw that the building was several stories high, twisting upward to a pointed spire. Like everything in M'tainla, it appeared to be made of ice, its walls a bluish white color and sort of translucent.

Taye pushed a few buttons on a discreet keypad beside the door and it slid open. "Your door code will be included in the welcome packets in your rooms," he told them.

"We will see you at dinner this evening," said Zachary. "And many more times throughout the summit."

"Be careful," said Carly.

The pair of them began making their way down the street.

Trevor and Sister Margaret waved goodbye and followed Taye into the building, walking briskly toward a wide ramp that spiraled upward.

The speedy pace they were moving at made it difficult to get a good look around, but since they'd be there for a full month, that was probably okay.

Trevor was eager to get to a room with a bed and hopefully a coffee maker as well.

The one motif he did notice was a certain starkness to the inside of the building that matched the outside. The ramp they ascended was made out of the same pale blue material as the exterior building, and Trevor was a little surprised when he pulled off his mitten and touched the banister to find that it was actually warm to the touch, not icy cold.

In fact, he was beginning to overheat in his heavy winter gear, a feeling that felt almost luxurious after so long in the blistering chill.

The floor felt like stone beneath his boots, and if it was a little bit slippery, that could be because of the snow crusting the soles, not because the ramp itself was icy.

They emerged into a curved hallway, unsurprisingly formed from pale blue material. "What are these buildings made of?" Trevor asked as he followed Taye down the hall.

"Ice," said Taye. "But altered by dragon magic. My great grandmother used to tell stories of fire dragons and their wonderful palaces made of magical flame." His voice sounded wistful. "But of course the fire dragons went extinct long before she was born. She got the stories from her ancestors. This icy city is not as hospitable for my kind, but that is not the dragons' fault, so we don't hold it against them."

"There were once fire dragons as well?" asked Sister Margaret. "What happened to them?"

"Humans happened," said Taye. "Your ancestors moved into their territory and decided they were a threat. They invaded dragon lands and then hunted them in the name of chivalry, sport, and land disputes."

"So the tales of dragon-slaying knights are true," said Trevor, softly. "I'm so sorry."

Taye shrugged. "Not your fault. Wasn't even *your* ancestors, as I understand it. The fire dragons lived in Europe."

"Humans as a whole still aren't amazing," said Sister Margaret softly. "We have a lot of growing up to do."

"As do many cryptids," said Taye. "You're here, and that's progress. I and many others believe that the cryptid races began to evolve more rapidly once we started these summits. Something about meeting and cooperating with other people, people who seem dissimilar to you but truly aren't so different in their souls, gives you a wonderfully beneficial perspective."

"The summits began around the fifteenth century, right?" said Trevor.

"Correct." Finally, Taye stopped in front of a door and punched a code into the pad beside it. "Sister Margaret, this will be your room." He opened the door and held it for her to push past into the room. "And Trevor, this one is yours."

Taye stepped to his left, entering the code for the next door over. "There is another door between your rooms for your convenience. I will return at six o'clock sharp to escort you to the banquet hall in the capitol building. If you have any questions for me, feel free to text me — my number is in your welcome packet, and your phones will function here in the city thanks to cell towers set up by the dragons and connected to a wireless network that works similarly enough to your networks. It has been a pleasure to meet you both, and I look forward to working with you over the next few weeks."

And with that, he pivoted on his heel and strode back down the hallway.

Chapter 20: Sister Margaret

Sister Margaret watched Taye leave and then closed her door and leaned her forehead against it for a moment with a huge exhalation. "Welp," she said to herself. "We made it. Didn't die. Didn't get injured. Didn't let Trevor die or get injured."

She pushed herself up and turned around, shedding her backpack and her mittens and leaving them on the floor next to the door. "We've got until six o'clock," she muttered to herself. "I don't know even know what time it is. Or what day it is. Didn't even bother to ask."

Spotting an alarm clock on the nightstand, Sister Margaret made a beeline for it. Before she could get there, a door to her left opened, and she whirled around, throwing star ready.

She relaxed when she saw Trevor making his way into the room, sans parka and lugging her two duffel bags. "Thanks," she said. "How about these rooms, huh?"

"Much swankier than we usually get," said Trevor with a laugh.

The rooms weren't particularly fancy, but they were certainly nicer than the cubby holes that were typically set aside for the warriors at the Vatican libraries their usual gigs sent them to.

And they were clearly designed for humans, much to Sister Margaret's relief. There were probably rooms for each type of cryptid, and witches had been coming to these summits for years. Oh, and vampires. Probably others who were shaped like humans too.

"Hey, do you know what day it is?" she asked. He probably would. Stitchers had a better sense of time than seers, since they were more detail-oriented.

She picked up the alarm clock. Ten o'clock. Good, they had hours to get situated and get some rest.

"I'm pretty sure we were only out there for one day," said Trevor. "I know we slept twice—"

"Well, we tried anyway," Sister Margaret interrupted.

"Right," said Trevor. "But I think we only slept for about six hours or so, and we definitely didn't walk for an entire day before we set up our second camp."

"So, that means tonight is the welcome banquet," said Sister Margaret. "And we didn't really miss anything by getting in late."

"We missed the opportunity to take our time preparing and exploring the city." Trevor sighed and set her bags down on the queen bed in the center of her room. "I need a nap. I'll see you later, okay?"

"Sure." Sister Margaret followed him to the adjoining door and shut it behind him, then set about divesting herself of her cold weather gear, stripping down the layers without bothering to fold or hang anything, just tossing down parka, sweater, jeans, long underwear all around the room with uncharacteristic abandon.

Finally, down to her black tank top and underpants, she turned toward the bed. Picking up the alarm clock again, she set it for three o'clock and collapsed onto the bed without bothering to turn off the light or get under the covers.

Chapter 21: Trevor

Trevor felt like he had barely closed his eyes when somebody pounded urgently on the door. "What the fuck?" he mumbled. Glancing at the clock on the solid wood nightstand, he saw that he had, in fact, been asleep for a good four hours. "Still not enough."

Stumbling out of bed, he grabbed his jeans and pulled them on as he made his way to the door. Whatever monster was outside banged on the door again just as he reached it. "I'm coming. Jesus. What is your problem?"

Buttoning up his pants, Trevor wrenched the door open and blinked sleepily at the grinning young man standing out in the hallway, his left hand still poised to knock, the right sleeve of his lavender button-up shirt hanging empty.

"Oh, my," said the man, running his eyes over Trevor's bare torso. "It is so nice to see you again, Trevor."

"Sammy?" Trevor blinked at the other mage in confusion. He had last seen Sammy West shortly after the epic battle that had cost the speller his right arm, over a year ago. "What are you doing here?"

An older man with dark skin, a long beard, a pale blue turban, and a fatherly air about him stepped out from behind Sammy. "Hello," he said in a dignified British accent. "I'm Ari. I'm Sammy's co-delegate from Pala."

"Pala, right." Trevor remembered the name from the bishops' debriefing. "You're the mage organization focused on social justice issues, right?"

"Social justice, public health improvements, reversing climate change, yes. Our mission is to use our mage powers and political influence to make the world a better place." Ari smiled at Trevor. "Sammy has told me much about you and Sister Margaret."

Sammy. Right. Trevor turned his attention back to Sammy. "What are you doing here?"

"Representing my people!" said Sammy. "And I'm very glad to see you alive. We were worried when you didn't show up."

"So, you knew I'd be here?"

"No, actually," said Ari. "But Taye told us you were late, and then Sammy recognized your names and we then realized that was probably why the dragons had specifically requested we send him."

"Right," said Trevor. "They specifically requested you? That's interesting. We were sent in case Coyote and Chameleon would be here." He shook head head abruptly. "Sorry, you guys can come in." He stepped back to make room for the others, and hurried to the couch that sat below the window, moving his still-unpacked bags to the floor beside it.

He pounded on the adjoining door to Sister Margaret's room.

"Coyote and Chameleon will be here too?" said Sammy. "Fantastic!"

"Now I'm wondering who the Illuminati sent — this feels like so many coincidences," said Trevor. "I mean, I don't *think* I know anyone who is an Illuminati, but—"

Sister Margaret's door opened and she poked her head around the corner, her hair coming out of its braid. "What's going on?" she asked.

"Put away your throwing stars," said Trevor. "Look who's come to see us!"

Sister Margaret's eyes wandered over to couch, following his gesture. "What the actual fuck?" She opened the door all the way, stepping into the room dressed only in her skivvies and a tank top. She set her throwing star down on the desk that stood beside the door.

Sammy stood up, beaming, and held out his arm for a hug.

As Sister Margaret whooped and rushed in for the embrace, Trevor glanced at Ari to gauge his reaction. He knew he didn't need to worry about Sammy being uncomfortable — or interested — and he certainly wasn't himself, but this wasn't exactly the ideal first impression on a potential political ally.

Fortunately, Ari's pleasant smile never wavered.

Sister Margaret stepped back and glanced over at the stranger, only then seeming to realize her state of undress and dishevel. She cleared her throat, but before she could say anything, Ari held out his hand for her to shake.

"Sister Margaret," he said warmly. "It's lovely to meet you at last. Ari Ahuja, of Pala."

"Oh, Pala!" She snapped her fingers. "See, I knew that sounded familiar." She turned to Trevor. "That's Sammy's group!"

"Sure." said Trevor. "Do you maybe want to put some pants on? You're a diplomat now."

"Right," she glanced down at herself. "Put a shirt on, yourself, before Sammy completely runs out of drool."

She turned and strode back to her own room.

Trevor grabbed the white t-shirt he'd shed earlier and pulled it on. "So, how long have you two been here?"

"We got in this morning," said Sammy. "Flew in from Argentina, but I guess since we came in from another direction, we didn't get the same welcoming committee. No lake on that side of the city."

"Have you had a chance to get your bearings yet?" asked Trevor. "We pretty much collapsed as soon as we made it to our rooms."

"A little bit," said Ari. "Of course, Taye was busy tracking you down, so a bigfoot showed us to our rooms — said he was the witch On'chala, so he knew where all the human rooms were — and we read through our welcome packets and then Taye showed up and introduced himself as the mage On'Chala, told us what happened to you, and we figured we'd give you some time to rest and then come check on you. You're not injured are you?"

Trevor shook his head. "Just rattled. It could have been really bad if Taye hadn't come after us. Turns out Antarctica is a tough place to navigate, especially when you weren't expecting to have to. I haven't had a chance to dive into any info about the summit. What did you learn?"

"It seems that much of the summit is about socializing," Ari observed. "When I asked Taye about it, he said many of the cryptids view it as one big party, while others do come for some political maneuvering. The general feeling is that this year, because of our presence, it will be more about politics than merriment, and that some of the cryptid species feel a bit resentful of that fact."

"Great," said Trevor. "Even the jolly ones are pissed at us."

"Hey, I'm always up for a party," said Sammy. "A banquet tonight, and you know I love getting dressed up all fancy, then some kind of tournament tomorrow afternoon. Not sure what squonkerball is, but I'm hoping it'll involve vampires in little shorts or something."

"Before the mysterious squonkerball tournament is the meeting carousel," Ari remind him.

Sister Margaret came back into the room, dressed in jeans and a clean tank top, her braid neatly redone.

"What is a meeting carousel?" she asked.

"Best I can tell," said Ari, "they split us into groups based on species. Some groups are assigned rooms, in which they remain stationary, while the others roam around and visit the conference rooms for fifteen minutes at a time, to feel out whether the two groups would like to open further negotiations for alliances."

"Like speed dating!" said Sammy, brightly.

Trevor stared at him. "What the hell is that?"

"You know, you get like five minutes to chat and then you move on to the next person? You've never done speed dating?" He looked around at the three blank faces. "Nobody?"

Trevor pointed to himself. "Ace and aro." He pointed to Sister Margaret "Celebate."

Ari pointed to himself. "Happily married with three children."

"Y'all are missing out," said Sammy with a shrug. "It's a hoot and a half."

"Well, anyway," said Ari. "It was very nice to meet you both. We'll leave you to prepare for the banquet. I'm looking forward to spending the next month getting to know you better."

"Thanks for checking in," said Trevor, following them to the door. "Bye."

"Bye!" Sister Margaret called as the other mages filed out. Trevor closed the door behind them.

"Well, now I feel like I did not, in fact, have to put pants on," said Sister Margaret. She shook her head with a laugh. "Sammy fucking West. What are the odds he'd be here?"

"It would seem that it's nothing to do with odds," said Trevor. "The dragons have arranged everything this way."

Sister Margaret sobered. "Which makes you wonder how friendly the dragons are after all. This feels a little bit manipulative, don't you think?"

Trevor tipped his head to the side. "I don't know. I think it feels more like they wanted us to come in with allies already in place. If they were trying to manipulate us and keep us off guard, you'd think they would have arranged for enemies to be here, not friends."

"Maybe," said Sister Margaret. "Speaking of enemies. We need a plan for dealing with the merfolk."

"I say we stick to our objective." Trevor walked over to the desk and studied the coffee maker. It looked like a standard machine, like you'd find in any hotel room in America. Where had the dragons gotten it? Witches, maybe?

Either way, he was glad to see it.

"Just avoid them?" said Sister Margaret. "You think they'll let us?"

Trevor removed the carafe and carried it to the small sink that stood just outside the bathroom door. "What do you propose instead?" he asked as he filled it with water.

"Let's kill 'em with kindness," she suggested. "Just be extremely friendly with what's-his-name."

"Bryan?" said Trevor as he poured the water into the tank. "That's what Carly called the leader of the school that attacked us."

"Yeah. Negotiate with Carly and Zachary, but just be super sweet and friendly anytime Bryan tries to attack us — which you just know he will, and then move on."

"I like it." Trevor put the coffee filter with grounds into the machine, shut the lid, and hit the button, waiting with bated breath for the scent of coffee to fill the air. It whirred on, and a moment later, he sighed with pleasure as the aroma began to emanate.

"You and your coffee," said Sister Margaret. "I'm gonna go make some tea and get ready for this banquet. My formal habit is elaborate, and takes some getting into. Might need you to help me buckle in a few places."

Chapter 22: Sister Margaret

Once her tea was made, Sister Margaret sat down at the desk, flipping through the welcome packet. Her eyes started glazing over a bit when she got to the list of cryptid races and the names of their representatives here at the summit.

There were significantly more races listed here than she'd known about. What the hell was an aqrabuamelu? Or a squonk?

She was familiar with the concept of a mothman, but hadn't realized they were real. Not only were they real, apparently she was about to meet four of them. And the plural was mothmans, not mothmen. Good to know.

Sister Margaret paused at the mages, looking to see if there would be any more surprises. Nope, she didn't know either of the mages sent as delegates from the Illuminati. Maybe they would turn out to be connected to Trevor or one of the Pala.

She couldn't imagine the Illuminati representatives would know Coyote or Chameleon, who had been raised in a secret society and had very little interaction with the outside world until recently.

Sighing, Sister Margaret realized she was stalling. She really, really didn't want to put on that formal habit. She didn't generally wear a habit at all in her day-to-day life, preferring her more practical leather armor.

Honestly, considering how many of her order also went around in brown leather armor, it might as well be their habit. But they did have an actual habit, mostly worn by those sisters who were positioned in more mainstream occupations like teachers and hospital workers.

And then there was the formal habit, which she would definitely have to wear at this stupid formal banquet tonight.

Sister Margaret opened one of her duffel bags and rummaged past weapons, first aid gear, armor, and toiletries. From the very bottom, she withdrew a garment bag.

Hanging it from the top of the bathroom door, she carefully unzipped it and regarded the habit with a sigh.

This was going to be very uncomfortable.

Chapter 23: Trevor

Trevor stared at himself in the full-length mirror that hung on the bathroom door. He had tried on the formal Warrior Mage Librarian uniform for lay people (which is apparently what the Church called anyone who wasn't a priest, monk, or nun) once before and at the time had fervently hoped he would never have to actually wear it.

As old-fashioned and elaborate as it was, he had to admit it did look good on him. He turned to the side and then the other side and then swiveled to check out the back.

It looked really good on him. Sammy was probably going to hit on him a lot.

And it probably wouldn't be that uncomfortable once it settled in a little. It was just so stiff. But it was designed to be able to move in — it was a warrior's uniform after all.

The heavy black canvas was discreetly thicker over his heart and other vulnerable areas and had a high, thick collar as well to protect his neck and throat. The black with its intricate white embroidered accents suited Trevor's brown skin, giving him a dark and mysterious air.

He buckled his sword belt over his hips. Oh, yeah. That looked bad-ass.

Trevor grinned at his reflection, then turned to the weapons he had laid out on the bed to finish filling in all the little sheaths, holsters, and pockets that peppered the uniform with weapons, lock picks, and first aid gear.

He finished arming up and glanced at the bedside clock. Twenty minutes still until Taye would come to collect them for the banquet.

Trevor was used to being early for things. He took a few minutes to run through some krav maga exercises, making a few adjustments of his weaponry as he did so to allow it to lie better. Then he sat down at the desk to review the page of cryptids again.

There was no real need to do so — he had an excellent memory, thanks to his stitcher nature — but he needed some kind of occupation. If he just sat there and waited, he'd drive himself crazy with worrying about how much he was going to fuck everything up, how little he was qualified for this post, and all the different ways in which he could let Sister Margaret down.

Finally, somebody knocked on the door, and Trevor leapt to his feet, rushing over to open it up.

As soon as the door opened, and he saw Sister Margaret's get-up, he burst out laughing.

"Shut up," she muttered, tugging on her headdress.

This was definitely the first time he'd ever seen his partner looking like a nun. But she was still the strangest looking nun ever.

She wore her usual brown combat boots, paired with loose black trousers and a sleeveless chainmail tunic that ended mid-thigh. Under the tunic was a long-sleeved black top. Over her forearms were black leather bracers.

But the crowning glory was the head dress. It resembled the wimples some of her sisters wore, but it was stiff like armor. Trevor squinted at it. "What is that hat made of?"

"Titanium." Sister Margaret glared at him. "It's titanium chain mail, like the tunic."

He giggled again. "That can't be comfortable."

She shrugged and sighed. "It's lined with some kind of super soft fabric," she said. "And at least it's not as heavy as they probably were back in the day. And I managed to get it all on by myself."

"Shall we get moving?" interrupted Taye, who stood behind her. He had abandoned his loincloth and wore a loose white suit with a colorful pattern across the chest and at the ends of the sleeves and legs. It was similar to pictures Trevor had seen of his Ethiopian grandfather, clearly influenced by the humans who lived nearby the salashifters' territory.

"Yeah, sorry." Trevor stepped out into the hallway and Taye immediately began to lead them briskly back down, the same way they'd come earlier that day.

"Where are the other mages?" he asked.

"I have elected to bring each group individually," said Taye. "In order to prevent some kind of bizarre parade-like situation. Aurora and the Illuminati are already seated. I will return for Pala next."

He led them down the stairs and through the bare lobby. As before, the desk off to one side was unstaffed.

The trio exited the hotel. Trevor expected Taye to have his hover barge waiting, but instead he simply turned and led them on foot up the alleyway.

When they reached the main thoroughfare, Taye led them up a set of stairs onto one of the broad causeways that crisscrossed the city above the roads.

The causeway was bustling, mostly with dragons, but a sprinkling of other cryptids walked past or sat at tables beside the buildings that lined the bridge, and Trevor looked around with interest.

He smiled at a pair of young dragons playing off to one side. One of the youngsters, noticing his regard, bounced over and roared, a blast of cold air smacking him right in the face.

The young dragon was immediately pulled away by the supervising adult. "I'm so sorry," exclaimed the dragon. "He was just saying hello, but he doesn't speak English yet."

"That's okay," said Trevor with a laugh. He wiped frost droplets from his eyebrows and hair. "He's adorable. How old is he?"

"One hundred and sixty-three," said the adult. "Still hasn't quite gotten his manners down, have you, T'Mani?" She roared gently at her offspring, and he bowed to Trevor, conveying extreme contriteness.

Trevor laughed again. "No problem." Looking around, he saw that Taye and Sister Margaret had continued walking. "But I need to catch up with my party."

"Thank you for understanding," said the adult dragon, herding T'Mani back to where his friend waited.

Trevor stretched his legs, hastening to catch up with the others.

Minutes later, they turned a corner and stopped abruptly, finding themselves at the end of a long line of a dizzying array of cryptids. The banquet was about to begin.

Chapter 24: Sister Margaret

As Sister Margaret waited in line, her anxiety grew. She couldn't help but feel out of her element among all these glamorously dressed cryptids. You'd think it would be incongruous to see a yeti in a formal ballgown, or a tuxedo designed to accommodate a large scorpion-like tail, but they pulled it off.

She couldn't help but wonder why all of the cryptids seemed to have had the same ideas about formalwear as humans.

There were regional variances. She noticed a group of humanoid cryptids with white hair and Asian features wearing kimonos, and a group of women in lovely embroidered dresses that evoked a South American feel.

"I will leave you here," said Taye. "Just check in with the person at the door."

Finally, they reached the door to the strange pyramid-like building — made of blue ice, of course, like everything else in the city —- and were met by a salashifter woman, who gave them a big, good-natured smile. "Hello!" she said. "You must be the Warrior Mage Librarians from the Vatican! I've been looking forward to meeting you."

"Yes," said Trevor, returning her smile. "I'm Trevor, and this is Sister Margaret."

"Wonderful! My name is Jahzara." She consulted a tablet on her podium and then turned her sunny smile on Taye. "Table Eighty-Five. There are four other mages already present." She pointed to a table toward the center of the room, where Sister Margaret could see two familiar faces and two men she hadn't met.

"Thank you," said Trevor.

"Yeah, thanks." Sister Margaret waved to Jahzara as Trevor led the way into the ballroom.

Jahzara gave her another bright grin and turned her attention to the next group.

Sister Margaret's eyes widened as they walked in a circuitous route between tables filled with every imaginable kind of person -– and a lot of people she never could have imagined in a million years.

She found her attention caught by the unicorns, grouped in a corner around a trough of some kind of golden liquid — beer, maybe? Their only concession to the formal nature of the banquet was multi-colored ribbons wrapped intricately around their horns, each one done in a pattern that coordinated with the colors of the horn itself.

Fortunately, they reached their table before her brain got completely overloaded, and she grinned at two of the mages already seated.

Coyote stood up as they approached, a broad smile splitting his face. "Hello, old friends." He stepped toward them, wrapping Trevor in a big hug, which Trevor returned enthusiastically.

He moved as though to hug Sister Margaret as well, but hesitated.

"I know, I know," she said. "This outfit isn't very cuddly."

"It's even less cuddly than your usual outfits," said Chameleon. She remained seated, but Sister Margaret had to raise an eyebrow at her remark. From what she could see of

Chameleon's ensemble, it was a navy blue version of exactly what Sister Margaret normally wore and pretty typical of her.

Chameleon must have noticed her regard and followed her thoughts. "I'm not trying to be cuddly," she said.

"Have you ever been cuddly?" said Sister Margaret.

"Once," said Chameleon serenely. She took a sip of her red wine. "February of 2018. I didn't care for it."

Spotting a card with her name on it, Sister Margaret sat down. Her chain mail jingled and she adjusted it so that it sort of bunched up at the small of her back and pooled down her sides. It was really not made for sitting down in.

"That looks very complicated," said Coyote. He was also wearing the ubiquitous leather armor so many warrior mages donned, his in a deep black.

Sister Margaret spared a pang of envy, then sighed. She loved her life and it was worth being told what to wear on occasion. Instead of dwelling on it, she turned her attention to the other two mages seated at the table.

Trevor gave the strangers a small bow. "Hello," he said. "Forgive me for not introducing myself immediately. We are the delegation from the Vatican. Trevor Harper and Sister Margaret Herrera, Warrior Mage Librarians."

Belatedly, Sister Margaret did a sort of half-stand and bobbed her head. Crap. She was already fucking up. She shouldn't have sat down so soon.

Then again, the other mages hadn't stood either.

"Nice to meet you," said the older man with what sounded like a Texas drawl. He sprawled in his seat in an expensive-looking suit paired with a tie that depicted cutesy purple dragons that bore little resemblance to their draconic hosts. Hanging in front of the tie, on a heavy gold chain, was a huge gold medallion divided into four quadrants, each with some kind of mystical symbol on it.

The other man gave Texas a slightly irritated look and finally stood, leaning forward and extending his hand to Sister Margaret across the table. He was clad more conventionally, in a black tuxedo, his blond hair slicked back with something that smelled strongly like shoe polish. He wore the same golden badge, but in a smaller, more discreet pin on his lapel. "Grand Master Henry Palmer at your service. My associate is Prince Gregory Pitts. We represent the Illuminati."

"Prince?" said Trevor. "You are American, are you not? May I assume the title is based within your society and not political?"

Prince Gregory made a gun with his fingers and shot an imaginary bullet at Trevor. "Bingo. You're a smart kid, huh? What are you, some kind of priest?"

Sister Margaret suppressed a laugh, and Trevor gave Gregory a tight, slightly pained smile.

"No, I just work for the Vatican," he replied.

Henry shook Trevor's hand as well, but Gregory made no move toward them, instead picking up a peanut from a dish in front of him and tossing it toward his face. It missed his open mouth and he picked up another one.

Sister Margaret watched, fascinated, as the man continued throwing three more peanuts in the general area of his gaping maw before finally landing one. He then proceeded to crunch down on it loudly as the other mages stared, unable to look away.

"So, where y'all from?" asked Gregory, either oblivious or used to the stares. "I come from Houston, myself, born and raised, and wouldn't live anywhere else in the world. God bless America, right?" He glanced at Sister Margaret. "Oh, no offense. I've been to Mexico, and it's nice, but you can't beat the good old U. S. of A." He raised his glass to Trevor. "This guy knows what I'm talking about, right?"

Henry's face was a blank mask, his eyes cold as he gazed at his colleague.

"Why do you mention Mexico?" asked Sister Margaret, softly. "Is somebody here from Mexico?"

"My great grandfather came from Guatemala," said Coyote. "Never been to Mexico, myself. You been to Mexico, Chameleon?"

"I have, actually," said Chameleon. "It is nice. Don't think anyone here is from there, though. Trevor? Are you from Mexico?"

"Not me," said Trevor.

"Well, I mean, you're clearly--" Gregory nodded toward Sister Margaret. "I mean, your accent is--" He waved his hands awkwardly. "Aren't you?"

"Born and raised in St. Louis, MO," said Sister Margaret sweetly. "I have an accent because I was raised by my grandmother."

"Who is Mexican!" said Gregory triumphantly.

"Who is Puerto Rican," Sister Margaret corrected him.

"I must apologize for Gregory," said Henry, cooly. "He is not as cosmopolitan as one might prefer."

"Huh?" Gregory gave Henry a sidelong glance, then shrugged and tossed another peanut in the general direction of his mouth.

Sister Margaret was actually feeling a lot more cheerful. She felt at home dealing with your standard American good ol' boy, and at least the other Illuminati representative seemed okay, if a little bit on the deadpan side.

"Well, anyway, glad to see we're all Americans here, then," Gregory charged on, completely oblivious to Henry's discomfort. "I'm sure we'll all get along splendidly." He beamed around the table and tossed another peanut at his mouth, miraculously getting it on the first try this time.

Chameleon leaned forward. "Did you see that Sammy West is a member of the other delegation? What are the odds?"

"Yeah," said Sister Margaret. "I hadn't seen him since just after Broken Bunker, and he was in rough shape. I guess he must be doing better."

"We invited him to join Aurora," said Coyote. "But he wanted to explore other options."

"He and Meerkat have kept in touch," Chameleon added with a faint smile and a little waggle of her eyebrows.

"Y'll have the queerest names," put in Gregory.

Sister Margaret blinked.

"What's that about?" Gregory continued. "Y'all born into some kind of bizarro cult?"

Trevor tilted his head. "You're a member of the Illuminati."

"Sure am." Gregory tapped his giant medallion and gave Trevor a proud smile. "Inducted when I was at Harvard, sponsored by my old man. My son joined up this year too, latest in a long line of Illuminati, going all the way back to Jamestown."

So, that's how he got chosen for this delicate posting. He probably bullied his way in based on his family line, leaving Henry to do all the actual diplomatic work, plus babysitting.

Just then, Sammy and Ari arrived. Sammy was dressed in a sharp black suit, his hair gelled in carefully artless spikes.

Ari wore a cream-colored suit with a matching turban on his head.

"Hello, hello," said Sammy with his trademark mischievous grin.

Coyote leapt to his feet. "Come here, you!" Contrary to his words, he rushed around the table toward Sammy, wrapping him up in a big hug.

Sammy lifted his arm to return the embrace.

Emerging from Coyote's exuberant greeting, Sammy waved to the rest of them with a grin. "Hiya, guys! Coyote,

Chameleon, great to see you! Damn, Trevor, you are looking fine in that uniform. Sister Margaret, you look super weird. What is that thing on your head?" Without giving her a chance to respond, he turned to Henry, who had stood up. He extended his hand. "How's it going? I'm Sammy; this is Ari. We're from a global organization called Pala, mages focused on creating good in the world."

"Hello." Ari sat down beside Sister Margaret as Henry introduced himself and Gregory again.

"So, how d'y'all know each other?" asked Gregory. "Seems like it's a big reunion, and we're at a disadvantage." He laughed heartily at his own thin joke.

"It's a long story," said Trevor.

"Sum it up," Gregory suggested.

Chameleon waved a hand to encompass Trevor, Sister Margaret, and Sammy. "These three destroyed the corrupt society we were born into. We helped."

Henry nodded and addressed Gregory. "You were briefed on this, sir. The Auditors were an international secret society focused on keeping mages as a whole from practicing multiple disciplines. Their governing body was attacked and dismantled last year, in large part due to the people at this table."

"I always thought they were a myth," said Gregory. "Some kind of bogeyman we tell our kids about to get them focused on learning the right kind of magery and not bother with trying to learn anything else that they can't damn well do anyway."

"Can't they?" Chameleon's eyes went white as she turned on her seer sight. Simultaneously, her hands glowed as she conjured a small fireball in her palm using a spell.

"It would appear that you can," said Henry, his eyebrows lifted.

"I can too," said Trevor.

"I've never done it any other way," said Chameleon, dismissing her spell and shifting her eyes back into their ordinary mode.

"I try not to, but I can in a pinch," said Coyote.

"I use all three as well," added Sammy.

The table turned toward Sister Margaret, who lifted her hands. "Don't look at me. I'm a seer and I have no desire to morph. But there have always been morphers in my Order. Although we don't call it that."

"What about you?" Gregory pointed at Ari.

"No," said Ari. "I only learned that it was possible when Sammy joined our group, and I am set in my ways. Some among us have begun to learn."

"A whole new era of magery," said Henry. There was a spark of something akin to excitement in his eyes, although his face as a whole remained neutral.

Just then, a bigfoot approached their table, this time with a tray of drinks. He placed a glass of beer in front of Sister Margaret, wine at Trevor's place, and some kind of fruity cocktail in front of Sammy. Ari appeared to be sticking with water.

"Thank you," said Sister Margaret.

"I'll take another beer over here," said Gregory, waving his nearly-empty glass.

The bigfoot blinked at him. "Certainly." He strode away.

"Jeez, what crawled up his ass?" said Gregory.

An awkward silence fell over the table, until Trevor turned to Coyote and asked, "Did you have any trouble getting in?"

"Yes, actually," he said. "Merfolk tried to ambush us on the lake." He lifted his right arm, which Sister Margaret saw belatedly was bandaged up at the wrist. "Got me with a trident, but Chameleon fucked him up good with a fireball."

"Apparently the merfolk are not fond of fire," said Chameleon.

"Good tip," said Sister Margaret. "So, they didn't disable your car?"

Coyote shook his head. "We were prepared for them. The dragonlord who met us mentioned what had happened to you all. I guess you had just been brought in out of the cold when we arrived."

"So we had a shield specifically over the car, and spells ready to fly." Chameleon bared her teeth in a bloodthirsty grin and mimed tossing a fireball from her palm.

"We didn't have any trouble," said Gregory. "Guess they knew better than to try and mess with us. We came in before any of you, hoped to do some sightseeing, but ended up just sleeping off the jetlag for a day and a half."

There was another awkward pause, before Sammy addressed Henry. "So, you're with the Illuminati? What's that like?"

"Oh, it's great," answered Gregory. "Only the best for us, you know. Cream of the crop. It's a good feeling, to be among the best."

Henry frowned. He spoke carefully, addressing the entire table. "We are moving in a new direction in the twenty-first century. Leaving the boy's club model behind. I believe you would agree that we, as a group, have a reputation for using our influence to cement the power of our members in the political arena. However, many of the younger members, myself included, would like to—"

"Buncha snowflakes, if you ask me," Gregory interrupted. He gave Henry a genial thump on the back.

Sister Margaret winced as the younger man froze in place, resentment clearly seething beneath the cold surface of his mask.

"I hope my son doesn't fall in with your lot. No offense, of course."

"Of course," murmured Henry. He sipped his water. "How could anyone take offense at that?"

Sister Margaret glanced over at Coyote and Chameleon, who had fallen silent. They had the look of two people who were settled in for a show. All they needed was a bucket of popcorn.

She had to admit to herself that the dynamic between the two Illuminati was a fascinating sort of shitshow, but she hoped it wouldn't interfere with the deals Cardinal Neubacher was hoping they'd be able to make, nor distract from her own mission to find Saint Joan's sword, which had been in the back of her mind during all the excitement.

She reminded herself to speak with Taye the next day about which dragon she should talk to about that.

"Please continue," Sammy invited Henry. "What direction are your younger members hoping to go in?"

"We would like to use our influence to improve the state of the world," he said, firmly, ignoring Gregory's eye roll. "In fact, I was pleased to learn that Pala would be represented here, and hope to forge a strong alliance between our two groups. We are ready to take on a new role in the global stage."

"I don't know about global," said Gregory. "I still think we should be focusing on–"

"Feel free to focus wherever you'd like," Henry snapped. "I will be making the most of this month."

Sister Margaret's eyes met Chameleon's across the table, and the younger woman lifted her eyebrows. Sister Margaret grinned back at her. She was starting to like this Henry guy. Gregory was clearly a joke who had no business even being here, and who apparently viewed the entire summit as some kind of exotic vacation.

But Henry? Henry they could work with.

Glancing around the room, Sister Margaret noticed a variety of cryptids lining up at a long, long table on one side of the hall, filling up plates of food.

Right on cue, Sister Margaret's stomach growled. She hadn't eaten all day, being too busy being stranded, rescued, and then napping.

She was definitely pleased to be at a banquet.

Just then, Taye silently and unexpectedly appeared at Sister Margaret's elbow. She had a dagger in her hand and halfway to his throat before she realized who it was and relaxed.

Taye cleared his throat, eyebrows lifted, but otherwise ignored the weapon as she tucked it away. "I am here to inform you that your table is welcome to approach the buffet."

"Buffet?" said Gregory. "Seems like a fancy do like this, we'd get table service."

"Yes, sir," said Taye. "But we do it this way to give the attendees more opportunity to mingle."

"Makes sense," said Trevor. "Shall we?"

The mages all stood and followed Taye in a single file line to the buffet table, winding between tables of cryptids.

Sister Margaret paused beside one table, eyes widening at its occupants. They looked human, but beside each stood another person with a needle in their arm and a tube running from the needle to a wine glass on the table.

One of the needle people, a white woman with short, artfully tousled brown hair and a large nose, smiled at her. "You're a mage, right?"

"Yeah," she said. "Sister Margaret. I work for the Vatican."

"I'd love to talk to you sometime about how to become a mage. I never knew people could do magic until I heard you guys would be here."

"Really?" Sister Margaret looked into her eyes. "You knew about vampires, but not mages? That's so odd to me; I was raised with magery, but always thought vampires were a myth.

How did you—" She paused. How the hell did you diplomatically ask someone how they ended up hooked up to a vampire's wine glass?

The woman's smile widened and, with her unencumbered arm, she reached into a purse that hung at her side, pulling out a small cream-colored card. She handed it to Sister Margaret.

On it was written a bulleted list:

- *Yes, it's consensual*
- *No, it's not sexual*
- *No, it's not addictive*
- *No, it's not generally life threatening; deaths are rare and always accidental*
- *I will not become a vampire from this*
- *They pay really well, plus benefits*

Sister Margaret laughed. "Thank you for this. I would be happy to talk to you later on about magery, and point you in the direction of a good mentor."

Turning, she hurried to catch up with the rest of her party at the buffet, where they were lined up behind a group of bigfoots. Sammy was at the head of the line of mages, chatting animatedly with the two bigfoots at the end of their line.

As Sister Margaret took her place behind Gregory and Henry, another group arrived, lining up behind her. These were humanoid in shape with tan skin, black hair, and noble bearing, but she quickly realized that their eyes were slitted and there was something odd about their tongues. They chattered among themselves in a language she didn't recognize.

Slitted eyes. . . . These must be the kallanpa amaru.

The story behind these cryptids was actually fascinating. They were a fungus-based life form and had been accidentally created when an overworked Incan priestess in ancient times had been preparing a plate of mushrooms as an offering to her local snake god.

The priestess also happened to be a witch and her preparations had somehow turned into a spell.

The result had been a race of immortal sapient cryptids who were capable of shifting into any form they wanted. They tended to prefer the shape of a human with some snake-like characteristics, and for their territory they had claimed an island off the coast of modern-day Brazil, which had earned the moniker Snake Island because it was full of highly venomous snakes, which the kallanpa amaru had bred as their pets and protectors.

Well, if the whole point of the buffet was for guests to be mingling, she better start getting diplomatic or whatever.

Sister Margaret gave the nearest kallanpa amaru a bright smile and stuck out her hand. "Hi. I'm Sister Margaret, mage, representative of the Vatican."

The kallanpa amaru blinked at her and their forked tongue flicked in and out of their mouth a couple of times.

Another of their party stepped forward and shook Sister Margaret's hand. "Sorry about that," they said. "Killa is one of the ancient ones, set in their ways. Many of the older of our kind speak only Quechua or Spanish."

"Oh." Sister Margaret switched to Spanish. "No problem. I will have to learn Quechua at some point. That's the language of the Inca, isn't it?"

The ancient one beamed at her and responded in Spanish as well. "It is, yes. You are human?"

"*Sí.*" She introduced herself again, in Spanish this time, as the line moved forward and she arrived at the food.

Sister Margaret busied herself with filling a plate, pleased that she had managed to make a connection so easily. Two, if you counted the vampire's . . . employee.

Maybe not getting killed wouldn't be so difficult after all.

But as she returned to her table, the other mages already seated and beginning to eat, she saw trouble approaching.

She nudged Trevor. "Merfolk. Ten o'clock. The unfriendly kind," she murmured. She picked up her steak knife. As a weapon, it wasn't ideal, but she figured it was better than nothing, and wouldn't automatically be construed as aggression unless she needed to use it.

And if she did need to get weapony, she had plenty of others too. This would just be the starter weapon.

The green mer, Bryan, stalked up to them, his short legs looking oddly disproportionate to his long torso. Somehow he made it work — maybe it was his overall aura of aggression that forced you to take him seriously.

Sister Margaret saw with satisfaction that the orange mer behind him had a bandage on his shoulder from her throwing star. Another mer in the entourage, a silver shark like creature, had more bandages covering half of their face, and she wondered if that was courtesy of Chameleon.

Before any of the mages could greet Bryan, he lifted his arm and flung something down onto Gregory's plate, which happened to be the closest to him.

Gregory recoiled in horror. "Ew. What the hell? Is that a fish head?"

It was, in fact, a raw fish head, nestled in the center of his mound of mashed potatoes.

"Don't touch it!" Taye stepped up beside Gregory and picked up his entire plate. "Go and get a new plate of food, sir. I will take care of this."

A stunned look on his face, Gregory rose to return to the buffet.

Taye bowed to Bryan. "The Illuminati have no quarrel with your school. Leave them be."

"This is a grave insult on your part," said Bryan. "The mage should be left free to react as he would. This will not be forgotten."

"Please do not attempt to bully me," Taye retorted. "I know your laws. No insult has been given here on either part. Your challenge has been rebuffed in standard form. Return to your table now."

A kallanpa amaru stepped forward and placed a hand on Bryan's arm. Had they been there the whole time? They must be the mer's On'Chala. "Come," they said. "He is right. No laws were violated. You may try again tomorrow or work your differences out via talks."

Reluctantly, Bryan turned and followed the On'Chala away, taking a seat at a table of merfolk about a hundred yards away.

Sister Margaret set down her knife and picked up her fork, hesitating over her potatoes. Too soon. She just kept picturing the fish head on top of Gregory's. Better start with the broccoli instead.

Somehow, she managed to polish off the whole plate, keeping quiet as the mages around her dissected the incident with the merfolk.

Gregory was all for greeting aggression with more aggression, but Sister Margaret couldn't help but notice that Henry was as quiet as she was. What was going on behind those cold, blue eyes?

Chapter 25: Trevor

The next day, Trevor's alarm went off far too early. And far too shrilly. With a groan, he groped around for his phone without opening his eyes. He grasped it and held it up in front of his face, finally opening his eyes just enough to find the off button.

Then he rolled back over and groaned again. He was a diplomat now. An important person with important speed carousels to get to. Sleeping in probably wasn't an option.

With a sigh, he tossed the covers off the bed and got up, stretching and yawning as he wandered over to the desk to check the schedule. The carousel started in an hour, and the mages were supposed to be in Conference Room B.

He was glad they'd be staying still for this first morning round. It would feel less awkward to be the approached than the approachers.

With another yawn, Trevor wandered over to the dresser and pulled out an outfit for the day. This one didn't need to be formal, just presentable, so he settled on black slacks and a white button-up shirt. He sighed again and added a gray tie to the ensemble. It would appear that he was becoming a tie person, and he wasn't really sure he cared for it.

But that was growing up, wasn't it? He was in his late thirties at this point, so it was probably about time for it.

It sure had snuck up on him, though.

Examining himself in the mirror, he nodded with satisfaction. It might not be what he would have chosen a year ago, but he did look sharp.

He knocked on the door between his room and Sister Margaret's, and she opened it right away, giving him a grin that was far too cheerful. She had always been more of a morning person than he was.

"Ready for breakfast?" she asked. She had also foregone her formalwear, opting for her standard brown leather pants, tank top, and brown leather armor, bandolier across her chest and twin swords at her side.

Without waiting for a response, she bounced into his room and headed for the door, leading the way out into the hallway.

Taye had told them after the banquet last night to return to the same building for breakfast and the carousel, so they headed down the alleyway toward the stairs up to the causeway.

The causeway was quiet this early, only a few cryptids, mostly dragons, eating at the sidewalk cafes. Most of these were solitary, sitting beside the table and staring down at tablets or smartphones in front of them, which was both strange and familiar at the same time.

Trevor briefly wondered how they used the phones and tablets without hands; then he noticed a dragon lift a claw which delicately held a stylus between two of the digits. She was actually quite dexterous with it.

Another dragon typed away at an oversized keyboard hooked up to a lap-top-sized screen.

He found it so interesting how cryptids had evolved alongside humans, adapting to human technology without humans ever really figuring out they were there.

Oh, sure, some humans had caught glimpses here and there, but they were always dismissed as lunatics. Probably others had figured it out and kept it to themselves or convinced themselves it couldn't be real.

Sister Margaret held the door open and Trevor slipped past her into the building. A sign had been set up with the word "Breakfast" on it and an arrow pointing off to the left, so he turned in that direction.

"How about this merry-go-round or whatever it's called, huh?" said Sister Margaret. "I wonder how eager cryptids will be to chat with us. I figure we're either going to be super popular, as a novelty, or just bored as everyone skips us and goes to talk to their friends instead."

Trevor nodded. "I would give my right arm to know who else is stationary, and whether we're going to have to deal with merfolk in this thing."

"Be careful what you wish for," said a cheerful voice behind them.

Oops. Trevor felt his face warm as Sammy slung his remaining arm around his shoulders. "Hey, I didn't mean to--"

Sammy laughed. "Oh, for goodness sake, of course you didn't. You're all good. It's a common expression. How'd you guys sleep last night?"

"Fantastic," said Trevor. "Yesterday was a long day. Hello, Ari." He gave a friendly nod to the other member of Sammy's party.

"And a late night," added Sister Margaret.

"Yeah, same," said Sammy. "Could have used another five hours or so, but here we are."

The four of them paused outside an open set of double doors leading to a room only slightly smaller than last night's ballroom.

Ari whistled. "Dragons don't do anything by halves, do they?"

"Well, we're very large, ourselves, aren't we?" said a jovial dragon standing inside. "Welcome, mages. Come on in; we won't bite! I am Dragonlord On'Klanka, and I'm looking forward to getting to know you better."

They stepped inside the room.

"Very pleased to make your acquaintance, Dragonlord," said Trevor with a bow.

She laughed. "So formal. I know we may seem a bit intimidating at first, but really, there's no need for all the bowing and 'make your acquaintancing.' I'm very approachable once you get to know me." She winked one huge eye and continued on her way toward a table, a tray of food balanced easily on one elbow.

"It just feels like someone who introduces themselves as 'Dragonlord such and such' should be bowed to, right?" Trevor remarked to Ari.

"I know what you mean," he said. He lowered his voice. "And it's unclear to me whether all of the dragons are Dragonlord such and such or whether some are just dragon such and such."

"Oh, I know that one!" said Sister Margaret. "It's age-based."

"Thank you." Ari bowed. "We must compare notes at some point; swap whatever information we've been able to glean."

The group arrived at the buffet table, which was full of a dizzying array of food for all kinds of appetites. As they had at last night's banquet, the mages headed for the section that looked designed for humans, which in this case held trays of pastries and warmers filled with oatmeal, scrambled eggs, and bacon.

Trevor loaded up on eggs and looked around for coffee, spotting a samovar at the very end, just past what appeared to be an entire roasted pig, complete with an apple in its mouth.

By the time he'd amended his coffee with cream and sugar, the other mages had claimed half of a long, rectangular table, sharing with a cluster of bigfoots at the other end.

He wove his way through the room, nodding amicably to various cryptids he passed along the way, including two tables of merfolk. Zachary gave them a friendly wave of one of his tentacles.

Bryan and his school just looked at him with cold eyes as they dined on what looked like whole raw fish.

Trevor shivered and slid onto the bench beside Sister Margaret. "Those merfolk are making me nervous."

He glanced over at them and saw to his dismay that a group of large, hairy mammalian cryptids — chupacabra, maybe? — had joined the merfolk and were glaring at the humans as well.

"It seems to be spreading," Sammy observed.

"I think the best strategy will be to ignore any groups that are actively hostile," suggested Ari. "And focus on making alliances with the cryptids who are interested."

Sammy pointed his fork at Ari. "Listen to this guy. He's done this kind of thing before."

"Only with humans," said Ari, eyes lowered modestly.

"Don't listen to him," Sammy insisted. "Ari was involved in the 2016 Climate talks in Paris, and represented—"

"Hey!" A familiar voice shouted.

Trevor turned toward the commotion and saw that the Illuminati were making their way through the room and had stopped beside Bryan's table.

Gregory glared at the mer. "You did that on purpose." The man wagged a finger dangerously close to Bryan's shark-like beak.

One of the chupacabra growled and stood up.

"I'm sure that's not true," Henry intervened smoothly, his face and voice flat and expressionless as he took Gregory's arm and continued onward toward the buffet table, pausing for just a second to throw a cold glare at first Bryan, then the chupacabra.

Gregory frowned, but followed Henry's lead.

The angry chupacabra took a step forward as though to follow, but Taye and a kallanpa amaru stepped in front of him and gestured back toward his chair, murmuring something Trevor couldn't hear.

Whatever they said, it worked. The chupacabra resumed his seat and the On'Chalas backed off, sitting at a table off to the side with a wide range of cryptids.

Trevor recognized the bigfoot who served as On'Chala to the mer — it must be a table full of the On'Chala, watching carefully to intervene in case of impending violence.

"Might be tricky to ignore that Bryan," Sister Margaret observed. "He seems determined to make his presence known."

"That Henry makes me kind of nervous too," said Ari. "Best to lock down an alliance with the Illuminati quickly."

"I like him," said Chameleon. "He seems like he has a good head on his shoulders. So he's not that personable? Neither am I, and you like me, right?"

"Fair enough." Trevor sipped his coffee and looked around the room. His gaze fell on the merfolk table again. Zachary and Carly were nowhere to be seen, but the others had been joined by another chupacabra and a witch.

This might be a very long morning.

Chapter 26: Sister Margaret

After breakfast, Sister Margaret, Trevor, and the delegates of Pala and Aurora made their way to Conference Room B. The Illuminati had chosen to eat their morning meal alone, and Sister Margaret mulled over the implications of that.

She had been assuming that making alliances with the other mage groups would be the easiest. She already considered Aurora to be her own allies and figured it wouldn't be difficult to negotiate with them, and certainly Sammy's group seemed amenable to working together, but the Illuminati were more complicated.

She wasn't sure what she'd been expecting from them. Actually, now that she thought about it, she'd been expecting *either* bumbling, entitled idiots like Gregory or cold-eyed secret society types like Henry, but not one of each.

Probably one or the other would be the one to approach, but she couldn't decide which. Maybe Trevor had some ideas. She'd have to ask him at lunch time. First, though, they needed to get through the morning.

The six of them arrived at the door to the conference room, and Sammy pushed open the door, holding it open for everyone with a smile and a flourish.

Sister Margaret returned his grin as she brushed past him and followed Ari toward the empty seats on one side of the massive table that dominated the room.

The mages arrayed themselves on one side, leaving the other empty for other groups to face them.

A couple of minutes later, the Illuminati arrived as well, seating themselves at the end of the table.

"Sorry we're late," said Gregory. "I was hoping to get in a round of golf this morning, but this party pooper insisted I had to be here. Couldn't figure out where the course is anyway. You guys know where the nearest golf course is?"

"I don't know that there is one," said Sammy. "I think the dragons have other games."

"No golf?" Gregory shook his head. "That can't be right."

Taye arrived and took a seat at a separate smaller table off to the side.

"Oh, good," said Gregory to Taye. "Can you tell me where the golf course is?"

The salashifter blinked at him. "The what?"

"Golf is a game a lot of a certain type of human play," said Chameleon. "It's played on a large lawn of several acres with strategically placed holes, hills, sand pits, and ponds, called a course."

Taye frowned. "That sounds like a waste of space."

"Very much so," Sammy agreed. His eyes flashed with anger. "Wasted space, wasted water, giant swathes of land with only grass growing and no other plants, covered in pesticides."

"Oh, you're one of those—" began Gregory.

"There's nothing like that here," Taye interrupted.

Sister Margaret hid a smile. Apparently Taye's job extended to ensuring the mages didn't kill each other too.

"If you enjoy sports, however, you should definitely check out the squonkerball tournament this afternoon. I would advise watching this round to get a feel for the rules and strategies, but perhaps you can play in the next tournament. It's a lot of fun, and hardly anyone dies anymore."

"Hardly anyone?" echoed Trevor.

"Yes, they've adjusted the rules considerably to make it safer," Taye enthused. "Do a lot of people die from playing this golf?"

"Hardly anyone," said Coyote.

Just then the door opened and four witches filed in, arraying themselves along the table across from the mages.

"Oh, good," Trevor murmured. "Jumping right into hostile territory."

Sister Margaret gave the witch across from her, the oldest of the group, a sunny smile. She glared back with narrowed brown eyes.

So, it was going to be like that.

Refusing to be intimidated, Sister Margaret widened her smile and leaned forward to include the other witches in its glow.

Another witch, a strawberry blonde dressed in a plum pantsuit returned the smile. "Hi," she said. Her voice had a slight accent, too light to easily place. Scandinavia, perhaps? "I'm Eva Nilson. You must be Margaret."

"Sister Margaret, yes," she replied. She gestured toward the other mages. "My associate, Trevor Harper, and the delegates from Pala, Sammy West and Ari Ahuja. The delegates from Aurora, Chameleon and Coyote. And the Illuminati, Henry Palmer and Gregory Pitts."

"*Prince* Gregory Pitts," said the Texan mage, leaning back in his chair.

Ignoring him, Sister Margaret glanced expectantly at the grumpy witch again, but the woman just crossed her arms and pursed her lips.

Eva nudged the other witch, who finally responded in a deep, strident voice, her French accent heavy. "Matriarch Monin."

The next witch looked about midway between the others in age, maybe in her fifties, with dark hair streaked in gray. She was dressed an emerald dress that accentuated her pale skin and matched her eyes almost exactly. "Matriarch Welch," she said. Her voice was deep and her accent was musical. "Of the Cornwall Council of Matriarchs."

The final witch crossed her arms and swept a scornful glance over the mages before introducing herself. "Alyssa Torres. San Antonio, Texas. United States of America."

"That's what I'm talking about!" said Gregory. "Texans unite!"

Alyssa stared at him, her black eyes flinty and cold. "I've been considering moving to South Carolina," she said.

"Oh." Gregory's eyes widened and he fell silent, slumping back slightly in his chair.

Sister Margaret couldn't help but be impressed. It seemed there was one thing that could pierce Gregory's sunny shield of oblivion, and that thing was someone being ever so slightly scornful of Texas.

Matriarch Monin tossed her curtain of iron-gray hair behind her and addressed a spot in the middle of the table. "Shall we get this over with?"

Eva's lips tightened and she laid a hand on Matriarch Monin's arm. The Matriarch shrugged it off with an angry frown.

"We'd like to open up a dialogue," said Matriarch Welch smoothly. "Some of us have seen witches and mages getting along in these modern times and—"

"And the rest of us are waiting for the other shoe to drop!" snapped Alyssa.

"I, for one, find it hard to believe that any of my sisters—" said Matriarch Monin.

"More like your daughters," interrupted Eva. "Matriarch, this ancient feud is pointless."

"Mages have no wish to reconcile either," said Matriarch Monin, her glare roving around the room, fixing each mage for a moment before moving on.

Sister Margaret was last, and she held her eyes as she spoke. "I have no fight with witches. I have, in fact, been instructed to sound out your group and see if any would be interested in working with us for the Vatican. We've already got a few witches on our payroll and witch and mage magic working together has been beneficial to all."

Trevor nodded beside her. "I am new to magery, and honestly have no idea why there's such enmity between our groups," he offered. "Maybe if you shared your objections we could help ease your concerns."

Matriarch Monin ignored him, instead staring at Gregory, who appeared to be doodling on the notebook in front of him. "This one isn't even paying attention."

Gregory looked up. "Huh?"

Giving him a sweet smile, Matriarch Monin leaned forward. "Will you welcome witches into your organization?"

"I mean, we don't really have a lot of girls," Gregory began.

Henry put a hand on his arm and interrupted smoothly. "I think what my associate is trying to say is that while we have traditionally been a male-dominated group, we have lately been initiating more and more women. Most of those are hereditary members at this point, as many of our established members bring in daughters as well as sons. But I do anticipate a growing number of women applying to our ranks from outside as well, and we would be honored if some of those applicants were witches and other cryptids."

"Huh." Alyssa snorted. "Sounds like a boys' club right now."

"Regrettably," Henry agreed. "But the future does not belong to Gregory and his ilk."

"Huh?" said Gregory.

Henry held Matriarch Monin's gaze as he stitched in a box of crayons and handed it to Gregory who began happily coloring in his doodle. "I think maybe we understand each other, yes, Matriarch?"

Matriarch Monin crossed her arms and leaned back in her seat, a thoughtful look on her face.

Matriarch Welch spoke up. "We've heard from the Vatican and the Illuminati. What about you?" She nodded toward Sammy and Ari. "How does your group see the future of witches and mages?"

"We are likewise eager to repair the rift between our numbers," said Ari. "In fact, like Sister Margaret, I too have instructions to court an alliance with witches."

"See?" said Eva. "It's time we put this behind us. Remember what happened in Oregon last year?"

Matriarch Monin shook her head. "I cannot."

Eva's brow furrowed. "You cannot remember or you cannot put this behind you?"

"I cannot put this behind me!" Matriarch Monin thumped her fist on the table. "There is nothing wrong with my memory." Her voice grew soft. "My memory is long, and if you'd heard some of the tales from before even my time—"

"That's just it, though, Matriarch," said Eva. "You have walked this earth for centuries, but even in your lifetime there has been no need for this enmity."

Alyssa interjected. "I remember what my great grandmother told me. She spoke of seeing her sisters tortured and burnt." She stared at Sister Margaret. "Your kind did this. You Church mages couldn't stand the thought of sharing power, of witches having magic that rivaled your own, so you spread lies and taught everyone to fear us. To kill us."

Sister Margaret bowed her head. "Yes. That's true. To our shame."

"What does your shame mean to us?" Matriarch Monin demanded. "Will it bring back the lives of the witches burnt?"

"No," said Sister Margaret. "Nothing can do that."

"And you!" Matriarch Monin pointed a bony finger at Henry. "The Illuminati was just as bad."

"Yes," Henry agreed. "I wish it weren't so."

"It's all in the past," said Gregory, waving an airy hand. "Can't you just move on?"

"What can we do to make it right?" said Henry before the elderly witch could respond. "How can our organization help you and yours?"

"You can't." Matriarch Monin abruptly stood and stormed out of the room.

Alyssa stood as though to follow, but Matriarch Welch grabbed her hand and pulled her back into her seat with a glare and a shake of her head.

Eva stood, bracing her hands on the table as she leaned forward. "Now is the time. We will end this ridiculous feud and usher in a new era of peace and cooperation. The stars are aligned. Look at the positions of Jupiter, Mars, and Venus." She lifted her hands and smacked them into the table, her voice rising as she continued. "The time is now!"

Matriarch Welch stood up as well, glancing at the clock over the door of the conference room. "Agreed. I think we've made our point." She looked around the room, smiling and nodding at the mages. "I look forward to working with your further to cement the alliances between our two—"

Eva's voice spiraled up another octave. "I will do whatever it takes to end this feud!"

Alyssa jumped to her feet and opened her mouth, lunging toward Eva, but Matriarch Welch, standing between them, held out her arms, gently restraining them both. "Well, it's just about time to switch rooms," she said. "Thank you for your time, mages. Ladies? Let's head out."

She turned toward the door, carefully keeping the two younger witches separated as she ushered them out of the room.

Sister Margaret looked around at the stunned faces of her fellow mages. "Well, I think that went pretty well, overall," she said.

Her gaze fell on Gregory, who was still happily coloring in his doodles.

"Could have been worse," said Chameleon. "I've never met a witch before."

"Some of them seemed nice," said Coyote.

"Maybe the next group will be more friendly," said Ari.

The door opened and Bryan stalked in.

"Maybe not," said Henry.

Chapter 27: Trevor

Trevor watched as nine merfolk filed into the conference room, arranging themselves across the table from the eight mages.

Those merfolk with legs were seated on chairs, while the tentacled variety pushed the chairs out of their way and floated above the ground.

The merfolk arranged themselves into three distinct groups, Bryan, the orange mer Sister Margaret had wounded, and two silver mer — including the one Chameleon had burned — were a clear group.

Another shark mer he hadn't met sat beside Zachary and Carly.

And then there were two other merfolk, one reddish mer with tentacles, and one sharklike with black and white stripes like a zebrafish who sat together in a separate grouping.

Trevor was a little amused to see Bryan, across the table from Sister Margaret, trying to intimidate her by staring directly into her eyes.

She returned the look, eyebrows raised. Did he think he was the first man — or at least male creature — to try to intimidate her? She was a warrior woman in a man's world, and he was going to have to do more than glare at her if he wanted to scare her.

Silence fell over the room as everyone waited for someone else to begin.

Finally, Ari stood up. "Let's begin with some introductions," he suggested. "My name is Ari Ahuja. My associate, Sammy West, and I are with a group called Pala."

Sammy belatedly stood up and gave the merfolk a friendly smile.

The mers' blank expressions didn't waver, so Ari continued. "Our organization is composed entirely of mages dedicated to improving our world through activism and political lobbying, and our main focus is currently on improving economical equity and on reversing climate change."

At this, Zachary and his school seemed to perk up slightly, as did the representatives of the unknown school.

Bryan and his group looked angrier than before, but none of them spoke.

Ari and Sammy sat down, and Chameleon and Coyote stood.

Chameleon spoke. "I am the leader of Aurora. We are a new organization that has sprung up in the wake of the destruction of the Auditors, a secret society in which I grew up. The Auditors were corrupt and power-hungry and we are determined to be the opposite and to undo as much of the harm caused by our predecessors as possible." She sat down again.

Coyote continued. "We are here because we would like to align ourselves with groups whose ideals line up with our own."

"And just to clarify," said Bryan. "Your so-called *ideals* are just to not be complete dicks."

"Essentially," Coyote agreed. He sat down.

"And your names?" asked the red octo-mer.

"Oh, right." Coyote stood up again, quickly introduced himself and Chameleon, and sat back down.

Trevor looked at Sister Margaret, and she nodded. The two of them stood up together.

"Trevor Harper and Sister Margaret Herrara," said Trevor. "Representatives of the Catholic Church, specifically the Warrior Mage dicastery. The Vatican is also interested in social justice issues and in reversing climate change. We welcome any cryptid alliances."

"Warrior mages?" said the zebra-striped mer. "Could you expand upon that?"

Trevor glanced at Sister Margaret and she happily took the reins. "In the Church, mages are divided into Warriors and Scholars. Many mages, especially lower-level clergy, are simply referred to as Warrior Mages or Scholar Mages with no specialty added, but as you get higher up in the hierarchy, various subcategories are added to your title. Trevor and I are Warrior Mage Librarians, which means our job is to defend and protect the Vatican's various archives, vaults, and libraries that are scattered around the world. These places are filled with rare books, dangerous artifacts, and the kind of knowledge that often attracts unsavory characters, so our job keeps us pretty busy. Other examples include Warrior Mage Scientists, Protectors, and Teachers."

The merfolk considered this for a moment, and then Bryan spoke. "So, you are highly ranked within your Church?"

"Yes," said Sister Margaret. "WMLs are considered one of the highest ranks within the Warrior Mage dicastery."

Apparently that was all they wanted to know, because as a group, the merfolk moved their collective gaze from her and Trevor to Henry and Gregory.

The two of them sat down, and Henry rose to his feet. Gregory remained seated, still working on his doodles, until Henry nudged him, and he hastily hauled himself upward. His eyes widened as he took in the merfolk, and Trevor tensed in anticipation of a blundering faux pas that might just get him killed.

He glanced over at Taye, who had been quiet thus far, but looked ready to stand up and intervene if needed.

Fortunately, Henry spoke, heading off anything Gregory might say. He introduced himself and his colleague and ran through a brief description of the Illuminati, wrapping up with, "Like Aurora—" he nodded toward Chameleon and Coyote, who nodded back, "—many among us are working to leave the old ways behind and use our power to advocate for real change." He sat back down, pulling Gregory with him.

Gregory opened his mouth as though to add to, or more likely, object to Henry's statement, but snapped it shut with a wince, shooting Henry a dirty look and reaching down to grab his shin.

Trevor cleared his throat as he desperately held back a laugh.

"We have heard a lot of pretty words," said Bryan after a moment. "But our kinds have been enemies for centuries."

"That's news to me," said Coyote. "We only recently found out that you exist."

"Humans have hunted in our territory," said Bryan. "You have polluted our waters, sailed through them without our permission, and now your reckless behavior is causing our oceans to heat up and storms to ravage our islands."

"Perhaps we would be better able to address your concerns if you would do us the courtesy of introductions," Henry cut in. "As we have done for you."

Bryan stared at him for a beat and then inclined his head slightly. He stood up, his short legs planted wide and his arms spread in a gesture that looked formal. The three merfolk on either side of him stood as well, echoing his posture. "I am Bryan, leader of the Agualadron School. Beside me are Kristen, Andrew, and Neal."

His fellow schoolmembers bowed slightly as their names were called.

"We are interested in eliminating humans from this planet," he concluded and then sat down.

Silence followed this proclamation. Trevor glanced at his fellow humans, gauging reactions.

Henry's expression remained predictably blank, while Gregory didn't appear to have heard anything at all.

Sammy and Ari looked shocked.

Sister Margaret was tense and her hands had fallen to her swords.

Chameleon and Coyote just looked thoughtful.

Before Trevor could say anything in response, the next school of merfolk was up for introductions, the octo-mer floating upward slightly, while the striped mer stood.

"I am Sally," said the striped mer. "Leader of the Herrnaudbault School. May I present my associate, Francine." The red octo-mer bobbed up and down once.

"If eliminating humans is what it takes, we will consider it," said Francine. "Our aim is to hold your kind accountable and to stop you from completely destroying our waters."

Trevor held back a sigh. He couldn't even entirely disagree with their words. Humans had been destroying the earth, and the oceans had taken a large portion of the brunt. He couldn't fault the mer with being skeptical that large portions of the human population were trying to do better and to reverse the damage done.

Finally, the Jeongsim School rose, and Zachary began their introductions. "I am Zachary," he said. "This is Carly and Helen, and we, the Jeongsim School, believe that our best chance lies in working with the humans to restore the waters to their former glory."

"You are fools," Bryan hissed. "Humans cannot change."

"We would like to try this way first," countered Zachary. "There are too many of them to fight them all."

"Fools and cowards," said Kristin. "You are unwilling to even challenge them in honorable battle. These two at least are warriors." She gestured toward Sister Margaret and Trevor and then toward Chameleon and Coyote. "And I can see these carry weapons as well. They have teeth — let us see how they bite."

"Enough." Henry stood up. "You cannot possibly win a war with humans."

"Says you." Bryan stepped toward Henry, malice in every inch of his body.

"He's right, though," said Sammy. "Surely you've seen submarines, torpedoes, all of the underwater weapons our governments could deploy. Then there are nuclear bombs. And don't underestimate the sheer stupidity of the people in charge — you bet your ass if you revealed yourselves, governments would start dumping oil into the water, and worse. They would destroy our entire ocean in the name of war."

"So, we will kill you off little by little," said Neal. "Guerilla warfare."

Trevor spoke up. "There are what, one hundred thousand merfolk alive today? There are eight billion humans."

"Cooperation is in our best interest," said Carly. She addressed the Herrnaudbault School. "Surely you must see that. The extremes these folk are talking about would mean the end of the mer or at the very least result in a far worse situation than we are currently facing."

"If we were to cooperate," said Sally. "We would need assurances that it would be on our own terms."

"You have to understand," said Ari. "That you would not be negotiating with humanity as a whole, but only certain groups of mages. Humanity as a whole has no idea that you exist, and it should be kept that way."

"Then what is the point?" Bryan demanded. "If, as you claim, a handful of humans can help us, then there is another handful of humans that we could simply slaughter and be done with it."

"Maybe," said Sister Margaret. "There are certainly some humans who are so filled with evil that it's a travesty that they are alive. But by adulthood, those people tend to fall into three categories — they're in prison and therefore mostly harmless to the world at large, they're smart enough to stay hidden so you cannot find them, or they're rich enough to be well-protected so you cannot kill them."

Bryan stared into her eyes, and she looked back, unflinchingly.

Finally he spoke. "Then perhaps you could help us kill those particular humans."

"If you're willing to work with us, perhaps," she agreed.

"Wait just a second—" began Sammy. He was cut off by a well-placed elbow in his ribs by Chameleon.

"Or perhaps," she continued. "We can work together to enact change in a more peaceful fashion. After all, everyone knows that the best warriors use force only when absolutely necessary."

"Is that what everyone knows?" Bryan crossed his arms.

"Yes," said Trevor. "Perhaps you are not as great a warrior as you seem to think."

Bryan lunged forward, pulling a fish head out of the pouch at his hip, and tossing it down in front of Trevor, getting slime all over his meticulously scribed notes.

"Ew!" He instinctively leaned backward, hands up and away from the fish head. Then he remembered that this was the first step in the ritual of challenging someone to a duel, and he carefully remained in position, careful to keep his hands away from the head.

If he touched it, he would be accepting the challenge.

Sister Margaret leaned over and grabbed the fish head, picking it up gingerly and tossing it back toward Bryan in a refusal gesture.

Out of the corner of his eye, Trevor saw that Taye and the merfolk's On'Chala were on their feet, watching closely.

Bryan glared, but picked up his fish head without comment, stowing it back in the pouch and then turning away.

"You have given us much to think about," said Sally. "I think it may be best that we part ways before violence begins." She leveled a stare at Bryan. "After all, this is the summit, and violence is frowned upon."

"Somebody is going to end up fighting that dickweed," Sister Margaret muttered to Trevor. "I just know it."

Chapter 28: Sister Margaret

Two hours later, Sister Margaret's head was whirling. In addition to the witches and merfolk, they'd met with chupacabra, squonks, aqrabuamelu, nittaewo, unicorns, kallanpa amaru, and finally dragons.

The dragons had been friendly. The kallanpa amaru seemed open to alliance.

The unicorns were awesome, and Sister Margaret had already made plans to watch the squonkerball games together that afternoon.

The others had ranged from wary to actively hostile.

"Well, that wraps up this morning's carousel," said Dragonlord On'Klanka, cheerfully.

Sister Margaret perked up. "Lunchtime now?"

"Lunchtime now," confirmed another dragon, one whose name she couldn't quite remember, but she bet it was mystical-sounding and hard to say.

The dragons shuffled out of the conference room, and Sister Margaret leapt to her feet, stretching and moaning.

"That was quite the morning," said Sammy.

"I think I'll go ahead and skip the next one of these meeting things," said Gregory airily. "Henry, you seem to have things well in hand."

Henry nodded, and Sister Margaret thought she detected a hint of relief in his expression. He had done some fancy wordplay a couple of times to keep his fellow Illuminati from being attacked, and at one point, Taye and the bigfoot who was assigned as On'Chala to the nittaewo had jumped up and physically restrained the diminutive cryptids to keep them from attacking Gregory.

Trevor turned to Taye. "Is lunch in the same place breakfast was?"

"It is indeed," said Taye. "Just down the hall from here."

Sister Margaret grabbed her notebook and waited for Trevor to finish gathering up his own notes before heading down the hall. "We've got two hours before the afternoon festivities," she pointed out. "Do you think we could eat quickly and then see if we can get a start on tracking down Saint Joan's sword?"

"Sure," he said. "As long as it's in that order. And I don't want to miss this tournament. It sounds fascinating."

"Right. How did that unicorn describe it? Like a cross between croquet and dodgeball?" Sister Margaret grinned. "Not sure how a unicorn knows what croquet and dodgeball are, but I'm intrigued."

"They must watch a fair amount of late night ESPN," said Trevor. "So, let's talk sword. Your boss thinks it's in a museum here in M'Tainla? Why, exactly, would the dragons have taken a human artifact like that?"

A passing dragon smiled at Trevor. "I'm afraid we're a bit like magpies," he said. "What artifact did you want to see?"

"The Sword of Saint Joan," said Sister Margaret. "Have you ever seen it?"

"Well," said the dragon, cocking his head as he pondered. "There are a lot of human and cryptid weapons at the World Heritage Museum on Tenth Street. You might start there."

"Fantastic! Where is Tenth Street?"

"Leave the building via the South Exit," the dragon instructed. "Then head west down the esplanade, and turn left when you get to the P'Tra'Tra Cafe. After about, oh, three blocks, you'll see a building that's shaped like two talons twined together. Turn right on the next esplanade and then take the stairs down. Go straight ahead for one and a half blocks, and the museum is on your left."

Sister Margaret stared at the dragon blankly.

"Got it," said Trevor.

"I knew there was a reason I kept a stitcher around," said Sister Margaret.

He grinned at her and led the way toward the dining hall. "Food first, though," he declared.

"Very much so," she agreed.

Upon arrival, Sister Margaret headed for the end of the smorgasbord, snagging a plate and tossing a tamale and a few tortilla chips onto it before heading for the nearest empty table, Trevor on her heels.

She was chomping at the bit to get to this museum, especially now that they had a real destination in mind. The sword was so close, she could taste it.

As she dug into the savory tomatillo sauce and chicken wrapped in a thick blanket of masa, she glanced around the room. It wasn't as full as it had been for breakfast; maybe some of the cryptids were lingering over their final carousel meet-ups.

"I actually think that the mer meeting went pretty well," Trevor remarked. He took a big bite of his sandwich, which was piled with veggies and what looked like salami and some kind of white cheese. "I mean, aside from all the death threats."

"They weren't threats, exactly," said Sister Margaret. She dipped a tortilla chip in the salsa verde on her plate, which was excellent. "More like declarations of intent."

"All right, well, aside from all of the declarations of intent to kill all the humans," he corrected. "We established a dialogue that was relatively civil. And at least they're not sneaky. I'd rather deal with someone who is open and honest and even polite about the fact that he hates me and wants to kill me than somebody going around being nice to my face but then plotting against me the rest of the time."

Sister Margaret paused, her fork halfway to her mouth. "You would? Then why did you take a job with the Vatican?"

Trevor raised an eyebrow. "Are you saying our co-workers want to kill me?"

"Not specifically that I'm aware of," she admitted. "But then again, they know we're friends, so they probably wouldn't tell me. But I assume at least somebody's out to get me around there, and you should probably do the same. Even if they don't want to kill you, somebody's probably gunning for our jobs."

"We're the most junior WMLs," Trevor pointed out.

"Nobody in our department." Sister Margaret resumed walking with a wave of her hand. "But others in the dicastery for sure. And they're probably resentful of your quick rise to this rank. I mean, two years ago, you weren't even a mage."

"Huh." Trevor thought about that as he chewed and swallowed. "Like who?"

Sister Margaret shrugged. "Like I said, I don't know anyone specifically. If I did, I would have already done something about it."

"Like killed them?" asked Trevor. "You were pretty agreeable back there with Bryan."

"What?" Sister Margaret stared at him. "You think I'd just assassinate someone in cold blood because I thought they might be after my job or yours?"

"Not really." Trevor shrugged and took a sip of his water. "I'm sorry. I think I'm just a little on edge. It was unsettling how many crytpids we've talked to today who seem at least amenable to the idea of killing all the humans."

"Fair," said Sister Margaret. "We'll just have to show them that some of us aren't so bad."

"I think it was smart to show a tough warrior front like that." Trevor pointed the butt of his sandwich at her. "That might be the tactic to take going forward. They respect toughness." He popped the final bite into his mouth.

"Damn," she observed. "You inhaled that thing."

He shrugged. "I know this sword is important to you. And I was hungry."

She laughed. "Well, thank you. If nothing else, a side quest will take our minds off of all these unfriendly cryptids, right?"

Trevor grinned and stood up as he finished swallowing. He grabbed his own plate and gave her an inquiring look.

Sister Margaret snagged one last bite and then pushed the plate toward him. He gathered up all the dishes and hustled toward the self-bus station situated next to the door.

Standing up, Sister Margaret followed Trevor out of the room.

Chapter 29: Trevor

Twenty minutes later, they stared up at the imposing Museum of World Heritage. The directions had been mostly correct, although it had been five blocks before they'd come to the twisted talon building.

The museum was enormous. Like all of the buildings in M'Tainla, it was made of magical blue ice. It was a blocky structure, much like you'd expect from a museum in human territory.

Trevor craned his neck and began counting the rows of windows. "Twelve stories," he said at last. "If the sword is here, it's going to be a bitch to find."

"Well, let's just hope there's a friendly guide who can help us," said Sister Margaret.

"Hey, you're not planning to steal this sword, are you?" Trevor asked, nervously.

"Mother Superior didn't say anything about stealing it," said Sister Margaret. "I'm like ninety percent sure I'm just supposed to report back to her that it's here. Or isn't. And then she'll handle negotiations to get it back."

"Okay, good." Trevor led the way forward, up the short, steep ramp — he was grateful for the cleated shoes Father Max had recommended he bring — and to the gigantic carved ice doors.

He grasped the handle, the icy cold of it biting through the thick knitted gloves he wore. The gloves had been a gift from an old friend, one of the last things she'd knitted before a mage battle had taken her life, and he felt her indomitable courage supporting him every time he wore them.

The door swung outward, and Trevor was obliged to step out of its way, slipping inside and pushing against it with his shoulder as Sister Margaret entered the building. He followed, letting the door slam shut behind him.

Inside, the entrance hall was vast and echoey, just like every large museum Trevor had ever been to. While human museums tended to have marble foyers, this one was more of that magicked ice.

That appeared to be the only difference, however. The atrium was lined with grand fluted pillars and there were benches scattered about and a fountain in the center. Directly in front of them about a hundred feet was a desk, behind which a dragon stood, busy at her computer.

There were a couple of bigfoots sitting on a bench beside the fountain and their low voices bounced around the space, converting the conversation into a low hum.

A dragon wandered across the room toward the back, moving from the south wing of the museum to the north, and then disappearing again.

A kallanpa amaru sat on another bench, bent over a tablet.

Trevor nodded toward the desk. "That seems like the best place to start."

An eager smile on her face, Sister Margaret practically danced her way over to the dragon. "Hi! I'm looking for a sword!"

The dragon's jaw gaped open in what Trevor by now recognized as the dragon version of a smile. "Looks like you've got some swords already," she observed. "You must be looking for a particular one."

"Yes," said Sister Margaret. "It's a fifteenth century sword from France, imbued with a bunch of magery—" she pulled out her phone and began to read. "'The Sword of Saint Joan was rumored to impart an ability to see what her opponent was about to do, the ability to heat up or freeze as its bearer chose, and the power to deflect magic from its bearer's opponent.'"

Trevor whistled. "I didn't realize this wasn't just a historically significant piece."

"I mean, it mostly is." Sister Margaret shrugged. "I wouldn't even know how to activate these spells, and I think that information is lost to our order too."

"I bet it's buried somewhere in a library," said Trevor. "Maybe we'll get to hunt it down." He did love a good puzzle.

The dragon behind the desk was typing something into her computer. "It looks like we have some human artifacts from the late medieval period on the second floor, including several weapons and pieces of armor. Two swords are listed as possibly magical."

"Fantastic!" said Sister Margaret. She bounced on the balls of her feet. "How do we get there?"

The dragon's jaw gaped again and she typed furiously for another few seconds. The computer beeped in response. "I have a docent coming down from that wing right now to guide you."

"Thank you," said Trevor. The two of them stepped aside politely to make way for a group of three salashifters behind them. He jerked his head. "Come on. I want to look around a little."

One of the salashifters touched his arm, the extreme heat of her hand reaching his skin even through the layers of his coat and long-sleeved shirt. "There's an exhibit of the art of my people right over there." She nodded off to the left. "I found it captivating."

"Sounds great," said Trevor with a smile.

"I'll send the docent to find you there," said the dragon.

Trevor hurried toward the salashifter art. He had always enjoyed exploring his Ethiopian heritage, and was fascinated by the existence of Ethiopian cryptids. Would the art be inspired by the culture of his mother's people? Or was the culture of Ethiopian humans influenced by salashifters? It was probably a little of both.

As soon as they passed between the pillars that marked the entrance to the salashifter exhibit, a wave of heat hit them like a brick.

"Holy shit," said Sister Margaret. "It's like walking out of the AC during a St. Louis summer."

"Not as humid," Trevor observed.

"Oh, right," said Sister Margaret with a roll of her eyes. "Everybody knows, it's not the heat; it's the humidity. Honestly, once you hit a certain temperature it's just fucking hot, and it doesn't matter if it's the ever-sought-after dry heat."

"Fair." Trevor peeled off his coat and hung it on one of a row of hooks hung on the wall. Unwinding his scarf, he hung it up too and then followed it with his mittens and hat. It was still hot. "I guess it's meant to replicate the conditions of the Dallol Valley."

"Hottest place on earth!" said a cheerful deep red dragon as he approached them from within the exhibit. "Welcome to the Gateway to Hell!"

"The Gateway to Hell?" Sister Margaret's eyebrows shot up.

"That's what some of the locals call the Dallol Valley," the dragon explained. "In fact, some human scientists use it to study whether life might be possible on hotter planets like Venus and Mercury."

"Fascinating." Trevor's eyes wandered to the first art installment in the gallery, a painting depicting a surreal landscape with yellow-brown rocky outcroppings surrounding colorful springs. "Is this it?"

"Beautiful, isn't it?"

"Yes." Trevor stared at the painting. "In a very stark kind of way." The piece was compelling, and he felt an intense longing to visit the place depicted. It looked inhospitable and desolate, and yet it called out to him.

He stepped forward, examining a certain spot. He pointed, careful not to let his fingers brush the painting. "What is this?" It looked like a small red lizard, emerging from one of the springs, caught in transition between the sulphuric water and the dry air. The edges of the lizard were sort of fuzzy, like it wasn't entirely solid.

"That is the artist," said the dragon. "This is a self-portrait, painted in human form, but depicting her fire form."

"That's what the salashifters look like in their other form?" Sister Margaret stepped up beside him, rising up on her toes a little to better see the lizard. "Where does all the bulk go?"

"That is a question many have pondered and nobody has been able to satisfactorily answer," said the dragon.

Trevor turned to ask more about the shifting process, and noticed another dragon approaching.

"Hello," called out the newcomer. "Are you the humans interested in the medieval swords?"

"Yes!" Sister Margaret whirled around.

"Hello, Sa'Ka," she said to the red dragon.

Sa'Ka addressed Trevor and Sister Margaret. "Are you sure you want to leave already? There are some wonderful pieces here, and you've barely scratched the surface."

"I'll be back, for sure," promised Trevor. He glanced at Sister Margaret. "But once she's got the scent on something like this, there's no stopping her."

Sister Margaret bounced on the balls of her feet. "It's the sword of Saint Joan!"

"Might be the sword of Saint Joan," said Trevor.

"Ah," said the new dragon. "I think I know the sword you're looking for."

"See?" Sister Margaret stared at Trevor with pleading eyes.

He laughed and raised his hands in surrender. "I will be back," he repeated to Sa'Ka. "Let's go."

They followed the docent, a smallish dragon with iridescent purple scales, back through the atrium. "I am Thr'Lo," she said. "You're humans, right? Here for the summit? I've never met any humans before."

"Yes," said Trevor. "We're the delegation from the Vatican."

"Ah." Thr'Lo turned to Sister Margaret. "Am I to understand, then, that you are a member of Joan D'Arc's order? Some kind of Knight of the Temple, wasn't she?"

Sister Margaret cleared her throat and glanced sideways at Trevor before admitting, "Knights Templar, yes. We don't call ourselves that anymore."

Trevor stopped short. "Wait, just a moment. The actual, mythical Knights Templar?"

"That seems like a contradiction," Thr'Lo observed. "How can this group be both actual and mythical?"

"My order is very old," said Sister Margaret. She unsnapped one of the compartments on her leather bandolier and withdrew a black and white cloth. Trevor had seen her use these cloths to clean off small blades after battle. She had larger ones that were almost identical that she used for her full-sized swords.

Sister Margaret unfurled the cloth, showing the words and symbol printed in white against the black background: *The Sisters of Saint Joan* above a silhouette of a sword, which he recognized as the same sword she had tattooed in more detail on her left forearm. Underneath, it read in smaller print: *The original Warrior Mages. Since 1025 AD.*

"Saint Joan lived in the fifteenth century," Trevor pointed out, frowning.

"Yes," said Sister Margaret, folding the cloth back up and tucking it away again. "And she wasn't granted sainthood until the twentieth century."

Thr'Lo led them onto an elevator, pressing a button as the doors slid shut behind them. Once again, Trevor was struck by how familiar the technology was here. He had been expecting either a more primitive facility or one run entirely by magic, but it seemed the dragons and other cryptids had embraced, or maybe influenced, human tech.

Again, it was probably a little of each.

"The order has only been known as The Sisters of Saint Joan since the 1930s, in fact," Sister Margaret continued. "We started in secret in 1025, the first known Church-approved order of women warrior mages. The Knights Templar."

"The Knights Templar were all women?" Trevor pondered that for a moment. "I guess I can see why that little fact would be lost to history. You know, given what history is like."

"Exactly," said Sister Margaret. "After about a century, as the Crusades really started heating up, the order's secrecy was abolished, which is why most historians believe we were founded in 1118, but even then it wasn't widely known that the Knights were women. In the fourteenth century, some French asshole found out and made a big stink, so the Vatican officially disbanded the order, covering up the reason for it. Which is why the end of the Knights Templar is so shrouded in secrecy and mystery."

The elevator came to a stop and the doors slid open again. "I would be very interested in interviewing you about all of this for the museum," said Thr'Lo.

"Sure," said Sister Margaret. She continued. "But unofficially, the order moved its headquarters to Portugal, changing its name for the first time. The Knights Templar became the very generic and pompous-sounding Knights of the Order of Our Lord Jesus Christ. After about four hundred years, someone decided that instead of hiding our gender, it would be easier to hide our warrior nature, so we became the Daughters of the Holy Spear, still hinting at our true purpose, but hiding behind the name of the spear that pierced Jesus' side during his crucifixion. And finally, after Saint Joan was canonized as a saint, we changed the name once again in order to honor our most famous and holy member."

"Huh." Trevor followed his partner as she trailed after Thr'Lo.

He chuckled, and Sister Margaret turned around, frowning. "What's so funny?"

"Oh, nothing," he said. "Just — not so long ago, secret societies were something to laugh about. The Knights Templar and the Illuminati were topics to speculate on merrily over a few glasses of wine with Mathilda. Cryptids were just tall tales and bad photo edits. Now, all of this—" he gestured vaguely at his surroundings " — is my life. And I absolutely love it. It's just wonderful and funny and unbelievable all at the same time."

Sister Margaret lifted her eyebrows with a wry twist of her lips. "Fair enough."

Thr'Lo turned, passing through a broad doorway into a room filled with transparent display cases. The blue tinge of the cases showed that they were made of ice, not glass.

Inside the cases, Trevor could see weapons, armor, and tools. Most of them he recognized as medieval human design. He smiled again at the way he automatically inserted the descriptor *human* in there.

That was new too.

Thr'Lo stepped to the side to let the human mages pass, and Sister Margaret moved unerringly toward one particular case with a large broadsword displayed.

It was an unassuming sword, about the same size as the one Trevor typically carried on his back, braced vertically, held with its point toward the floor and its leather-wrapped hilt at Trevor's eye level.

Sister Margaret reached out a hand toward the case, stopping short of touching it.

As Trevor stepped up beside her, he saw that her eyes were seer white. He turned on his own seer sight, curious to see what she was looking at, and stumbled backward at the shining brilliance of the layered spells on the sword.

"Holy crap," he murmured, turning his seer sight off again.

"Holy, indeed," Sister Margaret replied. "But this is no crap. This is the sword of Saint Joan of fucking Arc!"

"Wonderful!" said Thr'Lo. "We have it cataloged as *Mage-sword, European, Fifteenth Century.* It will be fantastic to have it properly identified."

Trevor and Sister Margaret exchanged a glance. It certainly wasn't his place to mention to the docent that the Sisters of Saint Joan were likely to try to negotiate the return of the sword to their community.

Sister Margaret seemed to feel the same way, because all she said was, "Thank you for showing it to us. Saint Joan is an important foremother to me. Figuratively speaking, of course. She never had any actual descendents."

Trevor's eye was caught by a bejeweled suit of armor to his left, and he wandered over to look at it. The card beside the display case read, *Human armor, probably royal, thirteenth century.* He gestured to Thr'Lo, waving the dragon over. "This isn't thirteenth century," he said. He pointed to the joints at the shoulders. "You see how that fits right there? This is eleventh century at the latest."

"Really?" Thr'Lo peered eagerly at the armor. "Thank you!" She reached out her foreleg to snag a rolling cart that stood nearby, pulling it toward her. On top of the cart was a tablet attached to one of the oversized, specially spaced keyboards the dragons used to accommodate their talons.

Thr'Lo typed into the keyboard, opening up a spreadsheet and amending a particular entry. "Please feel free to look around, and let me know if you see anything else like this. Are you an expert in human armor?"

Trevor shrugged. "I've studied a variety of medieval-age cultures," he said absently. "You seem to have a large collection of European things here."

"Medieval Asian goods are across the way," said Thr'Lo, pointing. "And the North African exhibit is beyond it. There are many other human exhibits on this floor, but my understanding is that American and Sub-Saharan cultures, even during that same time, were not referred to as medieval."

"Right," said Trevor. "I'd still love to see it all."

Sister Margaret cleared her throat, her phone in her hand and a regretful look on her face. "Unfortunately, we have places to be," she said. "The squonkerball tournament starts soon, and I want to get good seats."

Trevor nodded. "I have a feeling we'll be spending quite a bit of time in this place over the next month," he told Thr'Lo.

The dragon's jaw gaped open in a smile. "I look forward to seeing you again soon. Will you need me to guide you out?"

"I think we've got it," said Trevor. He led Sister Margaret back toward the elevator.

Chapter 30: Sister Margaret

Sister Margaret skipped ahead of Trevor as they exited the museum. She felt on top of the world. That sword! It was beautiful. Well, really, it was pretty plain, but when she'd looked at it with her mage sight, it was fucking gorgeous.

She'd counted at least five layers of spells, which was particularly exciting, since they'd only known about three, and Saint Joan had been a legendary speller.

If only she knew how to access the spells! Maybe her sword tattoo could help activate them. It was keyed to Templar energy, after all, and the sword's spells had to have some kind of connection to the Order still, even after centuries.

The sheer strength of the spells! Either it was completely undiminished, or Saint Joan was much, much more powerful than they'd known.

Maybe it was more than just the saint. Maybe she'd worked together with other spellers in the Order to layer those spells on there.

Then again, the Order had other swords from the same era and even earlier, and while they were imbued with spells, they didn't look like *that!*

She'd never seen anything like it, not in the Order vaults, not in the Auditor bunker, not even in any of the Vatican archives she'd been to.

She needed to contact Mother Eleanor as soon as possible.

Sister Margaret's feet slowed as she pulled out her phone, opened up her email app, and began composing a message to the leader of her order.

Dear Mother Superior,

I have found the sword, and it surpasses our wildest dreams. The dragons have it displayed in a museum and were happy to show it to us. I do not think they will be as happy to let it go, should you be inclined to move in that direction. But it is held safely for the moment. Please advise me on the next step to take. Until then, I will proceed with the summit and leave the sword where it is.

Your servant,

Sister Margaret Herrera

She read it over again and then sent it. The phone made its classic shooping sound, like one of those pneumatic tubes at the bank, and she tucked it back into her bandolier, still a little bit agog that she was getting cell phone service in Antarctica.

Then she hurried to catch up with Trevor as he was ascending up a ramp to the series of elevated esplanades in this multi-level ice city.

The pair of them hurried back to the cryptid council headquarters building.

As they entered, a sign pointed them in the direction of the squonkerball court.

Chapter 31: Trevor

Squonkerball, as it transpired, was played indoors in a square space about half the size of a basketball court with a wooden floor divided by red paint into quarters. Each quarter was then bisected diagonally in yellow paint.

Each side of the court was lined with four risers, which Trevor was surprised to see were made of mundane concrete rather than the ubiquitous ice. Each riser was deep enough to accommodate a throng of full-grown dragons, but cryptids of all species crowded the audience.

Down on the court, the first teams of the tournament were already gathered, stretching their muscles and swinging their mallets — which did look like croquet mallets.

Sister Margaret waved to her newfound unicorn friends, who were already seated alongside of Coyote, Chameleon, and Sammy.

Trevor followed her as she wove through the crowd to their front row seat.

"Oh, I'm so glad you got these seats," she exclaimed. "I was afraid I'd be stuck behind a larger cryptid and not be able to see anything."

"Speaking of 'seats,' said Trevor. "Where did you get those?" He nodded at the folding chairs Coyote and Chameleon were sitting on.

Coyote pointed off to the side. "They're free to borrow. Just right over there."

Trevor's eyes followed his finger, and saw a stack of lawn chairs leaning up against the wall across the court. He frowned. In order to get there, he'd have to walk right past Bryan and his school.

Bryan seemed to sense his attention and turned to stare directly at him. He looked at the chairs and then back at Trevor and smirked.

Trevor smirked back and moved his fingers in a stitching gesture. Two chairs disappeared from the stack and appeared beside him.

Still holding Bryan's gaze, Trevor picked up one of the chairs and tried to shake it open.

Unfortunately, it didn't open right away, and he was forced to look down. He quickly found the clasp and undid it, unfolding the chair, but by that time, Bryan had looked away, chatting with the other merfolk.

Trevor sighed. Not only had he missed the chance to pull a badass move, but now Bryan was talking to Sally, of the Herrnaudbault School, the ones who they thought they had a chance of swaying to their own side.

Oh, well. He turned his attention to the conversation beside him.

"So, where is Ari?" Sister Margaret was asking Sammy.

"I'm not sure, actually," said Sammy with a frown. "He was supposed to meet me here about—" he consulted his phone's clock. "Five minutes ago."

"I don't see the Illuminati either," Coyote observed. "I would expect Henry to be here at least, and actually this seems like something Gregory would be enthused about too."

Sammy opened his mouth to say something, but just then a dragon ran into the center of the court and began talking.

Trevor recognized the same dragon who had given them directions to the museum.

"Creatures sweet and scary," began the announcer. "Welcome to day one of the twenty-fourth annual Cryptid Summit Squonkerball Tournament!"

The stadium erupted in cheers, claps, stomps, howls, and other deafening sounds.

After a moment, the dragon held up a claw and the noise died down somewhat, although the excitement levels remained palpably high.

"I am your host and referee Pr'ana'lom."

More howls and hollers greeted this information, but it died down quickly on its own this time.

"You know how this works," shouted Pr'ana'lom. "Four teams of two, shifting alliances until the final quarter, when it's every cryptid for themselves!"

A few more whoops and hollers followed this statement.

"Magic can be used in the second and fourth quarters. First and third quarters are physical abilities only!"

Another punctuation of whistles and claps.

"If a player is hit by the ball, they gain two points, and the player who threw the ball gains three points. If a player is injured, their team automatically wins that quarter. And if a player is killed, their team automatically wins the entire match." He paused for effect, and a hush came over the room before he gleefully shouted. "LET'S PLAY SQUONKERBALL!"

And the crowd went wild.

Pr'ana'lom ran on all fours to one corner of the court, while eight cryptids holding mallets in hands, paws, or in the case of the unicorns, fitted over their horns, ran forward, taking places arrayed about the court, one cryptid in each section lined out on the floor.

With no further preamble, Pr'ana'lom thew a red ball into the court, straight at the head of a salashifter in human form, dressed in a tennis skirt and a matching white sports bra.

The salashifter watched the ball, mallet raised, until the last instant, when she moved lightning fast, smashing it toward a unicorn across from her.

Trevor winced at the sound of the ball hitting the mallet. The loud CRACK made it very clear that this was no soft, inflated dodgeball. This was a ball twice as large but just as hard as a croquet ball.

Beside him, Sister Margaret let out a whoop as the unicorn lobbied the ball back toward the salashifter, who sent it flying toward a bigfoot.

The crowd let out a collective, "Oooooh!" as the bigfoot missed the ball and it connected with his wrist instead.

"Two points to Team A," called out Pr'ana'lom. "And Three to Team C!"

It seemed that the bigfoot was not injured, as he grinned and tossed it into the air, smacking it with his mallet straight back toward the salashifter on Team C.

As the match went on, the crowd grew rowdier, especially during the next quarter, in which magic was allowed.

Each quarter lasted ten minutes, and the game went fast.

Trevor wasn't generally a big fan of sports, but he found himself caught up in the game, enthralled as the salashifters moved between forms with a flash of light each time, using their magic to dodge the ball and letting it bounce off some kind of forcefield that had been erected between the court and the crowd, and then setting it on fire before it winged back to the unicorns, who shimmered, making it impossible to tell exactly where they actually were.

The bigfoots' strategy didn't seem to change between the magic and physical rounds. Trevor surmised that their magic, whatever it involved, wasn't as effective as their pure brute strength.

The best moment, in Trevor's opinion, was when a kallanpa amaru shifted into the form of a second ball and their chupacabra teammate flung both balls at a unicorn, who ended up hitting the wrong one and getting beaned with the actual ball, resulting in a full five points to the kallanpa amaru and the chupacabra, aka Team B.

Between quarters, the teams changed positions, allying themselves with the team across from them, but in the final quarter, all teams were dissolved, and each cryptid just tried to hit all of the others.

Trevor's understanding was that in the end, those points still counted toward the teams' totals.

Finally, the game ended, and Team A — a salashifter and a unicorn — was awarded the victory.

To his surprise, Trevor found that he was on his feet, his throat hoarse from yelling and his hands sore from clapping. His heart was racing with excitement.

Looking around, he saw that everyone was in a similar state. Even cool-as-a-cucumber Chameleon was flushed with enjoyment.

Dropping into his chair, Trevor grinned at Sister Margaret. "Okay, that was pretty cool."

"That was amazing!" she said. She turned to the unicorn beside her. "How does one sign up for these things?"

The unicorn responded telepathically, broadcasting so Trevor and the others could hear the response. *Just tell your On'Chala. They'll get you on the roster for the next one. Do you want to be on a team with me?*

"Hell, yes!" said Sister Margaret.

Trevor moved back slightly to allow a bigfoot and a kallanpa amaru to pass in front of them, the pair of them chattering in rapid Spanish as they went in search of refreshment or the restroom or just to stretch their legs.

Turning his head, he realized that Gregory and Henry were now seated beside him. "Oh, hi," he said to Henry. "That was something, huh?"

Henry nodded. "I don't think I'll be playing anytime soon, but it was fun to watch."

"It wasn't so great," said Gregory. "Nothing beats a good old fashioned football game. I guess these creatures aren't advanced enough to know about football, huh?"

Trevor stared at Gregory, wondering yet again why he had come to the summit.

"You see?" Matriarch Monin's voice came from behind them.

Trevor turned to see her smirking at Gregory, but addressing Matriarch Welch.

"This is what mages think of us. Primitive creatures who can't kick a ball around a field into a net."

"Oh, I think you're confusing football with soccer," said Gregory, turning around with a patronizing smile. "Football, in America, is played by carrying and throwing an elliptical ball, and it's way better than soccer. A much more active sport, perfect for red-blooded American men. Maybe I could teach some of the guys around here how to play. I think you'd get a real kick out of watching it, ma'am. See a real sport."

Trevor winced as he noticed that cryptids all around them were quieting down to listen to this exchange.

"I have seen American football," said Matriarch Monin. "It is a ridiculous game."

"Hey, now!" Gregory stood up, but Henry pulled him back down.

Taye appeared as though out of nowhere, watching Gregory carefully.

"I agree," said Coyote. "American football is the worst."

"Those tight pants," said Chameleon. "How can anyone take them seriously?"

"Why you!" Gregory tried to stand again, but Henry was still holding onto his arm. Gregory angrily shook him off, and Taye took another step forward.

"Pah!" said Gregory. His face scrunched up, his lips working as though he was trying to work out what to say, but nothing quite fit in his mouth. Finally he threw his hands up in disgust. "If you're so into squinklyball, you just enjoy it on your own. I'm out of here."

And with that, he turned on his heel and stormed out, angrily shoving aside Eva and a salashifter woman on his way out.

"Ow!" He glared at the salashifter. "You burned me!"

"Sorry," she said. "I didn't mean—"

"Whatever." He kept going, Taye following behind him, murmuring apologies to anyone he ran into or pushed aside on his way out.

Chapter 32: Sister Margaret

After the game, most of the cryptids trooped upstairs in a giant, excited crowd to the dining hall for dinner.

As soon as they entered the cafeteria, Sister Margaret's eye was caught by the cluster of angrily muttering merfolk near the buffet. She recognized them as Agualadron School and two of the Herrnaudbault.

She frowned at them, wondering what got their kilts in a bunch this time. Hopefully they were pissed at someone else for once.

She piled a plate with human food, filled a pint glass with beer from a tap, and looked around for any friendly faces already seated.

Everyone she could see herself eating with seemed to be still in the buffet line, so she nabbed an empty table with plenty of room for all the mages and a space at the end in case the unicorns felt like joining them as well.

As soon as she sat down, Eva slipped into the chair across from her.

"May I sit with you?" asked the Scandinavian witch.

"Of course," said Trevor, as he pulled up a seat next to Sister Margaret. "I'm sorry things this morning didn't go as you were hoping."

"That's okay," said Eva. "I just wanted to—"

Her lips continued moving, but sound was no longer emerging, and Sister Margaret paused, fork midway to her face, blinking at her in surprise.

Eva pursed her lips and looked around, her eyes narrowed and brow furrowed. She stopped and stared over Sister Margaret's shoulder, her frown deepening.

Twisting around, Sister Margaret saw Matriarch Monin, a smug smile on her face, give Eva a tinkly little finger wave. Clearly, the older witch had spelled her quiet.

Sister Margaret turned back around just in time to see Eva make a vicious slashing motion in the air in front of her.

"I apologize for the immature antics of my colleague," said Eva, stiffly. Her breath came out ragged and harsh as she struggled to control her obvious anger.

Interesting. So a witch, unlike a mage, could break another witch's spell pretty easily. Sister Margaret filed away that information in case it came in handy later. It didn't seem terribly unlikely that she would find herself on the end of one of Matriarch Monin's vindictive spells at some point during this summit.

"No problem," said Trevor. "What were you—"

He was interrupted again by a fish head flying in front of him to land on Eva's plate of spaghetti.

The witch gagged and looked up at Bryan, who stood at the head of their table. Sister Margaret noted with irritation that he was standing right where she had intended the unicorns would sit.

"You would betray your own people to consort with these humans?" he demanded.

Eva's eyes narrowed. "Your outdated bullshit will end in—"

"You are a traitor to all of cryptid-kind," Bryan roared.

Matriarch Monin jumped to her feet, rushing to stand behind Eva. "What a witch does is none of your business, fish," she growled. She picked up the fish head and threw it straight at Bryan's face.

He caught it before it hit him, but didn't put it away, staring Matriarch Monin down instead. "I am surprised at you, madam," he said. "I thought you agreed that these *humans* don't belong here."

"I do agree with that," she conceded. "But Eva, misguided though she may be, is a witch nevertheless, and not a part of your machinations."

Bryan stared her down, and she met his gaze, lifting her chin. Her loose, iron-colored hair floated around her face, crackling with magical energy and her hands lifted, formed into defensive claws.

Deliberately, Bryan raised the fish head again, throwing it, without looking directly into Matriarch Monin's food on the table behind him.

"Oh, for fuck's sake!" Trevor thrust his chin forward, his jaw clicking, and his own chair clattered to the floor as he stood up abruptly.

This ought to be good. Trevor didn't lose his temper often, but Sister Margaret had learned that when he did, he could be absolutely savage. She grinned as she watched Trevor stride over to Matriarch Monin's table, shoving Bryan aside, and picked up the fish head. He shook the offending object in Bryan's face. "This again? What the fuck is your problem? You're just literally flinging dead things around like they're flowers and you're a tour guide in Hawaii!"

Time seemed to slow down as Trevor pulled his hand back and then moved it forward, smacking Bryan across the face with the fish head in a gesture Sister Margaret knew indicated that he was accepting the challenge on behalf of its original target.

The entire room, which had grown quiet during this exchange, inhaled in shock. There was a moment of silence as everyone looked at Bryan.

"I accept!" roared the mer.

And the crowd of cryptids, still pumped up from the squonkerball tournament, erupted into a new round of shouts.

Sister Margaret hesitated to join in the cheers. She watched Taye carefully as the On'Chala looked on with a grim face. It was his job — and to a lesser extent, hers — to keep Trevor alive, and he was not happy.

She wished she knew more about Bryan's fighting abilities, and about the rules of the duel. They knew how to avoid a challenge, but not what would happen if the challenge actually went through.

"You idiot," hissed Matriarch Monin. "You just volunteered to be my champion in the duel he challenged *me* to."

Trevor dropped the fish head and picked up a napkin, wiping his hands. "I'm aware of that, madam."

"Are you aware that Bryan has never lost a duel?" she asked. "Or that he is the reigning dueling champion of his school, a school that is known for its dueling prowess?"

"Um, no," said Trevor, his eyes flicking to the witch's face. "I was actually not aware of that."

"You have twenty-four hours to prepare," said Bryan. "The sequester shall begin in fifteen minutes."

Trevor lifted his chin. "Then I will see you tomorrow. You bastard."

Matriarch Monin threw back her head and laughed. Her electrified hair had dropped back down, cascading down her back, and she flung an arm across Trevor's shoulders.

Sister Margaret frowned. She could feel a headache coming on, and she wasn't sure if it was mostly because of this whole duel thing or because Matriarch Monin was suddenly being so confusingly chummy.

The adrenaline of the afternoon was wearing off, and she was abruptly very tired.

She glanced at Eva again.

Eva wore a wry smile as she watched the elder witch. She met Sister Maragaret's gaze. "This is actually very good for our cause," she said, quietly. "This is the fastest way you could have chosen to win over Matriarch Monin. She may be an old-fashioned beldame, but she respects courage and has always been appreciative of anyone coming to her aid. Very big on teamwork, she is."

"Huh." Sister Margaret turned as Carly sidled up beside her. "What can you tell me about this duel?"

"This is not good," said Carly. "Bryan is an accomplished duelist. He challenges a lot of people — I mean a *lot* — and he has never lost. Then again, I'm not sure he's ever fought a duel on land, so that might give Trevor an advantage. But he'll have brought his dueling trident, of course." She eyed the sword that hung at Trevor's hip. "What magics does your partner's weapon have?"

Sister Margaret frowned. Magic swords were no longer commonly used in mage society, mostly because the secrets to creating and unlocking the spells were largely lost to time. "None, but he is a powerful mage and is skilled in using all three of the mage disciplines in tandem."

"That won't matter," said Carly. "Use of magic during a duel is strictly prohibited. Magical weapons, on the other hand...."

"So, Bryan will have a magic weapon and Trevor won't even be allowed to shield against it, much less fling any spells?" Sister Margaret frowned. "That hardly seems fair."

"Maybe not," said Carly. "But that is the rule."

"What are the other rules?" asked Sister Margaret. "Will you help us prepare?"

Carly lifted her arms in a shrug. "There are many rules, and we will have to go over them all. We may as well get Trevor into his sequester. He will need to know more than you will."

Trevor approached, Matriarch Monin in tow. "Carly!" he said. "What is this sequester? I have to be alone?"

"No, it's a bit of a misnomer," said Carly. "You have to be confined to one place, but you may have as many visitors as you'd like, and you may choose where you're confined. I suggest someplace large enough that I can give you some basic training on how Bryan is likely to fight."

"Our rooms are pretty big," said Sister Margaret. "And that's probably easiest anyway."

"Let's go," said Carly.

Chapter 33: Trevor

Trevor's mind buzzed angrily as he marched back to his hotel room accompanied by Sister Margaret, Eva, Carly, and a bizarrely suddenly-friendly Matriarch Monin. As they walked, their group grew in number as the other members of Carly's school fell into step with them. At some point Trevor realized that Taye was also walking beside him, and a few minutes later, Sammy, Coyote, and Chameleon joined in as well.

By the time they finally began filing two-by-two up the ramp in the hotel, there were about fifteen mages and cryptids in their odd parade.

Trevor unlocked his room door and held it open as they all trooped in. He began to doubt Sister Margaret's assertion that their rooms were big enough for what they needed, especially when he noticed Pr'ana'lom, the dragon referee from the tournament among them.

Finally, everyone was in, and Trevor followed, closing the door behind him with a thud. He leaned against the door and surveyed the waiting crowd of friends, old and new, and vague acquaintances.

They all stared back at him, apparently waiting for him to begin.

Trevor cleared his throat. "Um. Thank you for being here to support me," he started. "I'm having some second thoughts, but I'm guessing there's no take-backs?"

Zachary stood up from his reclining position on the couch in the small living-room area and floated forward.

"If you do not fight, your life will be forfeit," he said with a shrug of one tentacle. "You may still die if you do, but at least you'd be able to fight for the right to live."

Trevor couldn't help but admire the way the merfolk managed to move so easily on land. He wished they didn't — it would help if Bryan was more of a, well, fish out of water, and he could use that to his advantage in the coming fight.

At least Bryan was working with arms and legs. It would have been far more difficult for Trevor to get used to fighting one of the octo-mer.

"The terms were set as follows," said Zachary without preamble. "The duel will occur twenty-four hours from the time of challenge, which was 6:15pm New Zealand Standard Time. Champion rules do apply, as Trevor volunteered instead of Matriarch Monin, who was the original challengee."

A ragged cheer broke out from the witches present, and Matriarch Monin clasped her hands in a double fist, pumping it in the air first on one side of her head and then the other.

Zachary solemnly waited until the cheer died down and then continued. "This means you are allowed one extra weapon."

"For a total of how many?" asked Sister Margaret.

"Three," said Zachary. "Bryan will only have two. Champion rules also dictate that the duel shall not be to the death. Please note that this does *not* guarantee that you will not die. It simply means that you or he may surrender at any time, ending the duel, and that the loser will not be put to death, nor must he forfeit any part of his body."

"Holy hell," said Trevor.

"The traditional dueling ring is a circle twenty feet in diameter," Zachary continued. He turned to Dragonlord On'Klanka. "Is there a dueling facility on site?"

"There is," he affirmed. "It has been used twice in the history of the cryptid collective's summits."

"Once in 1734, I believe," put in Carly. "Between Abigail of the Theriot School and a kallanpa amaru who inadvertently insulted the position of her dorsal fin. And again in 1986 between Jack of the Agualadron School and a witch. My understanding is that the witch was advocating for humans to be admitted to the Cryptid Collective, and Jack had the same objections Bryan does. Which makes sense, since they are from the same school."

"Who won those duels?" asked Trevor.

There was an awkward pause before Zachary spoke again. "There has never, to my knowledge, been a duel between a mer and a non-mer in which the non-mer won."

"Oh, good," said Trevor. "Wait, aren't the kallanpa amaru immortal? How could they have been killed in a duel?"

"We can be killed by fire and extreme heat," said the sole kallanpa amaru present in the room. Trevor recognized them; Sister Margaret had briefly chatted with them at the welcome banquet the night before. "Their name was Supay, and they fought well, but the mer knew our weakness and used it. The duel was quick and brutal."

"You make it sound like you were there," Trevor observed.

"As indeed I was." The kallanpa amaru bowed their head. "I witnessed the other as well. The witch's duel. She also fought well, and lasted much longer. If I recall correctly, she didn't have the advantage of a magical weapon. Do you have a magical weapon, young mage?"

Trevor locked eyes with Sister Margaret for a moment. He didn't have a magical weapon, but—

Sister Margaret stood up. "I know where we can get one."

Chapter 34: Sister Margaret

Without waiting for a response, Sister Margaret strode out of the room. She didn't know how, but she was going to get that sword for Trevor. There was no way in hell she was going to lose her friend and partner to a pointless duel just because some fucking mermaid — merman — merfolk person — whatever they called themselves — had it in for humans.

"Wait," said a voice behind her.

She turned to see a familiar dragon slipping from the room behind her. After a moment she realized he was the same young dragon who had given them directions to the museum earlier that day, Pr'ana'lom, who had also served as the announcer for the squonkerball games. Damn, it had been a long day. "Yes?"

"You found your Order's sword, didn't you? The one you were looking for? That's the weapon you're going to get?"

"What if I am?" she lifted her chin.

"I know someone who works at the museum," said the dragon. "I'll come with you."

"Oh. Thanks," said Sister Margaret.

"My name is Pr'ana'lom," he said.

"Sister Margaret," she replied. "Thanks for helping me."

"I really shouldn't be taking sides," mused Pr'ana'lom as they walked. "I'll probably get in trouble."

"Why?" said Sister Margaret.

"Why will I get in trouble?" asked the dragon. "Or why am I doing it anyway?"

"Both, I guess." She shrugged. "I meant the former, but I was probably going to ask the latter next anyway."

"I'll get in trouble because I'm supposed to play nice with the merfolk." Pr'ana'lom sighed, a great gust of ice that Sister Margaret felt the edges of. "This is the first summit in a long time that has seen any delegates from below the waves, much less from multiple schools. We were so determined to smooth things over with the merfolk. To truly bring them into the collective in a way that they have never really been."

"I don't think Bryan and his school had the same intention," said Sister Margaret drily as she began to ascent to the esplanade, her cleated boots crunching against the icy ramp. "You can't control the actions of others." She cocked her head as a thought occurred to her. "Actually, by helping Trevor, you might be cementing an alliance with at least one school of merfolk."

"What do you mean?" asked the dragon.

"Well, Zachary and Carly. Their school came along specifically to oppose and counteract Bryan and his mean little gang, right? So while you're opposing Bryan, you're actually allying yourself with Zachary."

"Maybe you're right. I hadn't considered that, which was a mistake. I'd forgotten that the mer are a deeply divided people." The dragon sighed again, and Sister Margaret stepped out of its chilly path. "We know so little about them, and they're so complicated. We don't know much about you and your kind either, but so far you have all been much friendlier."

"I think that's really just because you made good choices about who to invite," said Sister Margaret. "The Illuminati are an unknown element to me, but you did well to invite Pala, and Aurora as a group has the potential to be a big player in the mage world. If anyone can get them there, it's Chameleon. As far as inviting a delegation from the Vatican, well, you could have ended up with worse representatives than me and Trevor." She paused. "Can I ask you a question?"

"Of course."

"Did you, the dragons, I mean, invite me and Trevor specifically? Sammy said he was personally invited."

"Yes," said Pr'ana'lom. "You didn't know?"

She shook her head. "Why us? It can't just be because we knew some of the other mages."

"We knew it was a risk, bringing in humans. You, as a species, don't have a great track record for being diplomatic and open-minded. You know that there used to be fire dragons and water dragons, right? Humans hunted them into extinction."

Sister Margaret nodded. She was glad that at least her order hadn't been dragon-killers, even back in medieval times. They'd done some other things she wasn't too keen on, but not this. "I'm sorry," she said softly.

"Not your fault," said Pr'ana'lom. "But of course we wanted to be cautious. We did our research, choosing groups that had power and then looking within those groups in order to request specific representatives who we felt would fit in well, would be keen to participate fully, and would be assets to our summit."

"You kind of dropped the ball with Gregory, didn't you?" said Sister Margaret.

"We did not request Mr. Pitts, actually," the dragon admitted. "Nor Mr. Palmer. The Illuminati took our request more as a suggestion, unfortunately. It may have been a miscalculation to invite them. The Vatican, on the other hand, took our request seriously. We chose you and your partner specifically and emphatically. You are a unique pair, even among the specialized and elite mages who make up the ranks of the Warrior Mage dicastery."

Sister Margaret looked at him sideways. "We are? Are you sure?"

As they began to descend the ramp, the dragon returned her sideways glance, a twinkle in his big silver eye. "Quite sure. You're both multilingual and have a healthy respect for all cultures. You are an immensely skilled fighter and he is a brilliant scholar. Not only that, but he is also an adept fighter and you are intelligent and learned as well. It's rare to find anyone so well-rounded, much less two of you who work together. We watched the fall of the Auditors with interest, and the two of you were instrumental in bringing that about."

Sister Margaret nodded. "Fair enough."

"And finally, we thought it would be helpful to bring in mages who were familiar and friendly with each other."

"Again, the Illuminati seem like the odd ones out," Sister Margaret pointed out. "As far as I know, I don't know anyone in the Illuminati."

"Like I said, they didn't sent the requested delegation," repeated the Dragonlord.

Sister Margaret paused on the steps to the museum. "Are you saying I do know members of the Illuminati?"

Pr'ana'lom shrugged. "I said what I said."

"I see." Jogging the rest of the way up the steps, Sister Margaret ran through a list of all the people she knew who weren't affiliated with the Sisters of Saint Joan, dismissing most of them as potential members of one of the most secretive and yet somehow super famous clubs in the world.

"You're trying to guess, aren't you?" Pr'ana'lom laughed.

"No," Sister Margaret lied. "We should be focusing on how we're going to convince the museum to let us borrow the sword."

She tugged open the heavy door and braced it with her body to let the dragon in before her.

"Of course," said the dragon.

He clearly didn't believe her. Whatever. She'd figure it out later. Right now, Trevor was counting on her.

Chapter 35: Trevor

Trevor carefully tracked Helen's movements, circling opposite her, taking slow, cautious steps and waiting for the strike.

Helen lunged forward, her trident darting forward toward Trevor's shoulder and the oversized fishhook held in her other arm flying through the air on its filament line.

As the hook moved, a trail of sparks flew in its wake. Trevor was careful not to let any of the sparks touch him or his clothing — he already had a few tiny scorch marks on his armor and two spots on his skin that wouldn't stop itching.

Ducking the trident, Trevor spun to slice through the hook's tether. His sword failed to cut through the line, but succeeded in knocking it away. As Trevor whirled about again to face his opponent, Helen compensated for the new trajectory of the hook, lashing out with the butt end of the trident and swiftly tugging the hook back toward herself, its sharp point scraping along Trevor's arm bracer on its way, the magic sparks leaving more of those little black dots all along it.

Trevor gasped and fell to one knee as the trident's blunt end connected with his solar plexus. Instinctively, he thrust upward with the sword toward Helen's belly, but she twisted out of the way, bringing the trident's tines to his neck.

He sighed and raised his hands in surrender. "Again, please," he requested.

Helen was good, even on land, and she had assured him that Bryan was better.

Trevor itched to use his mage powers, at least to be able to stitch or to raise a shield. This wasn't the first time he'd had to fight without them, though, and he'd spent time every day practicing without them.

Never against a trident, a fish hook, and a non-human opponent, though. Helen had a similar form to Bryan's, so she was the logical choice of sparring partner.

Helen helped him to his feet and he got into a ready position once more, raising his sword and watching her closely.

Hopefully Sister Margaret would be able to get him the magical sword. Hopefully it would have a similar heft and balance to his own. Hopefully Bryan would be using similar weapons to Helen's.

Trevor forced himself to focus in the here and now. There was nothing to be gained from wishing, and everything to be gained from practice.

Helen spun suddenly, attacking once more with trident and fishhook simultaneously.

Trevor ducked and twisted, evading both. He tucked himself into a somersault, rolling across the circle delineated in tape on the floor and popping up behind Helen to tap her wrist in just the right spot that would have forced a human to drop their trident.

Helen simply spun her wrist around, bringing the tines of the trident toward his face.

He dove toward the floor to avoid it, grasping the fishhook's line, which was headed in an arc around his torso and pulling it downward with him. Sliding across the floor on his rear, Trevor began wrapping the line around his arm, careful to keep it over his leather bracer. After a couple of wraps, he stopped his slide with his heels and jumped back up to his feet, parrying with this sword against the trident that Helen was thrusting toward his face.

Then he tugged his arm back abruptly and Helen lost her grip on the handle of the filament. Trevor quickly unwrapped it, ducking her trident as he did so and then tossing the fishhook and its line over the edge of the circle so Helen couldn't retrieve it without breaking the rules.

She grinned at him in approval, but he han't won yet.

Trevor focused on the trident, which she was now wielding with both hands. Sweat dripped from his brow as he found himself fighting off a flurry of attacks. Finally, he found an opening and with a bellow, he charged in, his sword held to her throat.

Helen smiled broadly and raised her arms. "Good! You finally got one in!"

Lowering his sword with a sigh of relief, Trevor stepped back. "I need to take a break," he wheezed. "Can we take a break?"

Helen nodded, lowering her trident. She wasn't winded at all, which Trevor knew was an effect of the magic imbued in the trident; it conveyed unceasing stamina upon its bearer.

The mer had chosen the weapons Helen bore because they resembled weapons Bryan was known to possess and frequently use for duels.

Helen strode over to her hook and summoned it into her hand.

Trevor watched with interest as the handle flew upward and the line tidily arranged itself into a coil around her arm. "That must be a magic you have, and not something in the weapon," he observed. "Since you didn't do it in the circle."

"Correct," she said. "We can pull objects toward ourselves. It comes in handy in the water."

"And outside of it," he observed.

"True."

Trevor picked up his water bottle from the desk and sat down in his chair as he chugged. The water was lukewarm, but in his current state of sweaty exhaustion, it tasted like a miraculous elixir.

The supportive crowd that had been present earlier had left; many of them had arranged evening or early morning meetings during the morning's carousel. Even in the face of a duel, the Cryptid Collective's summit went on as scheduled.

All of tomorrow's afternoon and evening events had been canceled to make way for the duel and whatever aftermath would need to be dealt with, but tonight, the summit kept going.

Trevor couldn't help but wonder if the talking points had changed at all based on the events of the day.

Zachary approached with a towel and a jar of something yellow and oily-looking. "Let's take care of those itch-spots before they do any more damage," he suggested.

Trevor raised an eyebrow. "Damage?"

"You haven't been scratching them, have you?" said Zachary. He handed Trevor the towel.

"No," said Trevor, wiping the sweat from his face, careful to only dab the spot that itched from the sparks that had emanated from the magic fishhook. "Although now that you mention it, I think they're getting gradually itchier."

"Yeah, that'll keep happening until you start scratching," said Zachary. "And then it won't be so gradual." He opened the jar and a pungent sour salty odor sprang free.

Trevor flinched at the smell, but held still as Zachary slathered a healthy portion of the salve onto his cheek. The salve was surprisingly warm and the soothing effect was immediate.

"Were there any more?" asked Zachary.

Trevor held up his left hand, and Zachary applied the salve to the red dot that decorated Trevor's index finger.

"Okay, you should be good to wipe it off now," said Zachary.

With relief, Trevor used the towel to remove the salve from his face and hand. He had been concerned that this was a multi-step process and that he'd be smelling like rotten seaweed for days. "What the hell is in that stuff, anyway?" he asked.

"Rotten seaweed," said Zachary.

Ah. That explained it, then. He stood up and addressed Helen, who was spraying herself down with salt water. "You about ready for Round Two?"

Helen bared her teeth and set down the spray bottle. "Bring it on."

Chapter 36: Sister Margaret

"What's our move?" whispered Sister Margaret once the elevator doors slid shut. "Persuade someone to help us out or just take the sword and apologize later when we return it?"

Pr'ana'lom had bypassed the front desk already, heading straight to the elevator and pressing a button. Sister Margaret couldn't for the life of her remember if it was the same floor they'd gone to before or if her partner in crime was heading for another level to talk another dragon into letting them have the sword.

"Best not to steal from museums," said the dragon. "They're populated almost entirely by people who feel very passionately that everything in the world that's at least five years old belongs here."

"Sure, but those are the same people you'd have to talk into letting us take it," Sister Margaret pointed out.

"But we're talking them into letting us *borrow* it," countered the dragon. "Which is a whole different situation than when they think you're *stealing*."

Sister Margaret raised her eyebrows and crossed her arms. "Didn't they steal most of this stuff to begin with?"

"It's not the British Museum," said Pr'ana'lom. "And dragons in real life don't hoard wealth, like we do in your stories. Most of this stuff was purchased by various cryptids and then donated to our museum."

"Fair enough." The elevator door opened and Sister Margaret recognized the exhibit that contained Saint Joan's sword. "So, you're going to talk to your friend and they'll let us borrow it?"

"Hope so," said Pr'ana'lom.

"Pr'ana'lom! And Sister Margaret again! To what do I owe this pleasure?" The wing's curator greeted them from down the hall. She hurried toward them. "Here to see your ancestor's sword again?"

"She's not my ancestor, per se," Sister Margaret began.

"Not see it, exactly," said Pr'ana'lom at the same time.

Thr'Lo paid no attention to their words, instead simply herding the pair toward the display case. "Such an interesting piece, isn't it? I'm very pleased to have been able to update its description. Where is your scholarly friend?" She peered behind them as though suspecting that Trevor might have been lurking in a shadow.

"Well, that's really what we're here to discuss," said Sister Margaret.

"You have more information about the sword?" The curator snagged her computer cart again, and looked at Sister Margaret expectantly.

"No, we need to—"

"Ah, you're hoping for information from me, then," interrupted Thr'Lo. "I'd be happy to help, but I'm afraid I only know what I told you before, which, as you may remember was—"

"We need to borrow the sword," shouted Sister Margaret at the top of her lungs.

Thr'Lo froze mid-sentence, her mouth hanging open in surprise, displaying an array of teeth to rival a mer.

"If you don't mind," said Sister Margaret, more quietly. She licked her lips and tried to smile, but she could feel her face forming more of an embarrassed grimace than an actual friendly expression. Her teeth probably looked ridiculously tiny in comparison. At least Thr'Lo wouldn't feel threatened by her. "Please," she added for good measure.

Thr'Lo's jaw snapped shut with a click and her head twisted to stare at Pr'ana'lom who also wore an embarrassed expression. Thr'Lo's eyes narrowed and she glared daggers at her friend.

"Um, yes," Pr'ana'lom admitted. "That wasn't exactly how I had planned to bring it up, but it is a matter of some urgency."

Thr'Lo finally found her voice. "You want to *borrow* a priceless human artifact from *my* collection? And it's urgent?"

"I thought you said dragons didn't hoard," Sister Margaret muttered.

Thr'Lo's glare swung around to pin Sister Margaret in its beam. "I think it's reasonable to expect an explanation."

"Of course it is," said Pr'ana'lom, shooting a glance at Sister Margaret.

Great, now she had two giant teeth monsters pissed at her. Maybe she'd better let Pr'ana'lom do the talking.

She nodded mutely.

"Well?" said Thr'Lo.

"So, here's the thing," said Pr'ana'lom. He paused. "The thing is. Um. Well, so you know the merfolk?"

"I'm familiar, yes," said Thr'Lo.

"You know how they're always dueling?"

"Sure."

"And you know how when they duel—"

Sister Margaret couldn't take it any longer. "Some merfolk asshole challenged Trevor, the scholar you were so taken with, to a duel, or he challenged him on behalf of someone else anyway, and the non-asshole merfolk said that he needs a magic weapon, but we don't have any so we need to borrow this one, which honestly should belong to my order anyway, right? But we're not taking it for real, we're just borrowing it so Trevor can fight the damn duel, and then we'll give it back, at least for now, until my Mother Superior can figure out if she wants to try and buy it or whatever. I don't know; that's above my pay grade."

Thr'Lo stared at her again.

Sister Margaret tried for a smile again and got it mostly right this time.

"You want to take my priceless artifact and *fight with it*?" Thr'Lo was practically foaming at the mouth now.

"That is what it's designed for," Sister Margaret pointed out.

Thr'Lo flung her forelimb toward the elevator. "Get out! Get out of my exhibit! Now!"

"But—"

"Leave!"

"I can't just—"

"Go!"

"Can we please—"

"No!"

Sister Margaret raised her hands in surrender and began to back out. "Okay, okay. *Lo siento*. Sorry. Leaving. Going. Now." She turned around and walked the rest of the way back to the elevator. "So, what now?" she asked Pr'ana'lom as she stepped into the lift. "Do we maybe go—" A loud crashing sound came from the exhibit and she spun around, hands on her sword hilts, to find that the dragon was no longer behind her. "Pr'ana'lom?"

"Hit the button!" called Pr'ana'lom as he came careening around the corner, bounding on all four legs, the sword held in his mouth. "Go, go, go!"

Sister Margaret smacked the Lobby button and the doors began to close.

Pr'ana'lom skidded into the elevator, sliding through the doors just in time. He dropped the sword on the floor in front of Sister Margaret and she picked up, reverently running a hand down the center of the blade, careful to avoid the edges, which were still astonishingly sharp. Was there a spell on it to maintain the edge?

A siren sounded as they began to descend. Thr'Lo had activated a security alarm.

"Are we going to be able to get out of here?" asked Sister Margaret.

"I know a back way out," said Pr'ana'lom with a gaping grin. He nodded at the sword. "That is the one you needed, right?"

"Oh, yes." Sister Margaret sighed as she gazed at it. "This is it."

The elevator stopped, and she tensed as the doors opened, expecting to see a crowd of angry dragons, but the hallway in front of them was deserted.

Sister Margaret frowned. Where were their pursuers? Best not to question good fortune.

"This way," whispered Pr'ana'lom. He hurried down the corridor and she hastened after him, holding the sword up in front of her, since he hadn't grabbed its belt and scabbard.

She couldn't fault him for that; it wasn't exactly premeditated, nor had there been a lot of time. But it was still kind of a pain in the ass to carry around a huge bare broadsword, especially in a hurry.

Then again, the sword was not as heavy as she'd anticipated. More magic, probably. How many spells were on this beautiful bastard?

And how was Trevor going to be able to access the ones that would help him win the duel?

One problem at a time. First she had to get the sword to Trevor.

Pr'ana'lom paused in front of her, and she skidded to a halt, sword raised. Around them, the sirens still screamed.

"What's going on?" she hissed, trying to be quiet but needing to be heard over the claxons. "Why did you stop?"

"Nobody seems to be chasing us," said Pr'ana'lom. "Doesn't that seem odd to you?"

She shrugged. "So, let's go before they start."

"What if it's a trap?"

Sister Margaret turned on her seer sight. "There's nobody there," she said. "Come on." She pushed past the dragon and led the way down the hall. "It's all clear."

Pr'ana'lom followed, and Sister Margaret led him down the hallway, navigating the building by the simple tactic of following the images of her future self. That was the kind of thing that made novice seers' brains hurt as they tried to figure out how an image of themselves two seconds in the future would know where to go when they didn't know in the present and nobody was telling them, but Sister Margaret had been a mage her whole life, and she knew that wondering about shit like that would just drive you crazy and you'd never figure it out.

She trusted her mage powers and her trust was rewarded a few minutes later when she exited the building, Pr'ana'lom right on her heels.

"We did it," said Pr'ana'lom. "How did we do that?"

Sister Margaret shrugged and followed her future self up a ramp and along the esplanade until they reached a familiar spot. She thought about turning off the mage sight at that point, but there was still the possibility of pursuit, so she kept it on.

The pair of them traveled in silence until they reached the hotel and began ascending the ramp up to her and Trevor's rooms. She finally turned off her seer sight.

"What have I done?" moaned Pr'ana'lom suddenly.

Startled, Sister Margaret jumped and spun around, brandishing the sword at him.

"Hey! Watch where you're waving that thing!"

"Sorry." She lowered the sword. "Thanks for your help. What's going to happen to you for stealing this sword?"

"I don't know," said Pr'ana'lom. "Hopefully nothing terrible. We're going to return it, after all."

"I suppose someone will be coming after us soon," said Sister Margaret. "Maybe that's why they didn't chase us. They know exactly who took it, after all."

"My mom has got to be so pissed," said Pr'ana'lom behind her.

"Your mom?" Sister Margaret twisted her head around to frown at him.

"I may not have been entirely forthcoming about my relationship to Thr'Lo," he said. "I mean, I never said she was a friend. You assumed she was a friend."

"Are you fucking kidding me?" Sister Margaret stared at him. Then she began to laugh. Sometimes that was all you could do. Shaking her head, she turned around and kept walking up the ramp and then down the hallway to Trevor's room.

She knocked on the door, still chuckling to herself.

Zachary opened the door a crack and then flung it wide upon seeing her with the sword. "You got them to lend it to you!"

"Yeah, let's go with that," said Sister Margaret. "Where's Trevor? Might as well start practicing with this and hope nobody comes for it until after the duel."

Chapter 37: Trevor

Trevor stared at the sword Sister Margaret held out to him. He couldn't quite believe it was real. "You got it," he whispered. "I might have a chance at this."

"Maybe," said Sister Margaret.

He frowned. "What's that supposed to mean?"

"There are a lot of factors at play here," she said. "We don't even know if you can use the fucking thing."

"Or if they'll let you," added the dragon who came in behind her.

Trevor took the sword and hefted it. It was surprisingly light. Then the dragon's words hit him. "What do you mean? Why wouldn't they let me? I thought magical weapons were allowed."

"They are," said Helen.

"We didn't exactly get them to lend us the sword," Sister Margaret admitted. "We kind of sort of stole it."

Trevor sighed. "I can't condone that, but what's done is done. Let's hope they don't notice until after the duel and we can return it."

"Oh, they're aware," said the dragon. "They're probably on their way here right now to take it back."

"What?" Trevor turned to Sister Margaret, trying to make sense of the whole thing. "What is happening here?"

"Yes, please explain," said Zachary exasperation in his sibilant voice.

"Okay, so here's what happened." Sister Margaret ran through the whole story, starting with Thr'Lo's initial questions and ending with Pr'ana'lom's confession that he was Thr'Lo's son.

Stunned silence met the end of her story.

"I don't even know what to do with that," Trevor confessed. "I just— What do I do with that? Do I use the sword? Do we give the sword back? Do we— What do we do here?"

"Somebody will probably be pounding on the door any second now," said Sister Margaret. She seemed remarkably cheerful. "I guess the best we can do is hope they'll understand?"

"Actually," said Zachary.

He definitely sounded cheerful. Why the hell did everyone sound so damn cheerful?

"Nobody is allowed to take anything away from you while you're sequestered," he finished.

Oh. That was actually pretty cheerful. Trevor could feel himself cheering up very suddenly as well. "Really?" he asked. "So, we're good."

"In the sense that you have a magical weapon for the duel, yes," said Helen. "But once the duel is over, you'll presumably have to face the music."

"But I have a higher chance of being alive for the music," Trevor pointed out. "I can handle music, but only if I'm not dead."

"And if you are dead, you won't care about the music anyway," said Sister Margaret.

Trevor grinned at her. "You do have a way of putting things into perspective, don't you?"

She grinned back. "Always happy to help."

***

Trevor slept in the next day, but it still came sooner than he would have liked. Someday he was going to have to figure out if time travel was a thing. Then maybe he could just skip over the super stressful days like this. That could work, right?

Probably not — it seemed like the kind of thing that would open up a whole paradox situation.

It was moot anyway; today, he didn't have time travel. He'd have to stay in the present and fight Bryan. And the worst part was that aside from the passive magics, like the lightness, balance, and sharpness of the sword, they hadn't been able to figure out how to access any of its heavy-duty spells.

So, it was a fantastic sword, but essentially mundane. He had managed to beat Helen in sparring twice with the sword, but everyone agreed that Bryan was a better fighter than Helen was. And nobody was completely certain that he would be using the same kinds of weapons Helen had.

"So, you're probably going to die today," Trevor told himself in the mirror as he brushed his teeth. He did a different voice to represent his reflection arguing back at him. "But, Trevor, it's not a fight to the death!"

"If you think Bryan is going to hold back, you're an idiot," Trevor informed himself in his regular voice. "The whole not-to-the-death thing just means you don't have to kill him."

"That's nice, though, right?" said his reflection. "You don't like killing people."

"I doubt I'll get the chance to make that decision," said Trevor. He gave his back teeth one more quick polish, spit, and rinsed his mouth out. Then he sighed and stared at his reflection. One corner of his mouth quirked up. "At least I'll be a good-looking corpse. That's always an upside to dying young, right?"

"You're pushing forty," he said in his reflection voice. "That's hardly young."

"Well, it's young to die," he said. His small smile faded and he shook his head, sighing again.

A knock came from the main room, so he turned and strode out of the bathroom to answer it. Nobody stood in the hallway.

There was another knock, and he belatedly realized it was coming from the door that adjoined his and Sister Margaret's room.

Before he could answer it, Sister Margaret burst in, waving her phone around. "I think we may have cracked it!" she yelled. "We just might be able to unlock the sword!"

Trevor stared at her, not quite allowing himself to believe it. Maybe he wouldn't die today after all.

"Who did you talk to?" Trevor demanded.

"Sister Chantal; she's a scholar with my order, and she has been working on scanning and electronically cataloging some really old stuff from the order's archives."

"And she found a manuscript that goes into more detail about the sword?" Trevor's heart raced. This actually could be something.

"No, not exactly," said Sister Margaret.

Trevor resisted the urge to grab her by the shoulders and shake the answers out of her. If he got himself stabbed by his partner, that would make it harder to fight Bryan later. "Then what?"

"Well, what she did find was a book from the mid-fifteenth century, and it's the life story of a mage-blacksmith."

Trevor stared at her. "That's it? Some medieval peasant's memoir? How is that going to help us?"

"He may be the same blacksmith who made the sword," said Sister Margaret. "The book might contain technical details about the spells layered onto it."

"May be? Might contain?" Trevor could hear his voice spiraling up in octave, and didn't care. "I am fighting Bryan in eight hours, Sister. Eight. Hours. Has Sister Chantal even read the book? How long is it? What kind of shape is it in? What language is it in?"

Sister Margaret glanced at her phone as it chimed. "It's in medieval French. She's working on it. They were trying to restore the document before they read it, but I've managed to make them understand the urgency, so they're working with the computer, hoping they can make the pages clearer. She has a whole team of scholars all over the world; one is scanning it into the computer and using it to make the words clearer. Then the others are translating it in sections. They can get through it in time. I know they can. Hold on, let me read this." She unlocked her phone, but before she could read the text, Trevor snatched it out of her hand.

He peered at the screen. The text was in Italian, and for some reason his brain refused to translate it. "I can't deal with Italian today," he said, handing it back. Suddenly, all the energy drained out of him, and he staggered the two steps to the raw-edged wooden bench at the foot of the bed, thumping down onto its hard seat. "Ow."

Sister Margaret sat down beside him and put an arm around his shoulders. "Hey," she said. "We've faced uncertain battles before."

"This isn't an uncertain battle," said Trevor. "This is an almost-certain duel. I haven't done the math, but I'm pretty damn certain I have about a 1% chance of living to attend the after-dinner mixer tonight."

Sister Margaret didn't answer, as she was typing a response into her phone.

Trevor sighed again. He was doing a lot of sighing today. "What is she saying?"

"They found some information about the making of magical swords, and there's apparently hints in there about a special sword he's making for a French warrior woman."

Trevor sat up straight, interested in spite of himself. He wouldn't let himself hope. Just because this guy made the sword didn't mean there would be instructions on how to use it in his biography.

The phone chimed again. "A very special sword." Sister Margaret jumped to her feet, pacing back and forth. "Trevor, the order for the sword came from a holy military order out of Portugal and was backed by the Vatican."

Her eyes met his, and he caught his breath. This actually could be it. What was the harm in hoping, after all?

Trevor stood and walked over to the weapons rack, where he had stowed the sword the night before, once they'd decided rest would do him better than more rounds of sparring. Against all odds, the sword had fit perfectly in his own spare scabbard, which had been made specially for his custom broadsword.

He wasn't even sure why he'd brought along the empty scabbard, but he'd decided to take it as a good omen.

Somebody knocked on the door and then unlocked it without waiting for a response.

Taye slipped inside, carrying a breakfast tray. "How are you feeling about tonight?" he asked without preamble, setting the tray down on the desk and giving Trevor a searching look.

"I don't know," said Trevor. He nodded toward Sister Margaret, who was holding her phone at face level and staring at it intently as though she could influence the content of the next text message. "We may have a lead on the sword situation."

"Good," said Taye. "That's good." He pursed his lips and inhaled deeply through his nose, shifting his weight from foot to foot. "I'm sorry about all of this," he said, abruptly.

Trevor raised his eyebrows. "It's hardly your fault. I knew what I was doing."

"I'm still sorry," said Taye. "Somehow, I feel like I have let you down. Perhaps I should have briefed you better on the fighting skills of the other cryptids at the summit, or—"

"Honestly," said Trevor, dryly. "I should probably just not go around smacking people in the face with fish heads. As a general rule."

Taye stared at him.

Trevor set down the sword and walked over to Taye, putting an arm around him and guiding him over to the couch. "Have a seat. Lighten up a little. None of this was your responsibility. Bryan has had it in for us since before he even met us. Every day is a risk, no matter what we do."

He was surprised to realize that he was cheering himself up with his pep talk. Whether it was having an affect on Taye was hard to see; the salashifter didn't seem to have a huge range of facial expressions at the best of times.

Sister Margaret lowered her phone and smiled at him. "That's the Trevor I know and love," she said. "You beat Helen three times yesterday, remember?"

He nodded. "And the first one was before I even had a magical sword."

"Humans are optimists, then?" said Taye. "Like bigfoots. Always looking for something positive."

"Some of us," said Trevor with a shrug. He sniffed the air, catching a whiff of coffee and toast from the breakfast tray. "Might as well eat before this gets cold, anyway. Have to keep up my strength."

***

After breakfast, Helen came back and Trevor spent some time sparring with her. He found himself somewhat distracted, and only managed to win one bout.

After a couple of hours, he called a halt to it, not wanting to exhaust himself before the real fight.

Taye brought him some lunch and seemed to be in higher spirits, which in turn cheered Trevor up a little. He was starting to spiral mentally, and resolutely steeled himself. He knew from experience that he was more likely to lose a fight that he thought he would lose.

Trevor spent the afternoon alternating between reading a merfolk dueling manual Zachary had emailed him and stretching to keep his muscles limber.

He kept up an inner mantra, repeating whenever he needed it, *You are an experienced and skilled warrior. There's always a chance you'll win.*

The effectiveness of this strategy came and went in waves.

Every so often, Sister Margaret would poke her head in with an update on the translations of Sister Chantal's messages, none of which gave any concrete information. He knew she meant well, but with each time she interrupted him just tell him there was no real news, he felt a little bit more on edge.

Finally, around 4:45, Taye arrived again, carrying a light dinner of sushi and miso broth, with Zachary and Helen trailing behind him.

Sister Margaret must have heard them arrive, because she bounced in just after them. "Where's Carly?" she asked. "Are we heading down to the ring soon?"

"Carly is supervising the set-up in the dueling chamber," said Zachary as Trevor slurped his miso broth. "She'll make sure everything is done fairly and according to the rules."

"The Agualadron School will probably have a representative there as well," added Helen. "We should all head down there in about half an hour."

Trevor nodded, trying not to think about the fact that if Sister Chantal hadn't found anything yet, he was probably out of luck.

Hopefully Pr'ana'lom wouldn't be in too much trouble for stealing the sword for him. It would be a shame if he had ruined the dragon's life for no reason.

"It's still a better sword than mine, either way," he murmured around a mouthful of rice, seaweed, and spicy tuna.

"What?" said Zachary.

Trevor glanced up. "Nothing," he mumbled. "Just thinking out loud."

"You need to buck the fuck up," said Helen, sharply. "Mumble-boy isn't going to win against Bryan. Where's the warrior I fought yesterday? You seem to have given up already, and that will not do."

Trevor blinked at her, and she glared back. "Listen up, mage. You're not just representing the Vatican out there today. Nor even just mages or humanity. Our school has staked its reputation on the premise that humans, specifically mages, are worth allying with. Don't make us look like idiots."

He glanced at Zachary, who bobbed his head in agreement, his tentacles swaying. "You did good yesterday. You fought well. Even if you lose today, you must put up a good fight for our sake. Or our lives may be forfeit upon our return home."

Chapter 38: Sister Margaret

Sister Margaret's attention was about three quarters on her phone as she typed in a response to Sister Chantal's latest communique, and she was only sort of listening to the merfolk's conversation with Trevor.

Suddenly she felt like she had just heard something important, but couldn't put her finger on what it was. She turned to look at the three of them, her eyes narrowing. "What did you just say? Repeat that."

"We staked our reputation on the outcome of this summit," said Helen. "Merfolk take that very seriously. If it goes poorly, we will face a tribunal when we go home, and if they rule against us, our entire school will be outcast and the leaders executed."

"The leaders being you guys," said Trevor, his eyes darting between the two of them.

"And Carly, yes," said Zachary.

"So, if I die, so do you," said Trevor, slowly.

"Maybe not," said Helen. "If you die quickly, then yes, almost certainly. If you last a while, but are deemed to have been merely lucky, then we will probably be executed. If you fight well and honorably, even if you lose in the end, we will be applauded and our school rewarded for our foresight."

"Just the fact that you volunteered as champion helps, actually," said Zachary, helpfully. "As of right now, we are looking very good."

"As long as I don't fuck it up," said Trevor.

"Exactly," said Helen.

"He won't fuck it up," said Taye firmly.

Sister Margaret smiled at Taye's stoic vote of confidence.

It seemed to bolster Trevor's confidence as well. He straightened his spine and polished off his final sushi piece, following it up with a pungent dose of pickled ginger.

Trevor stood and took a deep breath. "Might as well head down there now."

"Wait." Sister Margaret stood as well and marched up to him. "Armor check."

Trevor held out his arms and Sister Margaret methodically tugged at each piece of leather strapped to his body, ensuring everything sat properly on his person.

She grunted with satisfaction as she found the dagger he had strapped to his thigh and then again when she came across the short sword, its point nestled at the small of his back.

Neither weapon was magical, of course, but he was allowed three weapons, and she was pleased to see that he was damn well doing that.

Finally, Sister Margaret stepped back. "Everything looks good." She studied his face. "You look good. You can do this. Remember, this isn't a fight to the death."

Trevor opened his mouth, but she held up a hand to forestall him. "I know. I know. But if you surrender, he has to allow it. He cannot kill you once you've surrendered. And as long as you've put up a good fight before that, your honor will be in tact." She glanced at Zachary. "Right?"

He nodded. "You surrendering won't affect your honor, provided you do not show cowardice."

"And remember that you have to utter the ceremonial words of surrender," put in Taye. "Do you remember the words?"

Trevor nodded and recited them. "'I concede the fight to you, my better-in-arms.'"

"Let's go." Sister Margaret jerked her head, and led the way to the door, her phone still clutched tightly in her hand. There was still a chance that Sister Chantal would find the answers in time to save Trevor.

When they reached the fighting ring, it turned out to be in a musty interior room in the cryptid collective headquarters, just down the hall from the squonkerball court.

Upon entering, their group was escorted to a sort of corral in one corner, encircled by a three-foot-high wall of ice with a swinging door that latched shut behind them.

Surrounding the ring were rows of bleachers, currently packed with cryptids of all species. Some of them gave her an encouraging wave when they saw her looking. Matriarch Monin held up a large poster with the words, "Go Trevor!" emblazoned on it in block letters with multicolored markers.

Sister Margaret could see Bryan and his crew occupying an identical enclosure kitty-corner from them, across the ring. "Oh, no," she murmured. "We practiced with the wrong weapons."

"What?" Trevor turned to look at her sharply.

She nodded toward Bryan, who was running through a series of lunges and thrusts with a pair of tridents, rather than the trident-and-fishhook Trevor had been practicing against.

Trevor shrugged. "That's actually fine," he said. "Remember last year, when we spent three months fighting off those demon-worshiping Satanic nuns in the sewers under New York City? They fought with sharpened staffs."

"That's right," she said. "You got really good against them."

"The trident is basically a pointy staff with extra points, right?" said Trevor. "No problem. Now, if it had been two fishhooks instead…." He trailed off with a shudder. "That fishhook was brutal, especially with the trail of itchy sparks. I'll be glad to not deal with those."

He turned back to Zachary, who was giving him some last-minute pointers.

Sister Margaret kept a close eye on Bryan, watching his form, looking for any weaknesses she could point out to Trevor. As she observed, she saw one of Bryan's lieutenants approach and grasp the tridents in his tentacles.

The mer examined the tridents and made some kind of adjustment to one of the tines. As he handed the trident back, a trail of sparks followed its movements. "Uh, Trevor?" she said. "I have some bad news about the tridents."

Trevor glanced over and winced. "Will those sparks be the same as the ones from Helen's fishhook?" he asked Zacharay.

"Most likely," said Zachary. "At least now we know what one of his weapons does. We'll have to wait and see the powers imbued in the other."

"Oh, good," said Trevor. "I do love waiting."

"Not for long," said Sister Margaret, glancing at her phone. "Duel starts in four minutes."

As though on cue, Dragonlord Ch'etwime stepped forward into the ring, rearing up into the air to gain everyone's attention. The chattering crowd quieted instantly.

Despite the similar size of the audience, the mood today was much more subdued than it had been for the squonkerball the previous afternoon. Maybe because in squonkerball, hardly anyone died.

That was not the case in dueling.

"As per merfolk law," he began, "I will cede to floor first to the challenger, and then to the challengee's champion. After each has spoken, the fight will begin. This is not a fight to the death."

Bryan opened the gate of his side's corral and glided forth until he stood, a trident in each of his outstretched arms, in the center of the ring. He turned slowly, his unblinking gaze roving over the crowd in sections until finally he faced Trevor. His beak gaped open and he bared his rows of sharp teeth. "I disagree," he said. "This *will* be a fight to the death. Your death."

Bryan pounded the butts of his two tridents onto the ground with a resounding THUD-thud, and then backed up, still holding Trevor's gaze, until he stood at the edge of the ring, waiting for Trevor to step out and speak.

Trevor heaved a great sigh, and Sister Margaret grinned. Trevor hated that kind of heavy-handed pretentious bullshit.

She watched as Trevor vaulted the enclosure's fence, Saint Joan's sword sheathed at his back, over the top of his short sword. He grinned at Bryan. "We'll see," he said. He reached back with both hands and drew the greatsword. "You ready?"

Bryan growled in response and darted forward, his tridents crossed, the one held in his left hand trailing sparks as he moved.

Trevor's grin widened and he bent at the waist, spinning around for momentum as he ducked beneath the tridents and swung his sword at Bryan's midsection.

Bryan twisted, dodging the blade. He reared backward, tossing the sparkly trident into the air over Trevor's head and then diving to the floor, sliding across the tile on his belly, slashing toward Trevor as he passed. He caught the trident before it hit the floor and heaved himself back up onto his feet.

Sister Margaret stared at the slash in Trevor's pant leg. Was his ankle cut or had the slash only been cloth-deep?

Trevor didn't seem to be bothered at all, circling around Bryan, looking for a way in.

Bryan's style was more gung-ho than Helen's. He darted around, swinging his weapons, feinting and thrusting, willing to take risks in order to keep Trevor off-guard.

Sister Margaret was gratified to see that this tactic wasn't finding much success. Trevor was ignoring the feints and blocking the thrusts with ease.

Finally, Trevor jumped forward, swinging the sword.

Bryan blocked it easily, but Trevor landed an elbow to the sharklike mer's left eye.

Trevor danced back for a moment as Bryan reeled, and then struck again with a flurry of strokes, aiming the sword at various seemingly vulnerable points in the mer's defense.

Bryan parried the first few automatically and then seemed to regain his composure as he began to fight back in earnest, using one trident — Sister Margaret still didn't know its magical properties — to defend and waving the other in Trevor's direction.

Trevor dodged the sparks with ease, keeping his bare face and hands out of harm's way, but ignoring any that landed on his clothing or armor.

Sister Margaret's phone chimed and she checked the text. Sister Chantal had found more information on the making of the sword, including a lengthy list of the spells imbued into it. Still nothing about how to access the powers it contained.

But — Sister Margaret's eyebrows rose as she read through the list. A lot of it was passive and wouldn't need activation. Awareness would help, though.

"Hey," she said to Zachary. "I probably should have asked this before the fight started, but are there designated breaks in the action or anything like that? Can Trevor call a time out?"

He tilted his bulbous head. "Time out?"

"Can he request a short break? I just got some new intel on the sword's powers. I need to tell Trevor."

Zachary lifted a tentacle in a shrug. "You'll just have to shout it to him. There are no breaks in a duel."

"Then Bryan will hear it too," said Sister Margaret. She paused. "Do you know how many languages Bryan speaks?"

Zachary shrugged again. "I would guess probably English, Spanish, and Mandarin. Those are all the standard ones most merfolk learn."

Of course, Trevor hadn't been feeling the whole foreign language thing that morning. Sister Margaret wished she spoke Amharic; she knew he had learned the Ethiopian language alongside English as a child, much as she had grown up speaking Spanish.

What would be the next easiest for Trevor to translate in his head while not distracting him too much from the duel? Probably medieval Latin or something ridiculous like that, but she sure as fuck couldn't speak Latin. She could barely read it.

Damn, she wished Bryan didn't know Spanish. Fuck it; Italian would have to do. At least that way she could just read it directly from Sister Chantal's text.

She looked up to find that Trevor was on the opposite side of the ring. He was also bleeding from a cut on his forehead and favoring his left leg.

"Fuck, fuck, fuck, fuck, fuck," she muttered. He needed this information, but she was going to have to wait until he came closer. There was no way she could shout over the sound of the crowd, which was getting rowdier as the fight went on.

Her phone chimed again, and she read the text. "Mios Dios," she murmured. Had she read correctly?

"Trevor!" she screamed out.

Trevor glanced toward her. As he did so, Bryan thrust his crossed tridents forward, and Trevor stumbled amid a cacophony of jeers and cheers from the audience.

She had to get this information to him in the least distracting way possible. "It unlocks with its bearer's blood!"

she screamed in Italian. "Bleed on the sword, and its magic is yours!"

Sister Margaret held her breath, waiting for Trevor to regain his balance, hoping he'd heard and understood.

Trevor fell to one knee. Bryan thrust his sparkler trident, one side tine aimed directly at his throat to finish him off, but Trevor raised the sword just in time to fend it off.

Sister Margaret winced as she saw a spark fly toward his head, landing in his short black hair. At least it wasn't on his face; maybe his tight curls would protect his scalp from the itchiness.

"Come on, you magnificent bastard," she whispered. "Get up! Get up! Unlock the sword with your blood."

Bryan continued to attack, taking any opening, and Trevor just kept blocking and defending, all of his focus taken up with staying alive. He didn't seem to have heard her instructions.

Chapter 39: Trevor

Trevor was breathing heavily, and his arms felt weak. He was fading fast, but somehow every time the tridents came at him, he found one more burst of energy, lifting the sword with heavy arms to block it.

The sword.

How was he supposed to get his blood on the sword? He wanted to get Bryan's blood on the sword, not his own.

And when had it gotten so heavy? He moved again, almost instinctively, blocking the crossed double tridents. His head itched and his hands itched, and he could feel blood and sweat dripping down his face, but at least kneeling like this, he wasn't putting any weight on his injured ankle.

Bryan backed off for a moment, and Trevor took advantage of the moment, moving his sword to one hand, and placing the palm of the other against the blade. With a wince, he cut into his hand, bloodying the blade.

The change was instantaneous.

So was Sister Margaret's reaction. "You were already bleeding from your forehead, you dumbass!" she yelled at him. "You didn't need to cut your hand!"

Oops.

But the sword felt lighter and his body was flooded with a new burst of energy, so he hardly even noticed the slice on his hand.

And something whispered to him inside his head, but he couldn't make out the words. What language was that?

As he listened, he kept blocking Bryan's blows. The stone on the pommel of the sword was glowing now.

Trevor looked up into Bryan's cold eyes. Smug bastard. Who did he think he was? Threatening humanity? Throwing fishheads around? What the actual fuck was this guy's fucking problem?

Trevor jumped to his feet.

Bryan stumbled backward with a startled shout, his left leg twisting slightly before he regained his balance.

"That's right," called Trevor. "You retreat from me!" He wasn't speaking English. What was that? French? He wasn't very good at French, or at least not modern French. He could read medieval French pretty well.

Trevor placed his thumb over the glowing gem on the pommel of the sword and the entire thing lit up like a laser weapon from a science fiction movie.

Gasps and exclamations surrounded him from the crowd, and he heard Sister Margaret, louder than any of them, yell, "Holy fuck!"

Holy fuck, indeed.

Suddenly, Trevor's mage sight activated. It must be the sword, which of course meant that it wasn't *him* doing magery, and was not against the rules. He grinned. He still couldn't stitch or spell, but at least he'd be able to see what Bryan was about to do.

One part of his mind wondered about that — hadn't the mer foiled Sister Margaret's seer sight when they'd first met? Either that had been an active magic on Bryan's part, which he wasn't allowed to use now, or it only worked if the seer sight was being wielded by the mage and not by a weapon.

He forced himself to focus on the fight. Watching the overlay of the future, Trevor began to take advantage of the new ability, blocking strokes before they reached him, dodging all of the magical sparks, and finally —- finally! — landing some hits of his own.

Damn, what he wouldn't give for the ability to shield against those sparks, though.

Suddenly, he saw with his mage sight a shimmering barrier form in front of his body, without the feeling of mage energy leaving him. He hadn't raised that shield. The sword had, at his request, and it wasn't blocking his weapon; only protecting his skin.

Now he didn't need to worry about the sparks.

But he still faced a formidable opponent with two tridents, one of which probably did something that it just hadn't shown yet.

A series of flurries later, and he found himself circling back around near the enclosure where Sister Margaret and their mer allies stood.

Sister Margaret called something out to him in Italian, but he didn't catch it. He didn't bother asking her to repeat herself, instead looking for an opening to disarm Bryan.

He remembered from sparring with Helen that the wrists were not the vulnerability that they were for a human, so instead he shifted his grip, holding the sword one-handed while he grasped the shaft of one of Bryan's tridents in his other hand, twisting it this way and that, trying to loosen his opponent's hold on it.

Bryan took advantage of his split focus to shove Trevor backward, toward the edge of the ring.

If Trevor left the ring, he would lose the duel. For a second, he considered simply following his momentum. He had already fought hard. If he lost now, surely his friends wouldn't be dishonored.

Something inside of him wouldn't let it end that way. Trevor regained his balance and pushed forward, abandoning his notion of disarming Bryan, instead hitting him with a flurry of thrusts and slashes and landing a kick to the mer's side that sent him spinning.

Trevor aimed another kick directly at Bryan's dorsal fin, and the mer howled in pain and dropped one of his tridents, the one with the mystery magic.

Both of them dove for the trident, Trevor reaching it just in time to pick it up and throw it away. This proved to the wrong move, as once the trident was airborne, it changed directions, snapping right back into Bryan's outstretched hand.

Well, that solved the mystery of what kind of magic the trident had. It was a magical boomerang.

Trevor changed tactics, now attacking with the sole purpose of hitting Bryan's fins. If the dorsal fin was that sensitive, the others might be too. He thrust his sword into a gap below Bryan's arm, straight into one of his pectoral fins.

The mer let out a stream of words in a language Trevor didn't recognize. Some kind of Asian language, maybe?

Taking advantage of Bryan's distraction, he darted forward, gripping the trident again. This time, Bryan's hold on it weakened, and he was able to grab it. Trevor skipped backward toward the edge of the ring and dropped it on the ground before kicking it over the edge. It skittered across the floor, but did not return to Bryan.

Bryan charged forward, favoring his right leg, and Trevor stood steady, just inside the ring, and sidestepped neatly just before the mer reached him.

Trevor spun around to see if his ploy had worked, but Bryan had managed to stop himself just in time, balancing precariously on just the tips of his unshod feet, arms windmilling and pectoral fins flapping, just barely on the inside of the ring.

Deliberately pushing one's opponent outside was strictly prohibited, so Trevor watched breathlessly as Bryan caught his footing and stepped forward again.

Trevor darted in and slashed at Bryan's belly, forcing him to jump back.

Outside of the line.

The crowd erupted into mayhem and the occupants of the corner corrals boiled out, Trevor's friends surrounding him with congratulations, Taye attacking his head wound with a stinging, sterilizing alcohol pad and a bandage, then following up with the slice on his palm.

After a few minutes, Trevor managed to extricate himself from Sister Margaret's hug and Sammy's excited chatter. He approached Bryan, who was sitting on a chair, his pectoral and dorsal fins being tended to by his orange lieutenant as he held an ice pack on his left knee.

Bryan stood and extended a hand toward Trevor, dropping the ice pack to the wooden floor. "Well fought, mage," he said, a grudging admiration in his hissing voice.

Trevor stopped, wary of this abrupt about-face. After a moment, he shook the mer's pale hand. It was scaly and slightly damp, which felt very odd. "Thank you," he said. "You were a daunting opponent."

Bryan inclined his head. "I did not think you would be able to beat me. You have proven me wrong. I would like to fight more of you, and I'm sure in the coming years, as we battle your kind, I will have ample opportunity." He leaned to one side to peer behind Trevor. "I would particularly like to fight your partner. She has a warrior's demeanor, even more than you."

So, the mer still wanted to take out humanity. He supposed it would have been too much to think that one duel would change his mind. "I hope you will never have that opportunity," said Trevor. "I would still like to work out the animosity you feel toward my species without resorting to war."

"I would not trust your negotiations," said Bryan stiffly. "There has been so little honor seen from your kind."

"Honor?" Trevor narrowed his eyes. "Honor is a very convenient word, isn't it? You can talk about honor and it sounds very noble. But what does it mean, really? To me, honor encompasses a wide range of qualities, and very few of them involve challenging everyone who crosses your path to fights. In fact, it doesn't involve fighting at all unless it's actually necessary."

Bryan opened his mouth as though to argue, but Trevor held up a hand to forestall him. "No, you're going to listen to me. Honor encompasses kindness. It encompasses flexibility, the ability to give people a chance. It precludes bigotry, the need to judge all of a certain kind of person based on your perception of some people like them. We have been trying to meet you halfway, this entire time. Trying to talk to you, to show you that we share your concerns and want to help negate the actions of people who have harmed you and would continue to do so. And we've been met by scorn, insults, and fish heads. Fuck your honor."

Trevor turned on his heel and returned to the corral where his friends waited.

Chapter 40: Sister Margaret

Sister Margaret looked up as Trevor approached, his face angry. "You look less happy than I would assume," she observed.

"That guy's a dick," Trevor muttered. "I don't want to talk about it."

Before she could agree, Ari, Sammy, Coyote, and Chameleon surrounded them, Ari grasping Trevor's uninjured hand and pumping it enthusiastically. "What a fight! Well done, sir!"

"Thank you." Trevor managed a grin.

Henry approached. "You fought well," he said.

"Is Gregory still off sulking?" asked Ari, looking around for Henry's associate.

Henry shrugged. "I haven't seen him all day."

"Not at all?" said Chameleon with a frown. "Doesn't that seem odd?"

"Odd, maybe, but not unwelcome," said Henry with another shrug.

"Gregory?" said Zachary. "That's one of the other mages, right? He's the one who is sort of…."

"Annoying?" suggested Sammy. "Idiotic? Obnoxious?"

"Yeah," said Zachary. "That's about right."

"He's probably wandering around, looking for a golf course," Sammy snickered.

"Alone?" said Chameleon. "He can't play by himself, can he?"

"He could practice," said Henry. "Or find the course and then try to cajole someone into playing with him later."

"Does it matter?" asked Trevor. "I could really use a change of clothing and a drink."

"Fair point," said Sister Margaret. "Let's go back to the hotel and then there's that mixer in the banquet hall."

Before she could head toward the door, a heavy hand landed on her shoulder, and she spun around.

Bryan raised his hands, and she relaxed, her eyes narrowing. "What do you want?"

He looked past her toward Trevor. "You made some interesting points a minute ago."

Trevor's eyes widened. "Seriously? Suddenly you're ready to listen to reason?"

"I am quite reasonable, actually," he said. "I'm known for it among my school."

Sister Margaret looked at Zachary, raising a questioning eyebrow. "Is that true?"

He lifted a tentacle in a shrug. "I have no idea. I am not of his school. He's certainly not known for it outside of his school, but his school in general is not known for reason. They're known for duels and fighting and radical ideas."

"Yes, well." A note of irritation entered Bryan's voice, which is really how Sister Margaret was more used to hearing him speak. "I would like to speak further of this."

He glanced around the room, which was still full of excited cryptids. "Someplace quieter, maybe?"

"How about the squonkerball court?" suggested Coyote. "Should be empty, right?"

"Yes." Bryan led a strange procession down the hall to the squonkerball court — Sister Margaret noticed Eva and Matriarch Monin fall into place behind the mages and merfolk as they left the dueling chamber.

"Where are we going?" asked Eva.

"Someplace we can talk," said Ari.

"At last," she said. "We can begin to usher in— Wait, why are we stopping here?"

Bryan pushed open the door to the squonkerball court and stepped into the room, triggering a motion-sensor light. He immediately stepped backward, nearly smacking right into Sister Margaret.

"What's going on?" she demanded.

"An excellent question," he replied. He stepped forward again and Sister Margaret pushed her way past him.

Then she stopped short and Sammy, in turn, nearly ran into her. "What's going on?" he echoed.

"Well, I found Gregory." Sister Margaret approached the center of the court, which should have been as empty as the rest of the room but was instead occupied by Gregory's gruesomely butchered corpse.

"Oh, shit," said Sammy. He turned away, holding his hand over his mouth and nose.

Ari moved away as well, gagging, but the others crowded in for a closer look.

"What is that carved into his forehead?" asked Chameleon. She crouched beside the body, peering at the head.

"I think it might be an American football," said Matriarch Monin. She cleared her throat, and Sister Margaret glanced at her, suspiciously.

Yep. The witch was holding back a laugh.

Sister Margaret pressed her lips together as a sudden urge to chuckle came over her too. She met Matriarch Monin's eyes, and had to look away almost immediately lest her mirth overcome her.

This was hardly appropriate, given the circumstances.

Hastily, Sister Margaret turned her attention back to the body.

"Who could have done this?" asked Ari.

"I feel like it's a pretty long list, actually," Coyote muttered. "The only ones I can rule out is myself and Chameleon."

"Wasn't either of us," said Trevor. He gave Sister Margaret an enquiring look, and she had to hold back laughter again as she shook her head.

Trevor gave her another kind of look that said that he knew exactly what was going through her head. Then his lips twitched too, and she had to look away again.

Okay, focus on the body.

Eva stepped closer and bent to look at Bryan's throat, which was cut. "This was done with the point of something," she said. "Rather than an edged blade."

She didn't say anything more, but glanced sidelong at Bryan, her gaze lingering on the trident he carried slung on his back.

"What are you suggesting?" Bryan took a step toward her, his teeth bared.

Zachary stepped between them. "We know you didn't do this."

Eva stood up and crossed her arms. "We know no such thing. Why wouldn't he have done it?"

"Wanton violence is prohibited at the summit," said Bryan. "Why the hell do you think I've been challenging all of the humans to duels? If I could have simply slit their throats, I assure you, I would have."

"He makes a good point," said Sister Margaret. She paused and cleared her throat. "No pun intended."

Turning on her seer sight, she looked around for signs of magery and then looked deeper, accessing the body's energetic qualities. "I don't see any lingering spell residue. There's an interesting . . . tint to the body's aura."

"Aura?" said Eva with a frown. "A dead body shouldn't have an aura, would it?"

"Maybe aura isn't the right word," she said, absently. She studied the body. "Mages don't use it in the same way as, say, a New Age healer would."

"We don't not use it in that way either, though," said Henry. "It's complicated."

Sister Margaret glanced sideways at the remaining Illuminati.

He caught her looking at him and raised his hands. "Wasn't me."

"These auras," said Eva. "What can you tell from this interesting tint?"

"I wonder if it indicates a form of magic that I'm not familiar with," Sister Margaret mused.

"Like a cryptid's magic?" suggested Trevor. His eyes were seer-white as well, but not being a natural seer, he probably wasn't seeing the same nuances she was, just the general oddness of it.

"A corpse typically has a static aura," she said absently, as she crouched down to look more closely at the body. "While a living person's aura is composed of colorful swirling eddies connected by flowing rivers of energy, a freshly dead body's energetic overlay is usually just a still pall of a dull sickly yellow. It turns kind of grayish as it decomposes, which is helpful for figuring out exactly when someone died, if you haven't seen them around in a while."

"And Gregory's is atypical? How?" asked Ari.

"Yeah. It's almost green." Sister Margaret sat back on her heels. "I've never seen this before. And even weirder, I could swear that it's—" she paused, searching for the words. "Crawling. Slowly. Like a swarm of injured beetles."

She glanced around. Was there another natural seer in the room? Her eye fell on Coyote. "Do you see it moving?" she asked.

Belatedly, he turned on his sight as well. He whistled. "Damn, that is creepy."

"What does this mean?" asked Bryan impatiently.

Sammy put his hand on Sister Margaret's shoulder. "Let me show them," he suggested, and she mentally tossed him a tether. His hand glowed as he projected her vision onto a blank space on the wall.

Matriarch Monin gasped softly. "That is a useful spell," she murmured.

Trevor turned off his seer sight and stepped closer to the wall to look. "Ugh. It does look like it's moving. Not in a good way, though. Not like it should move."

"Well, he is dead," Bryan pointed out, impatiently. "Would you like to explain to the rest of us what the fuck this could mean?"

"I've never seen anything like it," said Sister Margaret again. "This is what a healthy living human's aura looks like." She swiveled her head to stare at Coyote so that his aura was projected on the wall instead.

A variety of oohs and aahs sounded from the assembled cryptids.

"In an unhealthy human," she continued. "There might be blockages of the flow. Some of those swirls, which we call chakras, might be swollen or depleted or the colors might change a bit. We encountered a spell a while back that was cast over multiple people that caused their eyes to turn black and their auras went all kinds of crazy. The spell turned everyone's energy body this weird red color and the energy moved very erratically through it."

"What about cryptids?" asked Bryan. "I would like to see my aura!"

Sister Margaret shrugged and moved her eyes over to Bryan. "Oh, wow. That's cool."

Bryan's energy body looked like the ocean at the beach, all crashing waves with still tide pools in place of swirling chakras. She could see sharp red spots here and there on his fins, with dark red liquid emanating from them before it mingled with the deep blue of the rest of his aura, dispersing as it moved further from the injury.

Sister Margaret moved to look at Helen, whose aura looked the same, but without the red spots. "You can see that Bryan's injuries show in his aura, where Helen has none." Turning again to look at Zachary, she was surprised to see a very different flow, much slower and a deep green color, more like how she imagined the depths of the ocean looked.

"Different types of mer have different auras," said Eva. "Fascinating."

"Perhaps we shall now answer the age-old question of whether witches are human or cryptid," said Matriarch Monin with a low cackle.

Obligingly, Sister Margaret turned to look at the matriarch. "I guess you are human," she said. Matriarch Monin's aura looked very similar to Coyote's, although it moved more slowly. "The slowness might be accounted for simply by your advanced age," she observed. "Since non-witchy humans don't typically live so long, I've never seen the aura of anyone of your age. But what are all of these tendrils coming out of your aura?"

"Active spells, perhaps?" suggested the witch. She pointed to one of the lines that was particularly thick. It passed from her aura and went about ten feet out before fading away. "This one is purple, and I recently cast a spell that required amethyst and violets." She touched another one. "Last month, I used a sapphire to influence my garden to grow faster. This blue one is less prominent, so it may be from a longer time ago."

"Interesting." Sister Margaret pivoted to look at Eva, curious if the younger witch would look more like Trevor, and whether she could identify any color-coded spells. "Oh."

Sister Margaret stared at the younger witch. Her aura did, indeed, look like a healthy human's. Except for the tendrils. One of which ran directly from Eva's hand to Gregory's corpse. And the line was the same creepy green shade that covered the dead mage.

"Uuurgh!" Bryan's bellow was astonishingly deep, considering his typical hissing voice, but Sister Margaret didn't have time to ponder that as he leapt toward Eva, rage boiling out of him.

Not wanting another dead body in the room, Sister Margaret drew the pepper spray from her bandolier and gave a quick spurt into Bryan's wide, bulging eyes. She turned off her seer sight to better see what was happening, rather than everybody's auras.

"Argh!" He shouted again, flopping to the floor, his fins flailing.

At that moment, he looked nothing like the warrior he was, and just like a giant fish in distress.

"Sorry," said Sister Margaret.

Trevor stitched in a washcloth from the bathroom and quickly spelled it damp.

"Make sure it's cold water," Sister Margaret cautioned. "Salt water is best for pepper spray. For humans, at least."

"What did you do to me, mage?" Bryan hissed as Trevor helped him to the couch and began dabbing his face with the wet cloth.

"It's just pepper spray," she explained. "It's not lethal and shouldn't do any permanent damage. But I could see you were going to kill Eva, and—"

"Where is Eva?" Matriarch Monin interrupted. "Where did she go?"

Shit. Sister Margaret looked around and realized that the witch had left the room during the commotion. The door leading out to the hallway was ajar.

"I'll find her," said Sammy.

"I'll help," said Chameleon.

Sister Margaret nodded, satisfied, as the two mages strode out of the room, Chameleon already turning on seer sight, and Sammy's hand glowing with a spell.

"She tried to set me up," said Bryan, shoving Trevor aside and surging to a standing position and moving toward Sister Margaret. "You saw her earlier, with her sneaky insinuations and her sideways glances. She must pay!"

"Agreed," she said.

Bryan paused and stared at her. "Then why?"

"She should be brought to justice," said Trevor. He handed Bryan the washcloth so he could continue to soothe his face. "But not by you. You said yourself — no one is allowed to kill anyone during the summit unless in combat. Eva should stand trial for murdering Gregory. But you shouldn't kill her and stand trial yourself."

Bryan stared at Trevor for a moment and then bent in the middle, bowing briefly. "You have a point. I don't like it, but it's fair. I was angry and would have made a rash move." He turned to Sister Margaret. "That was well done and will not be forgotten."

Without another word, he marched toward the door.

"Put some salt water on your eyes," Sister Margaret called after him as he left. She sighed and met Trevor's gaze. "Well, I don't think we managed to convince him we're worth allying with."

Trevor shrugged. "At least I don't think he'll be throwing any more fish heads for a while."

Sister Margaret turned her attention back to Gregory's body. "What about this situation? Are we sure he's really dead? His aura is moving, after all."

Matriarch Monin approached the bed. "I believe he is," she said. "Eva is smart and she is known for being thorough. If she wanted this man out of the way, she wouldn't simply put him to sleep. Besides the injuries are extensive. And there is the, erm, football carved into his forehead." She snorted and turned away for a moment.

"Why kill him at all?" asked Zachary.

The older witch regained control of her laughter. She lifted her hands in an expressive shrug. "You'd have to ask her. Whatever her reasons, I think I may be able to break the spell."

Sister Margaret's eyes widened. "You can bring him back to life?"

"*Mais non.*" Matriarch Monin shook her head vigorously, her cloud of black hair swishing back and forth around her face. "You misunderstand. I believe she may have trapped his spirit in his body, and that may be the cause of this strange aura. I can free the spirit so it will go . . . wherever it should go next."

"You mean he's a ghost?" Trevor's eyes darted around the room as though looking for Gregory's specter.

"Not yet," said Matriarch Monin. "But if nobody interferes, he will be. This is a complex spell, however, and I'll need some time. It will help if Eva can be persuaded to tell me the elements she used."

"Speak of the devil," murmured Coyote. Sister Margaret noticed that his eyes were seer white.

Sammy and Chameleon returned with Eva under a paralysis spell floating behind them.

"We've notified Dragonlord Ch'etwime," said Chameleon. "He'll be bringing some officers in to take her into Cryptid Collective custody soon."

"In the meantime," said Matriarch Monin, fixing Eva in a stern glare. "You will let this poor man's soul go."

The glow around Sammy's hands pulsed as he released her head from the spell, allowing her to speak.

Her expression turned fierce, and she spat on Gregory's corpse. "I will do no such thing," she hissed. "He was a menace, a harbinger of old, outdated ways, doing only harm to our vision of a brave new world of peace and cooperation."

"Peace and cooperation?" Sister Margaret raised her eyebrows. "You murdered someone because you thought *they* were getting in the way of peace and cooperation?"

Eva tossed her head. "Can't make an omelet without breaking eggs."

"That expression is absurd," Matriarch Monin murmured. "What has this man's life to do with eggs? Your new world is an omelet? A worldview is not an omelet. If you want to use food as your metaphor, a paradigm shift is a soup. It takes time to brew, time spent patiently stirring the pot, adding ingredients little by little, seasoning, stirring, adding vegetables and meat and salt and herbs and fat, and cooking them all together until what you have is a whole new thing that barely resembles the ingredients you started with. It is not an omelet to be made in a flash, a destructive omelet to be eaten once and forgotten. It is to be shared. To be savored. It is better after time."

Eva set her jaw. "My metaphor may have been flawed," she said stiffly. "But this sorry excuse for a man was flawed as well, and he needed to be taken out. He was in the way."

Matriarch Monin shook her head. "You are at the summit. That is sacred. You will let this man, this mage, this Gregory rest in peace. And then you will face the consequences of your actions."

After a moment, Eva nodded once, sharply. "I will. But know this: I regret nothing. Not this life nor others I have taken in the pursuit of the future this world deserves."

"Your words have been noted," said Matriarch Monin.

Eva glanced at Sammy. "I'll need my hands."

Sammy looked at Matriarch Monin, who nodded. His spell pulsed again and Eva's arms fell limp before she raised them again, reaching into her pockets and taking out something furry.

"Ew. Is that a dead mouse?" Ari's face squinched up in disgust.

"Yes," said Eva. She didn't seem to notice his discomfort as she pulled more oddities from various pockets and pouches on her person. She had as many hiding places in her clothing as Sister Margaret, but instead of weapons, she had rocks, bits of dried plants, animal parts, and other bizarre objects.

Then again, to a witch, maybe those were weapons.

Finally, once Eva's cupped hands were overflowing, she looked at Sammy again. "I need to get closer."

Matriarch Monin nodded to him again, and he pushed Eva toward the body.

She arranged her sundries beside Gregory's mutilated corpse and began to move her arms back and forth and bob her head up and down. It looked very odd, considering her legs and torso remained completely still and she was floating about six inches off the ground.

Sister Margaret turned her seer sight back on, curious about how the counterspell would look energetically.

Gregory's aura was starting to yellow, the green tint fading upward as a breeze wafted out from Eva's swaying arms.

For a split second, Sister Margaret swore she saw Gregory's shape, a puzzled frown gracing his florid face, before the greenish mist shot upward and disappeared into the ceiling.

Chapter 41: Trevor

The next day should have been a return to meetings and negotiations, but instead, Trevor found himself in the bleachers of yet another amphitheater filled with cryptids avidly watching an unusual spectacle.

He and the other mages had managed to snag a seat at the front of the courtroom, just behind a rectangular box, about six feet by eight feet, made of clear ice, through which he could see Eva and another witch seated at a table.

Another table a few feet away, this one sans box, hosted a dragon and a kallanpa amaru.

Facing the tables and the bleachers was a long dais with a high table, at which were seated seven cryptids of varying species.

The similarity of the set-up to the familiar American courtrooms he was used to seeing on TV was surreal, rather than comforting.

The dragon in the center of the presiding tribunal emitted a wordless roar, and the chattering audience quieted.

"Thank you," said the dragon. "We are here today to decide the fate of one Eva Nilson, a witch of the Oslo coven. Who is representing the accused?"

The witch beside Eva stood. She was a striking woman who looked to Trevor to be about twenty-five years old. Of course, with witches, you never knew; she could have been anywhere from twenty-five to seventy. Her strawberry blonde hair was pulled back into a severe bun.

"I am, your honor," she said. "Matriarch Sara Michaels of Boston."

"Very good," said the dragon. He turned toward the other table. "And who is advocating on behalf of the deceased?"

The two cryptids at the other table stood, as Matriarch Michaels resumed her seat.

"Dragonlord Uq'pin'och," said the dragon.

"Killa," said the kallanpa amaru.

"Excellent. You may begin." The dragon settled back into his seat, as several of the other tribunal members leaned forward.

"We cede the first statement to the defendant," said Killa in Spanish. They sat down, as did their dragon counterpart.

Trevor's eyebrows lifted, and he glanced around the room, but nobody else in the audience seemed at all surprised by the change in language. A few cryptids had phones held in front of them, and he wondered if they were using a translation app.

Matriarch Michaels stood again and walked straight through the wall of the ice box to pace gracefully in front of the tribunal, giving equal attention to the judges, the audience, and the opposing council as she spoke. "My client admits freely the difficult choice that she made by removing this human, but accedes no wrongdoing. After all, this is the *Cryptid* Collective, is it not? The humans are here on our sufferance, and this one, this *Gregory Pitts*—" her face twisted into a sneer, "— was not invited, nor did he behave in a way that indicated any respect for the event, his fellow representatives, nor the Collective as a whole. He was not fit to attend this summit, and so he was removed from it."

She spun on her heel to face the judges, her head turning to give each member of the tribunal a stare for a second or so in turn. Finally, she concluded. "This was not a murder, but an extermination."

Matriarch Michaels pivoted once again, strode back through the icy wall of Eva's pen, and sat down beside her, folding her arms and leaning back in her seat.

Dragonlord Uq'pin'och heaved herself to her feet and walked to the center of the room. "Gregory Pitts may not have been personally invited to the summit, but he was chosen by his organization, the Illuminati, a group of great political and financial power among the human mages to represent them at this summit. As you know, the inclusion of the mages here at this summit, this summit in particular, was not made lightly."

Trevor held his breath. Would they finally get some insight into why they were here? Sister Margaret prodded his ribcage with a sharp elbow. Her eyes were wide, her lips pressed rightly together.

"And we may have requested certain representatives, yes, but we did not *require* that these personages were sent. We gave the invited groups some leeway. Gregory Pitts was not our choice, but he was the choice of the Illuminati, and we must trust that they had reason for that. As the representative of an invited group, he was under the protection of the Collective, under the truce of the summit. This *murder—*" She shot Matriarch Michaels a pointed look as she emphasized the word, "was a direct violation of that truce."

Dragonlord Uq'pin'och made her way back to her table, seating herself on her haunches behind it.

Sister Margaret elbowed Trevor again. "What do you think she meant by that?" she hissed. "This summit in particular? Do you get the feeling everyone else knows why we're here, but we don't?"

"It's a little bit maddening," he murmured, easing his injured body away from her sharp appendages. "I don't know why you're taking it out on me, though."

"Sorry." Sister Margaret raised her hands in an apologetic gesture, tucking her elbows close to her sides.

Matriarch Michaels took the floor again. "I would like to call to witness one Henry Palmer, human mage."

Henry made his way to the front of the room, his back straight, his face under complete control. A podium of ice appeared in the middle of the open space, facing the tribunal, and he took his place behind it.

One of the judges, a witch seated a little bit left of the center spoke to him. "I understand that in your human courts, you are generally required to swear an oath of truth before speaking."

Henry nodded.

"We do things a little bit differently here." She made a gesture and the podium lit up from within with a bright white light. "If you tell any untruths, the color of the spell will change, and you will be known to have committed perjury. The penalty for this is death."

Henry nodded again.

The witch leaned back in her seat and waved to Matriarch Michaels. "You may begin."

Matriarch Michaels moved to stand near the podium, angling herself so she addressed both the witness and the audience. "Gregory Pitts was a member of your society, the Illuminati."

She paused and Henry nodded once more.

"How close were the two of you?"

"Not close at all," said Henry. "In fact, I met Gregory for the first time two weeks before we left for the summit."

"And did you hit it off right away?" asked Matriarch Michaels. "Did you become fast friends?"

"No," said Henry.

Matriarch Michaels seemed to be waiting for him to continue, but after a few seconds, she lifted her eyebrows and continued her questioning. "Why not?"

"Our personalities did not mesh well, in my opinion," said Henry smoothly. This must have been close enough to the truth, as the white light didn't waver.

"Why was he chosen as a representative?"

Henry shrugged. "You would have to ask my superiors that."

She made a go-on gesture and leaned forward slightly. "If you had to guess."

"I would guess it was based on cronyism, to be frank," said Henry.

Trevor's brow creased. "Isn't speculating sort of frowned upon during a trial?" he whispered to Sister Margaret.

She shrugged. "In a human court, sure. Here?" She shrugged again.

"So you do not think he was qualified to represent the Illuminati here at the summit? But was sent anyway, because he knew a guy who knew a guy?" Matriarch Michaels' eyes bored into Henry.

Henry's face, of which Trevor could only see the right side, remained impassive. "I did not say he wasn't qualified."

"Do you believe he was qualified for the position?"

Henry pursed his lips. When he finally answered, the single word emerged in a clipped tone. "No."

"I have no further questions," said Matriarch Michaels.

Trevor looked around, but none of the cryptids present seemed to have any problems with the lack of focus strictly on facts.

As she returned to her seat, Killa, the kallanpa amaru attorney, glided to take her place.

"Gregory was not explicitly invited here, but you were, Henry. Did you know that?" The cryptid resumed the interrogation, once again speaking in Spanish.

Henry responded smoothly and fluently in the same language. "I was not made aware of that fact, no."

"Do you know why the Cryptid Collective chose you, out of the thousands in your organization?"

"No."

The kallanpa amaru tipped their head to the side, studying the mage for a moment before continuing. "Do you have a guess?"

Henry pursed his lips again, considering his response, then shook his head. "No."

The podium remained white.

"At least he's as clueless as we are," Trevor murmured to Sister Margaret.

"Do you know why the collective invited human mages to this summit for the first time?" asked Killa.

"No," said Henry.

Killa turned to face the judges. "But you do. You know the impact this change can make, has to make, on our world."

The judges nodded, and Killa turned back to the witness. "How will your organization react to the death of one of its representatives?"

Trevor hissed in frustration.

"Go back to why we're here, dammit," Sister Margaret muttered. She kept her elbows to herself this time, for which Trevor was infinitely grateful.

"That depends on a variety of factors," said Henry. "We are no stranger to the concept of political assassination. If apologies are made and the perpetrator dealt with in a satisfactory manner, I think it likely our leadership will be prepared to overlook it and maintain a positive relationship with the collective and its many members."

Killa raised their eyebrows. "And what would a satisfactory manner of dealing with Eva be, in the eyes of the Illuminati?"

"A life for a life would be customary," said Henry without hesitation.

"No further questions," said Killa.

Henry returned to his seat in the audience as Matriarch Michaels took Killa's place in front of the podium. "Bryan of the Agualadron School, please come forward."

Bryan came forward. His fins were bandaged, but aside from that and a slight limp, he seemed to be recovering from yesterday's duel.

"You were the first one to find the body, were you not?" asked the witch.

Trevor's mind began to wander as they rehashed the discovery of Gregory's body, only snapping back to the present moment when a question caught his attention once more.

"So, you agree that he deserved his fate?" Matriarch Michaels smiled at Bryan, a bloodthirsty glint in her eye. "He deserved to die, didn't he?"

"All humans deserve to die," said Bryan.

The podium remained white. The mer truly believed that. Trevor shivered.

"Do you feel that Eva Nilson was right to remove him from this earth?" asked Matriarch Michaels.

"Yes," said Bryan.

Eva jumped to her feet inside her box, gesticulating broadly, her lips moving. She tried to run toward the mer, but was stopped by the icy wall, which must have been spelled to allow only Matriarch Michaels to come and go. The Norwegian witch pounded on the barrier, but it dampened the sound.

Ignoring her client, Matriarch Michaels nodded, a small smile playing at the corners of her lips. "No further questions."

She walked back to her seat, still disregarding Eva as the accused witch slammed a fist down on the table and leaned over it, flinging indiscernible words in her face. Finally, the matriarch looked Eva in the eyes and said a single word.

Eva deflated, her head hanging as she walked back around the table and regained her seat, burying her head in her hands.

After a moment, Dragonlord Uq'pin'och stood and made her way over to the witness podium. "You believe all humans deserve to die," she said. It wasn't a question, but Bryan responded anyway.

"Yes."

"There are eight humans attending this summit. Well, seven now."

"Yes," said Bryan again.

"You have not killed any of them."

"No."

"Why not?"

Bryan's gray forehead creased. "It is the summit. I cannot kill them except in ritual combat."

"Clearly that isn't true," said Dragonlord Uq'pin'och. "Wouldn't you say?"

"I do not understand," said Bryan. "Isn't that the rule?"

"Ahhh." Dragonlord Uq'pin'och's mouth gaped open in a smile, revealing teeth just as sharp as Bryan's, but somehow less scary. "It isn't a question of *cannot*, you see. It's a question of *will not*." She addressed the tribunal. "You see, this cryptid, this honorable mer, will not kill a human at the summit, even though he adamantly believes they all deserve it. He will not do so, because he respects the rules, the sacred laws of this ancient gathering."

She paused. "I have no further questions."

Matriarch Michaels stood. "No further witnesses, your honors." Her voice carried through the walls of the box.

"Nor have we," said Dragonlord Uq'pin'och.

"Closing statements?" said the dragon who seemed to be the lead judge.

Matriarch Michaels strode forward as the witness podium disappeared.

"The Cryptid Collective has no general prohibition against killing anyone, much less humans," she began. "The sole argument against my client is that the killing occurred at the summit. And yes, there are rules against killing the diplomats invited to the summit, those of us who are here to peacefully strengthen the collective through treaties, trade agreements, and other useful accords. But was Gregory Pitts such a person?

"No. He was not invited to the summit. His own colleague admits that he was unqualified and unlikeable. He was not here to negotiate on behalf of his people, but to gawk at cryptids and insult us. So, I ask you to ponder this: do the rules of the summit, the rules against killing *representatives* of cryptid-kind, apply in this instance at all?"

Matriarch Michaels pivoted on her heel and strode back to her seat beside Eva, as Killa stood and glided to the center in her place.

"Of course the laws apply to the representatives of all invited groups." said Killa. "Gregory Pitts was sent here to represent the Illuminati, a group of human mages expressly invited by the Cryptid Collective to this summit. The reason behind that group's decision to send this man an not another is irrelevant. The personality of the representative is irrelevant. Who liked and disliked him is irrelevant." They paused and raised their hands. "This law is sacred. It has been broken. Justice must be served." With a dramatic downsweep of their arms, they turned and moved gracefully back to their seat.

There was a moment of silence in the courtroom and then the dragon judge nodded her head three times and spoke. "Thank you. We will reconvene in five minutes."

And with that, the tribunal stood and filed out through a door to their left.

"Only five minutes?" Trevor murmured to Sister Margaret. "Doesn't that seem like an absurdly short time to decide something like this?"

She shrugged. "For all I know, they're going into some kind of time warp and they'll be talking for twelve hours and only five minutes will pass here."

Trevor stared at her. "Is that a thing?"

"Probably not," she admitted. "But nothing I see here will surprise me at this point."

"Fair enough," he murmured.

The five minutes passed quickly and soon enough the tribunal filed back into the courtroom, arraying themselves behind their long bench.

The crowd quieted and the lead adjudicator spoke calmly into the silence. "We find Eva Nilson, witch of Oslo, guilty of disrupting the truce of the summit. We sentence her to death, to take place tomorrow morning at nine o'clock, in the city square, in a manner to be chosen by the present matriarchs of her people."

Chapter 42: Sister Margaret

"Have you ever seen an execution?" Sister Margaret asked Trevor. Her fingers danced over the daggers strapped to her arms, and she forced herself into stillness. "I've never seen an execution."

Trevor mutely shook his head. "You'd think it wouldn't be so—" He stopped and sighed. "I mean, we've killed before. Why should it be so—"

She nodded. "It's different. Battle is different from . . . this."

The crowd was significantly smaller today in the central square of M'Tainla than it had been the day before at the trial or the day before that at the duel.

"It would seem that others feel the same way," said Trevor, running a hand over his black hair.

Coyote and Chameleon appeared beside Sister Margaret, and she found herself holding a knife in each hand, pointed at her friends.

Chameleon raised an eyebrow. "Bit jumpy today, are we?"

Sister Margaret couldn't help but notice a slight cockney flavor to Chameleon's voice; the former spy was prone to adopting characters when she was nervous. "And you're perfectly comfortable?" She echoed Chameleon's raised eyebrow.

"Brings back some old memories is all," said Chameleon.

Coyote sat down heavily on the edge of a fountain. "We had plenty of this shit back in the Auditors. Sometimes for actual crimes. Usually for the whims of the Pontiff."

"My dad weren't a nice man," said Chameleon.

Trevor put a hand on Chameleon's arm. "You don't have to be here," he said, gently. "No one would blame you for going back to your rooms. Look around — half the representatives are absent."

Chameleon shook her head. "Nothing good ever came from hiding from your demons."

Henry stepped up on the other side of Trevor, Sammy and Ari trailing behind him. "We didn't miss it, did we?"

Sister Margaret shook her head and put her daggers away. "Nothing's started yet."

"Good." Henry nodded once. "I think it's important all the mages are here to bear witness."

Just then, across the square, the crowd parted as Eva was led toward the fountain in its center, head high. She was not restrained in any way, but simply followed behind Matriarch Monin.

Both witches wore equally grim expressions.

When they reached the fountain, Eva squared her shoulders and stared into her superior's eyes.

And then suddenly, with no fanfare, no flash of light or gradual shrinking, there was a tiny mouse on the ground in Eva's place, and an owl hovering in the air where Matriarch Monin had stood.

The mouse began to run.

The owl waited a moment and then swooped down, grasping the mouse in her talons and then sweeping back to land on the edge of the fountain. She transferred the mouse into her wickedly curved beak and then began rocking her head up and down, using gravity to force the mouse further and further into her mouth until only the tail dangled from her beak. And then the tail was gone too, and the owl's throat moved as she swallowed the mouse.

A moment later, Matriarch Monin appeared in the owl's place, perched on the side of the fountain. Without a word, the witch stood and strode back in the direction she'd come from.

In silence, the crowd began to disperse as well.

Sister Margaret stood for a moment, her eyes wide as she stared at the fountain. Then she turned and cocked an eyebrow at Trevor.

He nodded, and the two of them turned back toward their hotel, the other mages trailing behind.

What was there to say, after all?

About the Author:

Anna McCluskey is an Oregon-based, semi-nomadic, almost-entirely-feral fantasy author.

She is the author of the *Mathilda Holiday* series, the *Rhymes With Witch* series, and the *Warrior Mage Librarians* series. She has had several poems published in journals and anthologies, and her short fiction has been read by at least a dozen people, many of whom murmured appreciatively about it.

For information on upcoming projects, check out her website, www.annamccluskey.com.